'You could become my mistress.'

'Your mistress?' For a moment Averil did not seem to understand, and then her whole body went rigid with indignation. 'Why, you…! You don't think I am good enough to marry, but you would keep me for your pleasure!' She wrenched round. 'Let me go—'

Luc shifted his grip, afraid of hurting her, too aroused to release her. She thudded against his chest and he held her with one hand splayed on her back, the other in her hair, and kissed her. It was wrong, it was gloriously right, it was heaven. She tasted of wine and fruit and woman and he lost himself, drowning in her, until she twisted, jerking her knee up. If not for her hampering skirts she would have had him, square in the groin. As it was her knee hit him with painful force on the thigh and he tore his mouth free.

SEDUCED BY THE SCOUNDREL

Louise Allen

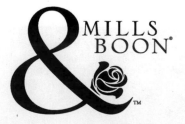

First published in Great Britain 2011
by Mills & Boon, an imprint of Harlequin (UK) Limited,
Eton House, 18-24 Paradise Road, Richmond, Surrey TW9 1SR

ISBN: 978 0 263 21827 5

Harlequin (UK) policy is to use papers that are natural, renewable and recyclable products and made from wood grown in sustainable forests. The logging and manufacturing process conform to the legal environmental regulations of the country of origin.

Printed and bound in Great Britain
by CPI Antony Rowe, Chippenham, Wiltshire

Dedication

With happy memories
of a wonderful week on the Isles of Scilly
and the kind staff in the tiny library

Author Note

Once I had chosen the treacherous seas around the Isles of Scilly as the setting for the wreck of the *Bengal Queen*, right at the end of her three-month voyage from India, I knew I had to go there to experience the islands for myself.

The heroine of this novel was going to be washed ashore on one of the uninhabited islands—but which one? On the Scillies small boats take the place of cars and buses, and I spent a happy week in the sunshine—criss-crossing from island to island, waving at seals, walking on sand so fine it was exported for use to blot ink in the eighteenth century. Finally I chose St Helen's, with its tiny old isolation hospital—a perfect base for the mysterious and dangerous man who will rescue Averil Heydon when she is washed, naked, onto the beach at his feet.

While I was there I was privileged to see the wonderful pilot gigs racing—their speed and the distances they can cover have not been exaggerated in this book. However, I have taken liberties with the Governor of the islands at the time, whose name and family are entirely imaginary and bear no resemblance to the real Governor.

Louise Allen has been immersing herself in history, real and fictional, for as long as she can remember, and finds landscapes and places evoke powerful images of the past. Louise lives in Bedfordshire, and works as a property manager, but spends as much time as possible with her husband at the cottage they are renovating on the north Norfolk coast, or travelling abroad. Venice, Burgundy and the Greek islands are favourite atmospheric destinations. Please visit Louise's website—www.louiseallenregency.co.uk—for the latest news!

Previous novels by the same author:

VIRGIN SLAVE, BARBARIAN KING
THE DANGEROUS MR RYDER*
THE OUTRAGEOUS LADY FELSHAM*
THE SHOCKING LORD STANDON*
THE DISGRACEFUL MR RAVENHURST*
THE NOTORIOUS MR HURST*
THE PIRATICAL MISS RAVENHURST*
PRACTICAL WIDOW TO PASSIONATE MISTRESS**
VICAR'S DAUGHTER TO VISCOUNT'S LADY**
INNOCENT COURTESAN TO ADVENTURER'S BRIDE**
RAVISHED BY THE RAKE†

*Those Scandalous Ravenhursts
**The Transformation of the Shelley Sisters
†Danger & Desire

and in Mills & Boon® Historical *Undone!* eBooks:
DISROBED AND DISHONOURED

Chapter One

March 16th, 1809—Isles of Scilly

It was a dream, the kind you have when you are almost awake. She was cold, wet… The cabin window must have opened in the night…she was so uncomfortable…

'Look 'ere, Jack, it's a mermaid.'

'Nah. Got legs, ain't she? No tail. Never got that. How do you swive a mermaid if she ain't got legs?'

Not a dream…nightmare. Wake up. Eyes won't open. So cold. Hurt. Afraid, so afraid.

'Is she dead, do yer reckon?'

Uncomprehending terror ran through her veins in the dream. *Am I dead? Is this hell? They sound like demons. Lie still.*

'Looks fresh enough. She'll do, even if she ain't too lively. I 'aven't had a woman in five weeks.'

'None of us 'ave, stupid.' The coarse voice came closer.

No! Had she screamed it aloud? Averil became fully conscious and with consciousness came memory and realisation and true terror: shipwreck and a great wave and then cold and churning water and the knowledge that she was going to die.

But she wasn't dead. Under her was sand, cold, wet sand, and the

wind blew across her skin and wavelets lapped at her ankles and
her eyes were mercifully gummed shut with salt against this nightmare and everything hurt as though she'd been rolled in a barrel.
Wind…skin… She was naked and those voices belonged to real
men and they were coming closer and they wanted to… *Lie still.*

Something nudged her hard in the ribs and she flinched away,
convulsed with fear, her body reacting while her mind screamed
at it to be still.

'She's alive! Well, there's a bit of luck.' It was the first speaker,
his voice gloating. She curled into a shivering ball, like a hedgehog
stripped of its prickles. 'You reckon we can get 'er up behind those
rocks before the others see 'er? Don't want to share, not 'til we've
had our fill.'

'No!' She jerked herself upright so she was sitting on the sand,
her arms wrapped around her nakedness. It was worse now, not to
be able to see. She dragged her eyes open against the sticky sting
of the salt.

Her tormentors stood about two yards away, regarding her with
identical expressions of lustful greed. Averil's stomach churned as
her instincts recognised the look. One man was big, with a gut that
spoke of too much beer and muscles that bulged on his bare arms
and calves like tree trunks. The one who had kicked her must be
the skinny runt closer to her.

'You come along with us, darlin',' the smaller one said and the
wheedling tone had the sodden hairs on her neck rising. 'We'll get
you nice and warm, won't we, 'Arry?'

'I'd rather die,' she managed to say. She dug her fingers into the
wet sand and raked up two handfuls, but it flowed out of her grasp.
There was nothing to use as a weapon, not even a pebble, and her
hands were numb with cold.

'Yer, well, what you want don't come into it, darlin'.' That must
be Jack. Would it help if she used their names, tried to get them
to see her as a human being and not just a thing for their use? She

struggled to get her terrified brain to work. Could she run? No, her legs were numb, too, she would never be able to stand up.

'Listen—my name is Averil. Jack, Harry—don't you have sisters—?'

The big one swore foully and she heard the voices at the same time. 'The others. Damn it, now we'll 'ave to share the bloss.'

Averil focused her stinging eyes along the beach. She sat on the rim of sand that fringed the sea. Above her a pebble beach merged into low rock outcrops and beyond that short turf sloped up to a hill. The voices belonged to a group of half-a-dozen men, sailors by the look of them, all in similar dark working clothes to the two who had found her.

At the sight of her they broke into a run and she found herself facing a semicircle of grinning, leering figures. Their laughter, their voices as they called coarse comments she could barely understand, their questions to Jack and Harry, beat on her ears and the scene began to blur as she closed her eyes. She was going to faint and when she fainted they would—

'What the hell have you got there?' The voice was educated, authoritative and rock hard. Averil sensed the men's attention turn from her like iron filings attracted to a magnet and hope made her gasp with relief.

'Mermaid, Cap'n.' Harry sniggered. 'Lost 'er tail.'

'Very nice, too,' the voice said, very close now. 'And you were about to bring her to me, I suppose?'

'Why'd we do that, Cap'n?'

'Captain's prize.' There was no pity in the dispassionate tone, only the clinical assessment of a piece of flotsam. The warm flood of hope receded like a retreating wave.

'That's not fair!'

'Tough. This is not a democracy, Tubbs. She's mine and that's an order.' Boots crunched over pebbles as the sound of furious muttering rose.

None of this was going to go away. Averil opened her eyes again and looked up. And up. He was big: rangy, with dark hair, a dominant nose. The uncompromising grey eyes, like the sea in winter, looked at her as a man studies a woman, not as a rescuer looks at a victim. There was straightforward masculine desire there, and, strangely, anger. 'No,' she whispered.

'No, leave you to freeze to death, or, no, don't take you away from your new friends?' he asked. He was like a dark reflection of the men she had come to know over the past three months on the ship. Tough, intelligent men who had no need to swagger because they radiated confidence and authority. Alistair Lyndon, the twins Callum and Daniel Chatterton. Were they all dead now?

His voice was hard, his face showed no sympathy, but for all that he was better than the rabble on the beach. The big man had his hand on the hilt of a knife and her rescuer had his back to him. 'Behind you,' she said, ignoring the mockery.

'Dawkins, leave that alone unless you want to end up like Nye.' The dark man spoke without turning and she saw his hand rested on the butt of a pistol thrust in his belt. 'There's no money if you're dead of a bullet in your fat gut. More for the others, though.' He raised an eyebrow at Averil and she nodded, lured into complicity. No one else was touching a weapon. He shrugged out of his coat and dropped it over her shoulders. 'Can you stand?'

'No. T-t-t-too cold.' Her teeth chattered and she tightened her jaw against the weakness.

He leaned down, caught her wrists and hauled her to her feet as she groped with clumsy fingers for the edges of the coat. It reached the curve of her buttocks, she could feel it chafing the skin there. 'I'll carry you,' he said as he turned from raking a stare over the watching men.

'No!' She stumbled, grabbed at his arm. If he lifted her the coat would ride up, she'd be exposed.

'They've seen everything there is to see already,' he said. 'Tubbs, give me your coat.'

'It'll get all wet,' the man grumbled as he pulled it off and shambled down the beach to hand it over. His eyes were avid on her bare legs.

'And you'll get it back smelling of wet woman. Won't that be nice?' Her rescuer took it, wrapped it round her waist and then slung her over his shoulder. Averil gave a gasp of outrage, then realised: like this he had one hand free for his pistol.

Head down, she stared at the shifting ground. The coats did nothing against the cold, only emphasised her essential nakedness and shame. Averil fought against the faintness that threatened to sweep over her: she had to stay conscious. The man she had hoped would be her rescuer was nothing of the sort. At best he was going to rape her, at worst that gang of ruffians would attack him and they would all have her.

Last night—it must have been last night, or she'd be dead of the cold by now—she had known she was about to die. Now she wished she had.

The sound of crunching stones stopped, the angle at which she was hanging levelled off and she saw grass below. Then her captor stopped, ducked, and they were inside some kind of building. 'Here.' He dropped her like a sack of potatoes on to a lumpy surface. 'Don't go to sleep yet, you're too cold.'

The door banged closed behind him and Averil hauled herself up. She was on a bed in a large stone-built hut with five other empty bed frames ranged along the walls. The rough straw in the mattress-bag crackled under her as she shifted to look round. There was a hearth with the ashes of a dead fire at one end, a wooden chair, a table with some crockery on it, a trunk. The hut had a window with threadbare sacking hanging over it, a few shelves, the plank door and a rough stone slab floor without so much as a rag rug.

Rather be dead... The self-pity brought tears to her eyes. The room steadied and her head stopped swimming. *No, I wouldn't.* Averil knuckled the moisture out of her eyes and winced at the sting of the salt. The pain steadied her. She was not a coward and life—until a few hours ago—had been sweet and worth fighting for.

An upbringing as the pampered daughter of a wealthy family was no preparation for this, but she had fought off all the illnesses life in India could throw at her for twenty of her twenty-two years, she had coped with three months at sea in an East Indiaman and she'd survived a shipwreck. *I am not going to die now, not like this, not without a struggle.*

She must get up, now, and find a way out, a weapon before he came back. Averil dragged herself off the bed. There was a strange roaring in her ears and the room seemed to be moving. The floor was shifting, surely? Or was it her? Everything was growing very dark…

'Hell and damnation.' Luc slammed the door closed behind him. The sprawled naked figure on the floor did not so much as twitch. He picked up the pitcher from the table, knelt beside her and splashed water on her face. That did produce some reaction: she licked her lips.

'Back to bed.' He scooped her on to the lumpy mattress and pulled the blanket over her. The feel of her in his arms had been good. Too good to dwell on. As it was, the memory of her sitting like a mermaid on the beach with the surf creaming around her long, pale legs was enough to keep a man restless at night with the ache of desire.

He poured water into a beaker and went back to the bed. 'Come on, wake up. You need water—drink.' He knelt and put an arm behind her shoulders to lift her so he could put the beaker to her lips. To his relief she drank thirstily, blindly. Tangled dark blond hair stuck to his coat, bruises blossomed on lightly tanned skin.

Long lashes flickered open to reveal dazed hazel-green eyes and then closed as though weighted with lead.

Then her head lolled to one side against his shoulder, she sighed and went limp.

'*Nom d'un nom d'un nom...*' This was the last thing he had planned for, an unconscious woman who needed to be cared for. If he put her into the skiff and sailed her across to St Mary's and said he had found her on the beach, just one more survivor of the shipwreck last night, then she would be safe. But what if she remembered? Her seeing him did not matter: he had a cover story accepted by the Governor. But he had been with the men and was obviously their leader.

Luc looked down at the wet, matted tangle of hair that was all he could see of her now. She sighed and snuggled closer and he adjusted her so she fitted more comfortably against him while he thought. She was young, but not a girl. In her early twenties, perhaps. She had not been addled by her experience; her reaction when she warned him about Dawkins told him that she had her wits about her. In fact, she seemed both courageous and intelligent. What were the chances that she would forget all about this or would dismiss it as a nightmare?

Not good, he decided after a few more moments holding her. She might blurt out what she had seen to anyone when she regained consciousness and he had no idea who he had to be on his guard against, even in the Governor's own household. Even the Governor himself.

His prudent choices were to leave her here with some food and water, lock the door and walk away—which would probably be as close to murder as rowing her out to sea and dropping her overboard would be—or to nurse her until she was strong enough to look after herself.

What did he know about nursing women? Nothing—but how different could it be from looking after a man? Luc looked at the slender figure huddled in the coarse blankets and admitted to himself that he was daunted. And when she woke, if she did, then she was not going to be best pleased to discover who had been looking after her. He could always point out the alternatives.

She had drunk something, at least. He would tell Potts to cook broth at dinner time and see if he could get that down her. And he supposed he had better wash the worst of the salt off her and check her for any injuries. Broken bones were more than likely.

Then he could get her into one of his shirts, make the bed more comfortable and leave her for a while. That would be good. He found he was sweating at the thought of touching her. *Damn.* He had to get out of here.

Luc stood on the threshold for a moment to get his breathing steady. He was in a bad way if a half-drowned woman aroused such desire in him. Her defiance and the intelligence in those bruised hazel eyes kept coming back to him and made him feel even worse for lusting after her in this state. Better he thought about the problem she would pose alive, conscious and aware of their presence here.

To distract himself he eyed the ships in St Helen's Pool, the sheltered stretch of water bounded by St Helen's where he stood, uninhabited Teän and St Martin's to the east, and Tresco to the south.

That damned shipwreck on the reefs to the west had stirred up the navy like a stick thrust into an anthill. Even the smoke from the endless chain of kelp-burning pits around the shores of all the inhabited islands seemed less dense today. They must have searchers out everywhere looking for bodies and survivors. In fact, there was a jolly boat rowing towards him now. If she had been dead, or unconscious from the start, he could have off-loaded her on them. But then, if his luck was good, he would never have been here in the first place.

He glanced round, made certain the men were out of sight and strolled down to the beach to meet the boat, moving the pistol to the small of his back. Eccentric poets seeking solitude to write epic works did not, he guessed, walk around armed.

A midshipman stood up in the bows, his freckled face serious. How old was this brat? Seventeen? 'Mr Dornay, sir?' he hailed from the boat.

'Yes. You're enquiring about survivors from the wreck, I imagine? I heard the shouting and saw the lights last night, guessed what had happened. I walked right round the island at first light and I didn't find anyone, dead or alive.' No lie—*he* had not found her.

'Thank you, sir. It was an East Indiaman that went down—big ship and a lot of souls on board. It will save us time not to have to search this island.' The midshipman hesitated, frowning as he kept his balance in the swaying boat. 'They said on St Martin that they saw a group of men out here yesterday and the Governor had only told us about you, sir, so we wondered. Writing poetry, he said.' The young man obviously thought this was strange behaviour.

'Yes,' Luc agreed, cursing inwardly. The damn fools were supposed to stay out of sight of the inhabited islands. 'A boat did land. A rough crew who said they were looking for locations for new kelp pits. I thought they were probably smugglers so I didn't challenge them. They've gone now.'

'Very wise, and you're more than likely right, sir. Thank you. We'll call again tomorrow.'

'Don't trouble, you've got enough on your plate. I've got a skiff, I'll sail over if I find anything.'

The midshipman saluted as the sailors lifted their oars and propelled the jolly boat towards the southern edge of Teän to find a landing place. Luc wandered back up the beach until they were out of sight, then strode over the low shoulder to the left, behind the old isolation hospital he was using as his shelter and where the woman now lay.

He did a rapid headcount. They were all there, all twelve of the evil little crew he'd been saddled with. There had been thirteen of them at the start, but he'd had to shoot Nye when the man decided that sticking a knife in the captain's ribs was easier than the mission they had been sent on. Luc's unhesitating reaction had sharpened up the rest of them.

'That was the navy,' he said as they shifted from their comfortable circle around a small, almost smokeless, fire to look at him. 'Someone on St Martin saw you yesterday. Stay round this side, don't go farther east along the north shore than Didley's Point.'

'Or the nasty navy'll get us?' Tubbs sneered. 'Then who'll be in trouble, Cap'n?'

'I'll be deep in the dunghill,' Luc agreed. 'From where I can watch you all be hanged. Think on it.'

'Yer. We'll think on it while you're prigging that mermaid we found you. Or 'ave you come round for a bit of advice on technique, like? Sir,' a lanky redhead asked, as he shifted a wad of chewing tobacco from one cheek to the other.

'Generous of you to offer, Harris, but I'm letting her sleep. I prefer my women conscious.' He leaned one hip against a boulder. Instinct told him not to reveal how ill she seemed to be. 'It could be four or five more days before we get word. I don't want you lot getting rusty. Check the pilot gig over this afternoon and we'll exercise with it some more tomorrow.'

'It's fine,' the redhead grumbled and spat a stream of brown liquid into the fire. 'Looked at it yesterday. Just a skinny jolly boat, that's all.'

'Your expert opinion will be a consolation as we sink in the middle of the bloody ocean,' Luc drawled. 'Dinner going to cook itself is it, Potts? My guest fancies broth. Can you manage that? And, Patch, bring me a bucket of cold water and a bucket of warm, as soon as you can get some heated. I don't want her to taste of salt.'

He did not bother to wait for a response, nor did he look back as he walked down to the little hospital building, although his spine crawled. At the moment they thought their best interests were served by obeying him and they were frightened enough of him not to push it, not after what had happened to Nye. That could change if the arrival of the woman proved to be the catalyst that tipped the fragile balance.

He needed them to believe her conscious and his property, not vulnerable and meaning nothing to him. He didn't want to have to kill any more of them, gallows'-bait though they were: he needed twelve to carry out this mission and they were good seamen, even if they were scum.

Chapter Two

The light was coming from an odd angle. Averil blinked and rubbed her eyes and came fully awake with a jolt. She was not in her cabin on the *Bengal Queen,* but in some hut. She had seen it before—or had that been part of the nightmare, the one that never seemed to stop but just kept ebbing and flowing through her head? Sometimes it had become a pleasant dream of being held, of something soft and wet on her aching, stiff limbs, of strong hands holding her, of hot, savoury broth or cool water slipping between her lips.

Then the nightmare had come back again: the wave, the huge wave, that turned into a leering hulk of a man; of being stared at by a dozen pairs of hungry eyes. Sometimes it became a dream of embarrassment, of needing to relieve herself and someone helping her, of being lifted and placed on an uncomfortable bucket and wanting to cry, but not being able to wake up.

She lay quite still like a fawn in its nest of bracken, only her eyes daring to move and explore this strange place. Under the covers her hands strayed, and found coarse sheeting above and below, the prickle of a straw-filled mattress, then the finer touch of the linen garment that she was wearing.

There was no one else there. The room felt empty to her straining senses, she could hear nothing but the sea beyond the walls. Averil sat up with an involuntary whimper of pain. Everything hurt. Her muscles ached, there were sore patches on her legs, her back. When she got her arms above the covers and pushed back the flopping sleeves to look at them they were a mass of bruises and scratches and grazes.

She was wearing a man's shirt. Memory began to come back, like pages torn at random from a picture book or sounds heard through a half-open door. A man's voice had told her to drink, to eat. A man's big hands had touched her body, held her, shifted her. Washed her, helped her to that bucket.

What else had he done? How long had she been unconscious and defenceless? Would she know if he had used her body as she lay there? She ached so much, would one more pain be felt?

Averil looked around and saw male clothing everywhere. A pair of boots stood by the window, a heap of creased linen spilled from a corner, a heavy coat hung from a nail. This was his space and he filled it, even in his absence. She twisted and looked at the pillow and saw a dark hair curling on it. This was his bed. She drew a deep, shuddering breath. For how long had he kept her here?

Water. A drink would make it easier to think. Then find a weapon. It was a plan of sorts, and even that made her feel a little stronger. She fumbled with fingers that were clumsy and stiff and threw back the covers. His shirt came part way down her thighs, but she was sitting on a creased sheet. Averil got to her feet, wrapped it around her waist, then staggered to the table. She made it as far as the chair before she collapsed on to it.

There was a jug beside a plate and a beaker on the table and she dragged it towards her with both hands. She spilled more than she poured, but it was clear and fresh and helped a little. Averil drank two beakers, then leaned her elbows on the table and dropped her head into her hands.

Think. It wasn't only him, there were those other men. They had been reality, not a nightmare. Had he let them in here, too? Had he let them…? No, there was only the memory of the dark-haired man they had called *Cap'n*. *Think*. The rough wooden planks held no inspiration, but the knife next to the plate did. She picked it up, hefted it in her hand. He'd be coming back, and she might only have that one chance to kill him when he was off guard. When he was in bed. Kill? Could she? Yes, if it was that or… Her eyes swivelled to the bed. Under the pillow. She had to get back there. Somehow.

Her legs kept betraying her as she tottered to the bed, but she made it, just in time as the door opened.

He swept the hut with a look that seemed to take in everything. Averil clenched her hand around the knife under cover of the sheet, but it had been on the far side of the plate, out of sight from this angle. Surely he wouldn't notice?

'You are awake.' He came right in, frowning, and looked at her as she sat on the edge of the bed. 'You found the water?'

'Yes.' *Come closer, turn those broad shoulders of yours, I'll do it now, I only need a second.* Where do you stab someone who is bigger and stronger than you? How do you stop them shouting, turning on you? High, that was it, on the left side above the heart. Strike downwards with both hands—

'Where is the knife?' He swivelled to look at her, a cold appraisal like a man sighting down the barrel of a weapon.

'Knife?'

'The one you are planning to cut my throat with. The one that was on the table.'

'I was not planning to cut your throat.' She threw it on the floor. Better that than have him search her for it. 'I was going to stab you in the back.'

He picked it up and went to drop it back beside the plate. 'It is like being threatened by a half-drowned kitten,' he drawled. 'I was beginning to think you would never wake up.' Averil stared at him. Her face, she hoped, was expressionless. This was the man who had slept with her, washed her, fed her, probably ravished her. Before the wreck she would have watched him from under her lids, attracted by the strength of his face, the way he moved, the tough male elegance of him. Now that masculinity made her heart race for all the wrong reasons: fear, anxiety, confusion.

'How long have I been here?' she demanded. 'A day? A night?'

'This is the fourth day since we found you.'

'Four days?' Three nights. Her guts twisted painfully. 'Who looked after me? I remember being washed and—' her face flamed '—a bucket. And soup.'

'I did.'

'You slept in this bed? Don't deny it!'

'I have no intention of denying it. That is my bed. Ah, I see. You think I would ravish an unconscious woman.' It was not a soft face, even when he was not frowning; now he looked as hard as granite and about as abrasive.

'What am I expected to think?' she demanded. Did he expect her to apologise?

'Are you a nun that you would prefer that I left you, helpless and unconscious, to live or die untouched by contaminating male hands?'

'No.'

'Do I look like a man who needs to use an unconscious woman?'

That had touched his pride, she realised. Most men were arrogant about their sexual prowess and she had just insulted his. She was at his mercy, it was best to be a little conciliatory.

'No. I was alarmed. And confused. I… Thank you for looking after me.' Embarrassed, she fiddled with her hair and her fingers snagged in tangles. 'Ow!'

'I washed it, after a fashion, but I couldn't get the knots out.' He rummaged on a shelf and tossed a comb on to the bed by her hand. 'You can try, just don't cry if you can't get the tangles out.'

'I don't cry.' She was on the edge of it though; the tears had almost come. But she was not in the habit of crying: what need had she had for tears before? And she was not going to weep in front of him. It was the one small humiliation she could prevent.

'No, you don't cry, do you?' Was that approval? He put his hand on the latch. 'I'll lock this, so don't waste your effort trying to get out.'

'What is your name?' His anonymity was a weapon he held against her, another brick in the wall of ignorance and powerlessness that was trapping her here, in his control.

For the first time she saw him hesitate. 'Luke.'

'The men called you *Captain*.'

'I was.' He smiled. It was not until she felt the stone wall press against her shoulders that Averil realised she had recoiled from the look in his eyes. *Don't ask any more,* her instincts screamed at her. 'And you?'

'Averil Heydon.' As soon as she said her surname she wished it back. Her father was a wealthy man, he would pay any ransom for her, and now they could find out who her family was. 'Why are you keeping me a prisoner?'

But Luke said nothing more and the key turned in the lock the moment the door was shut.

At about two in the afternoon Luc opened the door with a degree of caution. His half-drowned mermaid had more guts than he'd expected from a woman who had been through what she had, let alone the well-bred lady she obviously was from her accent. She must be desperate now. The table knife was in his pocket, but he'd left his razor on the high shelf, which was careless.

She was embarrassed as well as frightened, but she would feel better after a proper meal. He needed her rational and she was, most certainly, sharing his bed tonight. 'Dinner time,' he announced and brought in the platters and the pot of stew.

Averil turned from the stool by the window where she had sat for the long hours since he had left her, thinking about this man,

Luke, whose bed she had been sharing. The one who sounded like a gentleman and who was as bad as the rest of that crew on the beach. What was he? Pirate, smuggler, freebooter? The men were scum—their leader would be no better, only more powerful. She had dreamed about him, and in her dream he had held her and protected her. Fantasy was cruelly deceptive.

'Here,' he said as he dumped things on the table. 'Dinner. Potts is a surprisingly good cook.'

The smell reached her then and her empty stomach knotted. It was stew of some kind and the aroma was savoury and delicious. Luke had put the platter on the table so she would have to go over there to reach it, dressed only in his shirt and the trailing sheet. He was tormenting her, or perhaps training her as one did an animal. Perhaps both.

'I want to eat it here, not with you.'

'And I want you to use your limbs or you'll be as stiff as a board.' He leaned one shoulder against the wall by the hearth. 'Are you warm enough? I can light a fire.'

'How considerate, but I will not put you to the trouble.' The worn skim of sacking over the window let in enough light to see him clearly and she stared, with no attempt at concealment. If he had any conscience at all he would find her scrutiny uncomfortable, but he merely lifted one brow in acknowledgement and stared back.

He was tall, with hair so dark a brown as to seem almost black. He was tanned, and by the shade she guessed he was naturally more olive-skinned than fair. She had seen so many Europeans arrive in India and burn in the sun that she knew exactly how every shade of complexion would turn. His eyes were dark grey, and his brows were dark, too, tilted a little in a way that gave his face a sardonic look.

His nose was large, narrow-bridged and arrogant; it would have been too big if it had not been balanced by a determined jaw. No, it *was* too big, despite that. He was not handsome, she told herself.

If she had liked him, she would have thought his face strong, even interesting perhaps. He looked intelligent. As it was, he was just a dark, brooding man she could not ignore. Her eyes slid lower. He was lean, narrow-hipped…

'Well?' he enquired. 'Am I more interesting than your dinner, which is getting cold?'

'Not at all. You are, however, in the way of me eating it.' She was not used to snubbing people or being cold or capricious. Miss Heydon, they said, was open and warm and charming. Sweet. She no longer felt sweet—perhaps she never would again. She tipped up her chin and regarded him down her nose.

'My dear girl, if you are shy of showing your legs, allow me to remind you that I have seen your entire delightful body.' He sounded as though he was recalling every detail as he spoke, but was not much impressed by what he had recalled.

'Then you do not have to view any of it again,' Averil snapped. Where the courage to stand up to him and answer back was coming from, she had no idea. She was only too well aware that she was regarded as a biddable, modest Nice Young Lady who did not say *boo* to geese, let alone bandy words with some pirate or whatever Luke was. But her back was literally against the wall and there was no one to rescue her because no one knew she was alive. It was up to her and that was curiously strengthening, despite the fear.

He shrugged and pulled out the chair. 'I want to see you eat. Get over here—or do you want me to carry you?'

She had the unpleasant suspicion that if she refused he really would simply pick her up and dump her on the seat. Averil fumbled for the sheet and stood up with it as a trailing skirt around her. She gave it an instinctive twitch and the memory that action brought back surprised a gasp of laughter out of her, despite the aches and pains that walking produced and the situation she found herself in.

'What is amusing?' Luke enquired as she sat down opposite him. 'I trust you are not about to have hysterics.'

It might be worth it to see how he reacted, but he would probably simply slap her or throw cold water in her face—the man had no sensibility. 'I have been practising managing the train on a court presentation gown,' she explained, as she reached for the fork and imagined plunging it into his hard heart. 'This seems an unlikely place to put that into practice.'

The stew consisted of large lumps of meat, roughly hewn vegetables and a gravy that owed a great deal to alcohol. She demolished it and mopped up the gravy with a hunk of bread, beyond good manners. Luke pushed a tumbler towards her. 'Water. There's a good clean well.'

'How are you so well provisioned?' she asked and tore another piece off the loaf. 'There are how many of you? Ten? And you aren't here legitimately, are you?'

'*I* am,' Luke said. He returned to his position by the hearth. 'Mr Dornay—so far as the Governor is concerned—is a poet in search of solitude and inspiration for an epic work. I told him that I am nervous of being isolated from the inhabited islands by storms or fog, so I keep my stock of provisions high, even if that means stockpiling far more than one man could possibly need. And there are thirteen of us and we are most certainly here in secret.'

She stowed away the surname. When it came to a court of law, when she testified against the men who had imprisoned and assaulted her, she would remember every name, every face. If he left her alive. She swallowed the fear until it lay like a cold stone in her stomach. 'A poet? *You?*' He smiled, that cold, unamused smile, but did not answer. 'When are you going to let me go?'

'When we are done here.' Luke pushed himself upright and went to the door. 'I will leave you before the men eat all of my dinner. I'll see you at supper time.'

His hand was on the latch when Averil realised she couldn't deal with the uncertainty any longer. 'Are you going to kill me?'

Luke turned. 'If I wanted you dead all I had to do was throw you back or leave you here to die. I don't kill women.'

'You rape them, though. You are going to make me share your bed tonight, aren't you?' she flung back and then quailed at the anger that showed in every taut line of his face, his clenched fist as it rested on the door jamb. *He is going to hit me.*

'You have shared my bed for three nights. Rest,' he said, his even tone at variance with his expression. 'And stop panicking.' The door slammed behind him.

Luc stalked back to the fire. He wouldn't be on this damn island with this crew of criminal rabble in the first place if it was not for the attempted rape of a woman. Averil Heydon was frightened and that showed sense: she'd had every reason to be terrified until he took her away from the men. He could admire the fierce way she had stood up to him, but it only made her more of a damn nuisance and a dangerous liability. Thank God he no longer had to nurse her; intimacy with her body was disturbing and he had felt himself becoming interested in her more than was safe or comfortable. Now she was no longer sick and needing him, that weakness would vanish. He did not want to care for anyone ever again.

The crew looked up with wary interest from their food as he approached. Luc dropped down on to the flat rock they had accepted as the captain's chair and took a platter from the cook's hand. 'Good stew, Potts. You all bored?' They looked it: bored and dangerous. On a ship he would exercise them too hard for them to even think about getting into trouble: gun drill, small arms drill, repairs, sail drill—anything to tire them out. Here they could do nothing that would make a noise and nothing that could be seen from the south or east.

Luc lifted his face to the breeze. 'Still blowing from the nor'west.

That was a rich East Indiaman by all accounts—it'll be worth beach-combing.' They watched him sideways, shifting uneasily at the amiable tone of voice, like dogs who expect a kick and get their ears scratched instead. 'And you get to keep anything you find, so long as you don't fight over it and you bring me any mermaids.'

Greed and a joke—simple tools, but they worked. The mood lifted and the men began to brag of past finds and speculate on what could be washed up.

'Ferret, have you got any spare trousers?'

Ferris—known to all as Ferret from his remarkable resemblance to the animal—hoisted his skinny frame up from the horizontal. 'I 'ave, Cap'n. Me Sunday best, they are. Brought 'em along in case we went to church.'

'Where you would steal the communion plate, no doubt. Are they clean?'

'They are,' he said, affronted, his nose twitching. And it might be the truth—there was a rumour that Ferret had been known to take a bath on occasion.

'Then you'll lend them to Miss Heydon.'

That provoked a chorus of whistles and guffaws. 'Miss Heydon, eh! Cor, a mermaid with a name!'

'Wot she want trousers for, Cap'n?' Ferret demanded. 'Don't need trousers in bed.'

'When I don't want her in bed she can get up and make herself useful. She's had enough time lying about getting over her ducking,' Luc said. He had not given the men any reason to suppose Averil was unconscious and vulnerable. They had believed he was spending time in her bed, not that he was nursing her. His frequent absences seemed to have increased their admiration for him—or for his stamina. 'I'll have that leather waistcoat of yours while you're at it.'

Ferret got to his feet and scurried off to the motley collection of canvas shelters under the lea of the hill that filled the centre of the island. St Helen's was less than three-quarters of a mile across at its widest and rough stone structures littered the north-western slopes. Luc supposed they must have been the habitations of some ancient peoples, but he was no antiquarian. Now he was just glad of the shelter they gave to the men on the only flank of St Helen's that could not be overlooked from Tresco or St Martin's.

Stew finished, Luc got to his feet, took a small telescope from the pocket of his coat and turned to climb the hill. It took little effort, and he reckoned it was only about a hundred and thirty feet above the sea, but from here he commanded a wide panorama of the waters around the Scillies as well as being able to watch the men without them being aware of it. Beachcombing would keep them busy, but he did not want a knifing over some disputed treasure.

He put his notebook on a flat rock and set himself to log the patterns of movement between the islands, particularly the location of the brigs and the pilot gigs, the thirty-two-foot rowing boats that cut through the water at a speed that left the navy jolly-boat crews gasping. The calculations kept his mind off the woman in the hut below.

With six men on the oars the pilot gigs were said to venture as far afield as Roscoff smuggling, although the Revenue cutters did their best to stop them. They got their name from their legitimate purpose, to row out to incoming ships and drop off the pilots who were essential in this nightmare of rocks and reefs.

The gig he'd been given for this mission lay on the beach below, waiting for the word to launch with six men on the oars and the other seven of them crammed into the remaining space as best they could. Beside it was his own small skiff that he used to give verisimilitude to the story of his lone existence here.

For the men hunting amongst the rocks below him what happened next would bring either death or a pardon for their crimes. For him, if he survived and succeeded in carrying out his orders, it might restore the honour he had lost in following his conscience.

Luc shied a pebble down the slope, sending a stonechat fluttering away with a furious alarm call.

Scolding loudly, the little bird resumed its perch on top of a gorse bush. 'Easy for you to say, *mon cher,*' Luc told it, as he narrowed his eyes against the sunlight on the waves. 'All you have to worry about is the kestrel and his claws.' Life and death—that was easy. Right and wrong, honour and expediency—now those were harder choices.

Chapter Three

Averil sat by the window with the old sack hooked back and studied what she could see through the thick, salt-stained glass. Sloping grass, a band of large pebbles that would be impossible to run on—or even cross quietly—then a fringe of sand that was disappearing under the rising tide.

Beyond, out in the sheltered sound, ships bobbed at anchor. Navy ships. Rescue, if only they were not too far away to hail. She could light a fire—but they knew Luke was here, so they would see nothing out of the ordinary in that. Set fire to the hut? But it was a sturdy stone building, so that wouldn't work. Signal from the window with a sheet? But first she would have to break the thick glass, then think of something that would attract their attention without alerting her captors.

With a sigh she went back to searching the room. Luke had left his razor on a high shelf, but after the episode with the knife she did not think he would give her a chance to use it and she was beginning to doubt whether she had it in her to kill a man. That was her conscience, she told herself, distracted for a moment by wondering why. It was nothing to do with the fact that she kept wondering if he could really be as bad as he appeared.

Intense grey eyes mean nothing, you fool, she chided herself. When darkness came he would come back here and then he would ravish her. His protestations about not taking an unconscious woman surely meant nothing, not now she was awake.

Averil thought about the 'little talk' her aunt had had with her just before she sailed for England and an arranged marriage. There would be no female relative there to explain things to her before her marriage to the man she had never met, so the process had been outlined in all its embarrassing improbability, leaving her far too much time, in her opinion, to think about it on the three-month voyage.

Her friend Lady Perdita Brooke, who had been sent to India in disgrace after an unwise elopement, had intimated that it was rather a pleasurable experience with the right man. Dita had not considered what it would be like being forced by some ruffian in a stone hut on an island, surrounded by a pack of even worse villains. But then, Dita would have had no qualms about using that knife.

The light began to fail. Soon he would be here and she had no plan. To fight, or not to fight? He could overpower her easily, she realised that. She knew a few simple tricks to repel importunate males, thanks to her brothers, but none of them would be much use in a situation like this where there was no one to hear her screams and nowhere to run to.

If she fought him, he would probably hurt her even more badly than she feared. Best to simply lie there like a corpse, to treat him with disdain and show no fear, only that she despised him.

That was more easily resolved than done she found when the door opened again and Luke came in followed by two of the men. One carried what looked like a bundle of clothes, the other balanced platters and had a bottle stuck under his arm.

Averil turned her head away, chin up, so that she did not have to look at them and read the avid imaginings in their eyes. She was not the only one thinking about what would happen here tonight.

'Come and eat.' Luke pushed the key into his pocket and moved away from the door when they had gone. 'I have found clothes for you. They will be too large, but they are clean.' He watched her as she trailed her sheet skirts to the chair. 'I'll light the fire, you are shivering.'

'I am not cold.' She was, but she did not want to turn this into a travesty of cosy domesticity, with a fire crackling in the grate, candles set around and food and wine.

'Of course you are. Don't try to lie to me. You are cold and frightened.' He stated it as a fact, not with any sympathy or compassion in his voice that she could detect. Perhaps he knew that kind words might make her cry and that this brisk practicality would brace her. He lit a candle, then knelt and built the fire with a practised economy of movement.

Who is he? His accent was impeccable, his hands, although scarred and calloused, were clean with carefully trimmed nails. Half an hour with a barber, then put him in evening clothes and he could stroll into any society gathering without attracting a glance.

No, that was not true. He would attract the glances of any woman there. It made her angrier with him, the fact that she found him physically attractive even as he repelled her for what he was, what he intended to do. How could she? It was humiliating and baffling. She had not even the excuse of being dazzled by a classically handsome face or charm or skilful flirtation. What she felt was a very basic feminine desire. Lust, she told herself, was a sin.

'Eat.' The fire blazed up, shadows flickered in the corners and the room became instantly warmer, more intimate, just as she had feared. Luke poured wine and pushed the beaker towards her. 'And drink. It will make things easier.'

'For whom?' Averil enquired and the corner of his mouth moved in what might have been a half smile. But she drank and felt the insidious warmth relax her. Weaken her, just as he intended, she was sure. 'Who are you? What are you doing here?'

'Writing bad poetry, beachcombing.' He shrugged and cut a hunk of cheese.

'Don't play with me,' she snapped. 'Are you wreckers? Smugglers?'

'Neither.' He spared the cheese a disapproving frown, but ate it anyway.

'You were Navy once, weren't you?' she asked, on sudden impulse. 'Are you deserters?'

'We were Navy,' he agreed and cut her a slice of bread as though they were discussing the weather. 'And if we were to return now I dare say most of us would hang.'

Averil made herself eat while she digested that. They must be deserters, then. It took a lot of thinking about and she drank a full beaker of wine before she realised it had gone. Perhaps it would help with what was to come… She pushed the thought into a dark cupboard in the back of her mind and tried to eat. She needed her strength to endure, if not to fight.

Luke meanwhile ate solidly, like a man without a care in the world. 'Are you running to the French?' she asked when the cheese and the cold boiled bacon were all gone.

'The French would kill us as readily as the British,' he said, with a thin smile for a joke she did not understand.

The meal was finished at last. Luke pushed back his chair and sat, long legs out in front of him, as relaxed as a big cat. Averil contemplated the table with its empty platters, bread crumbs and the heel of the loaf. 'Do you expect me to act as your housemaid as well as your whore?' she asked.

The response was immediate, lightning-swift. The man who had seemed so relaxed was on his feet and brought her with him with one hand tight around her wrist. Luke held her there so they stood toe to toe, breast to breast. His eyes were iron-dark and intense on her face; there was no ice there now and she shivered at the anger in them.

'Listen to me and think,' he said, his voice soft in chilling contrast to the violence of his reaction. 'Those men out there are a wolf pack, with as much conscience and mercy as wolves. I lead them, not because they are sworn to me or like me, not because we share a cause we believe in, but because, just now, they fear me more than they fear the alternatives.

'If I show them any weakness—anything at all—they will turn on me. And while I can fight, I cannot defeat twelve men. You are like a lighted match in a powder store. They want you—all of them do—and they have no scruples about sharing, so they'll operate as a gang. If they believe you are my woman and that I will kill for you, then that gives them pause—do they want you so much they will risk death? They know I would kill at least half of them before they got to you.'

He released her and Averil stumbled back against the table. Her nostrils were full of the scent of angry male and her heart was pattering out of rhythm with fear and a primitive reaction to his strength.

'They won't know if I am your woman or not,' she stammered.

'You really are a little innocent.' His smile was grim and she thought distractedly that although he seemed to smile readily enough she had never seen any true amusement on his face. 'What do they think we've been doing every time I come down here? And they will know when they see you, just as wolves would know. You will share my bed again tonight and you will come out of this place in the morning with my scent on your body, as yours has been on mine these past days. Or would you like to shorten things by walking out there now and getting us both killed?'

'I would prefer to live,' Averil said and closed her fingers tight on the edge of the table to hold herself up. 'And I have no doubt that you are the lesser of the two evils.' She was proud of the way she kept her chin up and that there was hardly a quiver in her voice. 'Doubtless a fate worse than death is an exaggeration. You intend to let me out of here tomorrow, then?'

'They need to get used to you being around. Locked up in here you are an interesting mystery, out there, dressed like a boy, working, you will be less of a provocation.'

'Why not simply let me go? Why not signal a boat and say you have found me on the beach?'

'Because you have seen the men. You know too much,' he said and reached for the open clasp knife that lay on the table. Averil watched as the heavy blade clicked back into place.

'I could promise not to tell anyone,' she ventured.

'Yes?' Again that cold smile. 'You would connive at whatever you suspect we are about for the sake of your own safety?'

'I…' No, she could not and she knew it showed on her face.

'No, I thought not.' Luke pocketed the knife and turned from the table. 'I will be back in half an hour—be in bed.'

Averil stacked the plates, swept the crumbs up, wrapped the heel of the loaf in a cloth and stoppered the wine flask. She supposed it would be a gesture if she refused to clean and tidy, but it gave her something to do; if she was going to be a prisoner here, she would not live in a slum.

It was cool now. That was why she was shivering, of course, she told herself as she swept the hearth with the crude brush made of twigs and added driftwood to the embers. The salty wood flared up, blue and gold, as she fiddled with the sacking over the window. What was going to happen was going to be private, at least. She wiped away one tear with the back of her hand.

I am a Heydon. I will not show fear, I will not beg and plead and weep, she vowed as she turned to face the crude bed. Nor would she be tumbled in a rats' nest. Averil shook out the blankets, batted at the lumpy mattress until it lay smooth, spread the sheet that had been tied around her waist and plumped up the pillow as best she could.

She stood there in Luke's shirt, her hair loose around her shoulders, and looked at the bed for a long moment. Then she threw back the blanket and climbed in, lay down, pulled it back over her and waited.

* * *

Luke spent some time by the shielded camp fire listening to the game of dice in one tent, the snores from another, and adding the odd comment to the discussion Harris and Ferret were having about the best wine shops in Lisbon. Some of the tension had ebbed out of the men with their efforts all day hunting along the shoreline for wreckage from the ship. Nothing of any great value had been found, but a small cask of spirits had contained just enough to mellow their mood.

He was putting off going back down to the little hospital, he was aware of that, just as he was aware of trying not to think too closely about Averil. He wanted her to stay an abstraction, a problem to be dealt with, not become a person. None of them wanted to be there, most of them were probably going to die; he had no emotion to spare to feel pity for some chit of a girl who, with any luck, was going to come out of this alive, although rather less innocent than she had begun.

'Good night,' he said without preamble and strode off towards the hut. Ferret and Harris were on guard for the first two hours; they were reliable enough and had no need of him reminding them what they were looking out for or what to do under every possible circumstance. There was a lewd chuckle behind him, but he chose to ignore it; he could hardly control their thoughts.

The hut was tidy when he unlocked the door and stepped inside. There was a lamp still alight and the fire had been made up; Luc inhaled the tang of wood smoke and thought the place was as nearly cosy as it would ever be. But one look at the bed dispelled any thought that Averil had decided to welcome him and had set out to create an appropriate ambiance. She was lying under the blanket as stiff and straight as a corpse, her toes making a hillock at one end, her nose just visible above the edge of the covering at the other. He did not look at the swells and dips in between.

'Averil?' He moved soft-footed to the middle of the room and sat down to pull off his shoes.

'I am awake.' Her voice was as rigid as her body and he saw the reflected light glint on her eyes as she turned her head to watch him.

Luc dropped his coat and shirt over the back of the chair. As his hands went to the buckle of his belt he heard her draw a deep, shuddering breath. Well, he wasn't going to undress in the dark; she was going to have to get used to him—or close her eyes.

'Have you never seen a naked man before?' he asked, slipping the leather from the clasp.

'No. I mean, yes.' Averil found it was difficult to articulate. She cleared her throat and tried again. 'I was brought up in India—*saddhus* and other holy men often go naked.' And there were carvings in the temples, although she had always assumed they were wildly exaggerated. 'They smear themselves with ash,' she added. Now she had started talking it was hard to stop.

Luke said nothing, simply turned towards the chair, stepped out of his trousers and draped them over the back with his other clothes. Averil shut her mouth with a snap, but her eyes would not close. This was not an ash-smeared emaciated holy man sitting under a peepul tree with his begging bowl, watching the world with wild, dark eyes. Luke was… She searched for a word and came up with *impressive,* which seemed inadequate for golden skin and long muscles and broad shoulders tapering into a strong back, down to narrow hips and—

He turned round and her mouth dropped open again, although all that came out was a strangled gasp. 'You see what effect you have on me,' he said, coming towards the bed with, apparently, no shame whatsoever.

'Well, stop it,' she snapped, then realised immediately how ridiculous it was. Obviously *that* was necessary for the humiliating and painful business that was about to occur. 'Stop flaunting it,' she amended in the tone of voice her aunt used for rebuking the servants.

Luke gave a snort of laughter, the first genuine amusement she had heard from him. 'That part of the male body does what it wants. You could close your eyes,' he suggested.

'Is that supposed to make me feel any better? It will still be there.'

He shrugged, which produced interesting undulations in those beautiful muscles and made *that* bob in a most disconcerting way. She could well believe that it had a life of its own. She wanted to look away, but her neck seemed paralysed, as rigid as the rest of her.

Luke reached out and turned back the blanket. Averil forced herself not to grab it back. *Don't struggle, don't react. Don't give him the satisfaction.*

'Could you move over?'

'Wh…what?' She had been expecting something quite different, not this polite enquiry. He just had to get on top of her, didn't he?

'Shift across.' Luke stopped, one knee on the bed. Averil found she could move her eyes after all; she fixed them on the cobwebbed rafters. 'You aren't expecting me to leap on you, are you?' He sounded impatient and irritated, not crazed with lust. Perhaps he did this sort of thing all the time.

'I have no idea what to expect,' she flashed back. The anger and humiliation freed her locked muscles and she twisted round to sit up and confront him. 'I am a virgin. How would I know how to go about being ravished?'

Chapter Four

He closed his eyes for a moment. 'I am going to sleep in this bed with you, that is all. Did you not realise? Did you still think I was going to force you, for heaven's sake?'

'Of course I did! I am not a mind reader!' Fury flashed through her, obliterating the relief. She had been so frightened all day, she had tried so hard to be brave and now…now he was implying that she ought to have realised? That it was her fault she had been so scared?

'Oh, you—you infuriating man!' She lashed out, her hand hitting him across the chest with a dull thud. His skin was warm, the dark curls of hair surprisingly springy.

'You *want* me to make love to you?' He caught her wrists as she tried to hit him again. His hands were hard and calloused against her pampered skin and this close she could smell him—fresh sweat over traces of some plain soap and what must be the natural scent of his skin.

'Make love? Is that what you call it? No, I don't want you to *make love* or ravish me or anything else. I've been terrified all day and *now* you tell me you never had any intention—' She ran out of words and sat there in the tangle of blankets glaring at him, holding on to her temper because if she did not the alternative was to give way to tears.

'I do not ravish women,' Luke said flatly and released her hands. 'Unconscious or awake.' She had insulted him, it appeared. Good. She had not thought it possible.

'Then what are you doing with that?' Averil made a wild gesture at his groin and he recoiled before her flailing hand made contact.

'I told you, it has a life of its own. I don't have to take any notice of it.' Luc sounded torn between exasperation and anger. 'I am sorry you were frightened unnecessarily,' he added, with as much contrition as if he was apologising for jostling her elbow at a party. 'I thought you realised I had no intention of hurting you in any way. If you can just move over so I can get in, we can go to sleep.'

'Just like that? You expect me to be able to close my eyes and sleep with you in the bed?' She heard the rising note of hysteria and bit her lower lip until the pain steadied her. The relief of realising he was not going to take her had cracked her self-control; now it was hard to hang on to some semblance of calm. 'Why can't you put some clothes on?'

'I have no spare clean shirts to wear—you are wearing the last one. And one more layer of linen between us will make no difference to anything.'

She wondered what the grinding noise was and then realised it was her own teeth. At least if Luke was in the bed with the covers over him she couldn't see his naked body. It was an effort not to flounce, but she turned on her side with her back to him and lay against the far edge of the bed, her face to the wall.

The ropes supporting the mattress creaked, the blankets flapped. 'There is no need to rub your nose against the stones like that,' Luke said. 'Come here.' He put an arm around her waist and pulled her backwards until she fitted tight against the curve of his body. 'Stop wriggling, for heaven's sake!'

'We are *touching*,' Averil said with what calm she could muster, which was not much. He was warm and hard and her buttocks were pressed against the part of his anatomy that he said had a mind of its own—and was still very interested by the situation by the feel of it—and one linen shirt was absolutely no barrier whatsoever. Below the edge of the shirt her thighs were bare and she could feel the hairs on his legs.

'I am certainly aware of your cold feet,' he said and she thought he was gritting his teeth. 'Will you stop moaning, woman? You're alive, aren't you? And warm and dry and fed and still a virgin. Now lie still, count your blessings and let me sleep and you might stay one.' She thought she heard a muttered *If I can* but she was not certain.

Woman? Moaning? *You lout,* she fulminated, as she tried to hold her body a rigid half-inch away from his. But that only pushed her buttocks closer into his groin. The heavy arm across her waist tightened and she gave up and let her muscles relax a little.

Count my blessings. It was a distraction from the heat and solidity behind her and the movement of his chest and the way his breath was warm on her neck. She was alive and so many people were not, she was certain. She had kept their faces and the sound of their voices out of her mind all day; now she could not manage it any longer. Her friends, so close after three months, and her numerous acquaintances, even the people she glimpsed every day but had never spoken to, were like the inhabitants of some small hamlet, swallowed up entire by the sea.

Averil composed herself and prayed for them, her lips moving with the unspoken words. She felt better for that, the grief and worry a little assuaged. The long body curled around hers had relaxed, too; he was sleeping, or at least, on the cusp of sleep. *I am alive, and he is protecting me. For now I am safe.* But the dark thoughts fluttered like bats against the defences she tried to erect in her mind. These men were deserters, traitors perhaps, and she knew too much about them already. What might she have to do to maintain even the precarious safety she had now?

* * *

Luc felt Averil's body go limp as she slid into sleep. He let himself relax against her as her breathing changed and allowed himself to enjoy the sensation of having a woman so close in his arms. The softness and the curves were a delicious torment; the female scent of her, not obscured by any soap or perfume, was dangerously arousing. It was over two months since he had lain with a woman, he realised, thinking back over the turbulent past weeks. And then they had been making love, not lying together like this, almost innocently.

The tight knot in his gut reminded him that he was still angry that Averil had supposed he would take her by force. Luc thought back over the words they had exchanged—they hardly qualified as conversations—and tried to work out why she had thought him capable of rape. He had never once said he would make use of her body, he was certain of that, and he had explained why he needed to share her bed.

She had been tired and frightened by all she had gone through; obviously she had not been thinking clearly, he told himself. He supposed stripping off had not been tactful—but she could have shut her eyes, Luc thought with a stirring of resentment. If she wanted him to wear a nightshirt, then she could do some washing tomorrow; he had too much else to think about without worrying about Averil's affronted sensibilities.

It did occur to him as he began to drift off to sleep that he was not used to being with well-bred young women on an intimate level. He had been at sea, more or less permanently, since he had been eighteen; he had no sisters at home, no young sisters-in-law. No one, thank heaven, to have to care about. Not any more.

But this wasn't some society drawing room or Almack's. To hell with it, she was in his territory now and she would just have to listen to what he said and follow orders. His aching groin reminded him that something else was refusing to follow orders. It would be interesting to seduce her, he thought, toying with the fantasy as he let sleep take him. Just how difficult would it be?

Averil woke with an absolute awareness of where she was and who she was with. In the night she had turned over and now she half lay on Luke's chest with her naked legs entangled with his. One moment she had been relaxed in deep sleep, the next her eyes snapped open on a view of naked skin, a tangle of dark curls and an uncompromising chin furred with stubble. He smelled warmly of sweat and salt and sleep. She should have recoiled in disgust, but she had the urge to snuggle closer, let her hands explore.

Every one of her muscles tensed to fight the desire.

'You're awake,' he said, his voice a deep rumble under her ear, and moved, rolling her on to her back so his weight was half over her. 'Good morning.'

'Get off me!' Averil shoved, which had no effect whatsoever. 'You said you don't ravish women, you lying swine.'

'I don't. But I do kiss them.' He was too close to focus on properly, too close to hit, but ears were easy to get hold of and sensitive to pain. She reached up a hand, got a firm grip and twisted. 'Yow!' Luke had her wrist in his grasp in seconds. 'You little cat.'

'At least I am not a liar.' She lay flat on her back, her hands trapped above her head, her senses full of the smell and feel of him, her heart pounding. She had hurt him, but he had not retaliated and there was amusement, not lust or anger, in his eyes, as though he was inviting her to share in a game.

But she was not going to play—that was outrageous. Luke was too big even to buck against, although she tried. And then stopped as her pelvis met his and that rebellious part of his body twitched eagerly against her belly. Something within her stirred in response, a low, intimate tingling. She blushed. Her body wanted to join in with whatever wickedness his was proposing.

'Since when has kissing amounted to ravishment? I need us to go

out there looking as though we have just been making love.' There
was exasperation under the patience and somehow that was reas-
suring. If he was bent on ravishing her he would not be discussing
it. Still, it was wrong to simply succumb so easily.

'Making love?' She snorted at the word and he narrowed his
eyes at her.

'Do you prefer *having sex?* It will make life easier for both of us
if you can give the impression that you have been seduced by my
superior technique and are now happy to be with me.'

Averil was about to tell him what her opinion of his technique
was when his words the previous evening came back to her. *A pack
of wolves.* 'I see,' she conceded. 'I am safer if I do not seem like
a victim. If I am happy to be with you, then it is convincing that
I would be confident. And they will think I am unlikely to try to
escape and put you all in danger.'

'Exactly.' Luke breathed out like a man who had been braced for
a long argument. 'Now—' He bent his head.

This was not how it was supposed to be, the first time. This was
the antithesis of romance. *And I wanted romance, tenderness...*

'You don't have to kiss me. I can pretend,' Averil said as she
tried to move her head away. She only succeeded in clashing noses.
Luke had a lot of nose to clash with. But she did not want to pretend. She realised that it was herself and her own desires that were
the danger, not him.

'You *are* an innocent, aren't you?' That was not a compliment.
'Never been thoroughly kissed?'

'Certainly not!' She had never been kissed at all, but she was not
going to tell him that.

'You'll see,' Luke said, releasing her wrists and capturing her
mouth.

It was outrageous! He opened his mouth over hers, pushed his
tongue inside and...and... Averil gave up trying to think about
what was going on so she could fight him. But she did not seem to

have any strength; her muscles wouldn't obey her and the rest of her body was in outright mutiny.

Her arms were round his neck, her fingers were raking through his hair, her breasts were pushing against his chest—which had to be why they ached so—and her lips...

Her lips moved against Luke's, answering his caress, and it was, some stunned part of her mind that was still working realised, a caress and not an assault. His mouth was firm and dominant, but that dominance was curiously arousing. The heat and the moistness were arousing too and the thrust of his tongue was so indecent... and yet she wanted to echo it, move her own tongue, although she did not dare.

Against her stomach she felt his flesh pulsing and lengthening and sensed the restraint he was imposing on himself. Her legs wanted to open, to cradle him, and her aunt's words came back and made sense now of what had seemed embarrassingly ludicrous before. He only had to move a little, to thrust... Suddenly she was frightened again and he sensed it.

'Averil?' They looked at each other, noses almost touching. 'Have you *ever* been kissed before?'

Mute, she shook her head.

'I thought not.' He threw back the covers and got out of bed, the sudden cool rush of air as effective in cutting through her sensual daze as his abrupt words had been. This time she had the sense to turn her head away from his nudity and to stare at the wall. After a few minutes he came back. 'Averil?'

'Yes?' She kept her head averted.

'Look.' She risked a quick look. He was holding out a small mirror. 'You see?'

A wanton creature stared back at her in the scrap of glass. Its hair was a wild tangle, its eyes were wide and dark and its mouth—*her* mouth—was swollen and pouting.

'Oh,' she breathed. 'Oh, my. Does it last?'

Luke had moved away and was lifting some things down off the shelf, but at that he turned his head and studied her. 'For a bit. Then I have to do it again.' She felt the crimson flood up from breast to forehead and his lips quirked. He looked thoughtful. He had, thank goodness, put on his clothes. 'I'll get you some hot water. When you come out don't forget that you have been conscious these past four days.'

Averil sat up as the door banged behind Luke. One kiss and she felt like this—and she didn't even like the man, or want him. He thought it was amusing, the wretch. It was not amusing, it was outrageous and shameful, those were the only possible words for it. Her breasts still tingled, her stomach felt very strange—almost as though she was apprehensive, but not quite the same—and lower down there was the most embarrassing awareness and that strange little pulse stirring. He had made her feel like this—and he must have realised—and then he had stopped.

The door opened, Luc dumped a bucket inside and then closed it again. Whatever his morning *toilette* consisted of, he was performing it elsewhere. Averil climbed out of the tangled bedding and went to fetch the hot water. *Then I have to do it again,* Luke had said.

'Oh, my heavens,' she murmured. 'I had no idea.'

Luc stood on the shore, pocket watch in hand, as half-a-dozen of the crew fitted the oars in the rowlocks and pulled away towards the bulk of Round Island to the north. There were no other ships or boats out in the area and it seemed a good opportunity to work the excess energy out of the men.

Behind him the others lounged on the short grass, jeering at the rowers. 'You reckon you'll do better?' Luc asked. 'You drew the short straw—you'll be rowing with breakfast in your bellies to weigh you down and they're pushing to get back to eat.'

'Wot about the mermaid—Miss Heydon, I mean, Cap'n? I'll take her breakfast down to her, shall I?' Harris's tone could have served as a definition of the verb *to leer.*

'I—' Luc broke off as a figure walked over the shoulder of the hill. 'No need, Harris, Miss Heydon has come to eat with us.'

He had to admire her. From the set of her shoulders and the frown between her brows she was as tense as any sensible woman would be under the circumstances, but her back was straight, her chin was up and she had scraped back her hair into a plait down her back in a way that must have been intended to diminish her attractiveness. The fact that it simply showed off her bruised cheekbones and her wide hazel eyes was not her fault, Luc pondered appreciatively as she got closer.

He saw with satisfaction and a sharp pang of arousal that her mouth was still lush and swollen from his kisses. He had never kissed a complete innocent before and it had been…interesting. He wanted her. Was he going to have her? It was a stimulating fantasy, that and the thought that by the time he took her she would want it just as much as he did.

'Good morning,' she said, her voice as coolly polite as if they were all in a drawing room. 'Is that breakfast? You are Mr Potts— the one who cooks?'

Potts gawped, displaying his few remaining teeth, then, to Luc's amazement, touched a finger to his forehead. Goodness knew how long it had been since someone had addressed him as *Mister,* if they ever had. 'Aye, er…ma'am, I am and 'tis that. Got mackerel or bacon, unless you fancy porridge, but it's wot you might call lumpy.'

'I would like bacon and some bread please, Mr Potts.' Averil sat down on the flat rock Luc usually took for himself. He wondered if anyone else noticed the automatic gesture to sweep her non-existent skirts out of the way. 'And is there tea?'

'Aye, ma'am. No milk, though.'

'Really? Never mind.' She turned and looked directly at Luc for the first time, as haughty as a duchess at a tea party. 'Couldn't you have stolen a goat?' She was overdoing the confidence and completely forgetting that she was supposed to have just passed a night of bliss in his arms.

'We did not plan on company,' he said with an inimical glance at the cook. Potts might well decide that a raid on the neighbouring islands to steal some livestock would be amusing. 'And we will not be drawing attention to ourselves by stirring up the islanders and lifting their goats either.'

Potts grunted; he knew a warning when he heard it. Luc studied Averil and was rewarded by the colour staining her cheeks. So, she was still agitated by that kiss; it was strangely satisfying to know that he had unsettled her like that—and it would be a pleasure to do so again. He was not used to virgins and Averil's untutored responsiveness was unexpected. It was doubtful whether she realised she had responded—it was all very new to her and she had been too shocked to think.

The other men had been down by the water's edge, catcalling at their rapidly vanishing comrades. Now they turned and began to walk back to the fire, their focus on the woman in the badly fitting clothes. He saw her eyes widen and darken as the haughty young lady vanished, leaving a girl who looked ready to run. His hand rested on the hilt of his knife as he watched the men's reaction. Would they react as he intended or would they turn as a pack and attack to get at the girl?

Chapter Five

Luc saw Averil's eyes dart from one man to the other and the almost imperceptible relaxation when she realised that Tubbs and Dawkins, the two who had found her, were not there. He had sent them off with the first crew so they would be too winded for an immediate reaction when they encountered Averil again. In their turn the men stared at her with interest, but the mood was different from when they had found her on the beach. He took his hand from his knife and shifted his weight off the balls of his feet.

Time to mark his territory. Luc took two platters from Potts and went to the rock where Averil sat, legs primly together, hands clasped in her lap. 'You're in my seat,' he said and got a cool stare in return. In the depth of her hazel eyes fear flickered, but she tipped up her chin and stared him out. *'We're lovers, remember,'* he mouthed and she blushed harder and shifted to make room for him next to her, hip to hip.

Luc handed her a plate and touched her cheek with the back of his free hand. 'Hungry, sweetheart?'

'Ravenous,' she admitted dulcetly, her eyes darting daggers at him. She folded the bread around the slices of bacon and bit into it. 'This is good, Mr Potts.'

'Thank you, ma'am,' the cook said, then spoiled it by adding slyly, 'nothing like a bit of exercise to give you an appetite, I always say.'

'Quite,' Averil retorted. 'That hut was in a shocking state—it took a lot of work to tidy it up.'

Thwarted, Potts returned to his frying pan, glowering at the grins of the other men. They were good-humoured smiles, Luc noticed, neither jeering nor directed at the young woman on the rock. 'Well done,' he murmured. She narrowed her eyes at him, so he added more loudly, 'I've a pile of washing needs doing.'

'I am sure you have, Luke darling,' Averil said, then softened her tone with an effort he could see. 'I will need hot water, please.'

'See to it after breakfast, Potts.'

'Is she doing all our washing, Cap'n?' Ferret asked through a mouthful of herring.

'*Miss Heydon* is not doing anything for you, Ferret.'

'Are you the man who lent me these clothes?' Averil asked as Potts handed her a mug of black tea.

'Aye, ma'm.'

'Is Ferret your real name? Surely not.' She took a sip of tea and gasped audibly at the strength of it.

'Er…it's Ferris, ma'am.'

'Thank you, Mr Ferris.'

The man grinned. 'Pleasure to help the Cap'n's lady, ma'am.'

The others said nothing, but Luc sensed, with the acute awareness of his men any captain learns to acquire, that something in their mood had changed. They had stopped thinking of Averil as a nameless creature for their careless pleasure and started regarding her, not just as his property, but as a person. She was frightened of them still, wisely so—they had not forgotten that she was a woman and they had been celibate for weeks. He could feel the apprehension coming off her like heat from a fire, but she had the intelligence and the guts to engage with them.

Miss Averil Heydon was a darned nuisance and enough to keep any man awake half the night with lustful thoughts and an aching groin, but he was beginning to admire the chit. Admiration did nothing to dampen desire, he discovered.

'They're coming,' Tom the Patch said, his one eye screwed up against the sun dazzle on the waves.

Luc pulled out his watch. 'They need to do better than that.'

'Nasty cross-current just there,' Sam Bull observed with the air of a man determined to be fair at all costs.

'These waters are one big cross-current,' Luc said. 'You reckon you can do better?'

'Yeah,' Bull said, and nodded his curly head. 'Easy.'

They are training for something, Averil thought, watching the men as she sipped the disgusting tea. Her teeth, if they had any enamel left, would be black, she was sure.

The men were a crew, a real ship's crew, not a motley group of fugitives. They weren't hiding here because they were deserters, or waiting for someone to come and take them off. It was incredible how much more she was noticing now her terror had abated a little. Instinct had told her to try to treat the men as individuals and, strangely, that had been easier to do over the shared food than it had been to pretend an intimacy with Luke that she did not feel.

Or, at least, she corrected herself as she felt the warmth of his thigh through the thickness of their trousers, she felt an intimacy, just not one involving any sort of affection or trust.

He was a good officer though, albeit a rogue commanding rogues. She had seen enough army officers in her time in India, and she had watched how the *Bengal Queen* was run; she could recognise authority when she saw it.

The men were focused on the approaching boat while Luke ate his bacon, his eyes on the pilot gig, too. 'Why are you here?' she asked, low voiced.

He shook his head without looking at her.

'Deserters have no need to train for speed,' she carried on, speculating. 'And why steal one of those big rowing boats, why not a sailing ship? A brig—you have enough men to crew a brig, haven't you?'

'You ask too many questions,' Luke said, his eyes still trained on the sea. 'That is dangerous, be quiet.'

A threat—or a warning? Averil put down her empty plate and mug and studied his profile. She could believe he was a man of violence, one who would kill if he had to and do it with trained efficiency, but she could not believe now that he would kill her. If he had been capable of that, he would have been capable of raping her last night.

'It is less dangerous to tell me the truth.'

'For whom?' he asked. But there was the slightest curve to the corner of his mouth and Averil relaxed a little. 'Perhaps later.'

The rowers were close now and she could see Tubbs at the tiller and Hawkins heaving on an oar. Some sound must have escaped her lips for Luke turned towards her. 'They won't hurt you—you are mine now.' He dipped his head and the shock of his mouth on hers, here, where the men could see them, froze her into immobility. It was a rapid, hard kiss on the lips, nothing more, but it felt startlingly possessive and so did the way his hand stayed on her shoulder when he stood to watch the men land, his pocket watch in the other palm. That big hand would curl into a formidable fist in her defence. She could feel the pressure of each finger and shivered—how would it feel if he caressed her?

'Not bad,' he called down to the rowers as they splashed through the shallow surf and up the beach. 'You could do better. The rest of you, get going. On my mark—now!'

There was a scramble as the others heaved themselves aboard and began to back-water away from the shore. The first crew, without a backward glance, made for the fire and the food Potts had left for them. Then they saw Averil on her rock and they slowed like a pack of dogs sighting a cat, their eyes narrowing.

Luke left his hand where it was for a moment longer, then strolled down to meet them. 'Close your mouth, Tubbs, or something will fly in,' he said mildly. The man muttered and a snigger went round the group as their eyes shifted between Luke and Averil.

She wanted to run. Instead she got to her feet, picked up Luke's plate and walked down to the fire. 'More bacon, darling?' Somehow she produced the purr that her friend Dita had managed to get into the most innocuous sentence when she wanted to flirt. Dita, who was probably drowned. Averil blinked back the prickle of tears: Dita would have both charmed and intimidated this rabble.

Close now, they gawped at her and Averil remembered what Luke had said about the wolf pack. These men eyed Luke as much as they ogled her, on the watch for his reaction, edgy as if they waited for him to snarl and lash out if they encroached on his property.

'Will the others beat your time, do you think?' she asked, direct to Tubbs.

He blinked, startled, as if the frying pan had addressed him. 'I reckon we're better by a length,' he said when Luke did not react.

'The boat looks very manoeuvrable. At least it seems so to me. I have been on an East Indiaman for three months, so any small boat looks fast.' She sat on the grass by Luke who had hunkered down, apparently intent on the gig. Without looking at her he put out his arm and tugged her closer and the men's eyes shifted uneasily. Now what? Instinct told her to keep talking to them, make them acknowledge her as a person, not a commodity, but she dared say nothing that would seem as if she was probing into their purpose here.

'Had a lot of treasure on it, did it?' Dawkins said.

'Not bullion, I'm sure. But there would have been silks, spices, gem stones, ivory, rare woods—those sorts of things.' There could be no harm in telling them; the cargo would have gone down or been ruined by the water.

'You come from India, then?' one of the men asked. Luke began to stroke the side of her neck languidly, as a man pulls the ears of his gun dog while they sit and wait for the ducks to rise to the guns.

Averil found she was leaning in to him, her lids were drooping... She made herself focus. 'Yes, India. I lived there almost all my life.'

'Ever see a tiger?'

'Lots of them. And elephants and huge snakes and crocodiles and monkeys.'

'Cor. I'd like to see those. Did you ride on the elephants?'

They asked questions, and she answered, for almost twenty minutes. She felt better, safer in their presence now. Almost safe enough to be alone with them, she thought and then caught Dawkins's eye and almost recoiled. What the big man was thinking about was plain to see and her whole body cringed against Luke.

His hand stilled. 'What?' he murmured.

'Nothing.'

He stood, pulling her to her feet. 'Just time to show you that washing I want doing. Timmins, bring a bucket of hot water and one of cold from the well.'

'I suppose you realise I have never washed a garment in my life, let alone a male one,' Averil said as they walked back to the old hospital.

'Men's clothing ought to be easier,' Luke said. 'No frills, no lace, stronger fabric.'

'Sweatier, dirtier, larger,' Averil retorted. She lifted one hand and touched her neck where he had been stroking it. The skin felt warm and soft, and her own touch sent a shiver of awareness through her that was disconcerting. She had not wanted him to stop, she realised, shamed by her reaction. What was the matter with her? Was she naturally a complete wanton, or was it shock, or perhaps simply instinct to try to please the man who could protect her?

'You are a belligerent little thing, aren't you?' Luke said as they stepped into the hut.

'You would be belligerent under the circumstances,' she snapped. 'And I am not little. I am more than medium height.'

'Hmm,' he said, and turned, trapping her between the wall and his body. 'No, not little at all.'

'Take your hands off my...my breasts.'

'But they are so delightful.' He was cupping them in his big hands, the slight movement of his thumbs perceptible through the linen of the shirt.

'Don't,' she pleaded, as much to her own treacherous body as to him.

'But you like it. Look.'

Shamed, she looked down. Her nipples thrust against the fabric, aching, tight little points, demanding attention.

'I cannot help that reaction, any more than you can help *that,* apparently.' The bulge straining against his breeches was very obvious. Luke moved back a little and she remembered another of her brothers' lessons. But his reactions were faster than hers. No sooner had she begun to raise her knee that she was flat against the stones, his weight pinning her.

'Little witch,' he said and bent his head.

The kiss was different standing up. Even though she was trapped Averil felt she had more control, or perhaps she was just more used to the sensations now. She found she no longer wanted to fight him, which was disconcerting. She moved her head to the side and licked into the corner of Luke's mouth, then nipped at his lower lip, almost, but not quite hard enough to draw blood. He growled and thrust his pelvis against her, blatantly making her feel what she was doing to him.

Averil let him take her mouth again, aching, wanting, despite the part of her mind that was screaming *Stop!* She was going to have to sleep with this man again tonight—was he going to be able to control himself after this?

'Damn it,' Luke said. He lifted his head and looked down at her, his eyes dark, his breath short. 'I think you've been sent to try my will-power to the limit—'

The door banged open behind them, and he turned away so abruptly that she almost fell. 'Over there by the table, Timmins.'

The man put down the buckets and walked out while Averil hung back in the shadows behind the door. He must have guessed what they had been doing, she thought, her face aflame.

'I can't do this any more,' she said the moment they were alone. 'I cannot. I don't understand how it makes me feel. I am *not* wanton, I am not a flirt. I don't even *like* you! You are big and ugly and violent and—'

'Ugly?' Luke stopped sorting through the heap of linen in the corner and raised an eyebrow. Nothing else she had said appeared to have made the slightest impression on him.

'Your nose is too big.'

'It balances my jaw. I inherited it from my father.' He tossed the tangle of clothing on to the table. 'There is some soap on the shelf.'

'Did you not hear a word I said just now?' Averil demanded, standing in his path, hands on hips.

'I heard,' Luke said as he dragged her back into his arms and kissed her with such ruthless efficiency that she tottered backwards and sat down on the bed with a thump when he released her. 'I just do not intend to take any notice of you losing your nerve.

'You'll get over it. Make sure the collars and cuffs are well scrubbed. You can dry them on the bushes on the far side of the rise. Just make certain you keep the hut between you and the line of sight from the sea.'

Averil stared at the unresponsive door as it closed behind him and wished she had listened and taken note when she had overheard the sailors swearing on board the *Bengal Queen*. It would be very satisfying to let rip with a stream of oaths, she was quite certain.

Castration, disembowelling and the application of hot tar to parts of a certain gentleman—if he deserved the name—would be even more satisfying. She visualised it for a moment. Then, seized with the need to do something physical, if throttling Luke was not an option, Averil shrugged out of the leather waistcoat, rolled up her sleeves and went to find the soap. It was just a pity there was no starch or she would make sure he couldn't sit down for a week, his drawers would be so rigid.

She began to sort the clothing, muttering vengefully as she did so. None of it was very dirty—the captain was obviously fastidious about his linen. It also smelled of him, which was disconcerting. Was it normal to feel so flustered by a man that even his shirts made one think of the body that had worn them?

Averil searched for marks, rubbed them with the soap, then dropped those garments in the hot water. How long did they have to soak? She wished she had paid more attention to the women doing their washing in the rivers in India; they seemed to get everything spotless even when the water was muddy. And it was cold, of course…

She was scrubbing briskly at the wristbands of one shirt before she caught herself. What was she doing, offering comfort to the enemy like this? Let him launder his own linen—or do whatever he would have done if she hadn't been conveniently washed up to do it for him. But then, she was clad in his shirt and he said he had no clean ones, so if she did not do it, goodness knew when she would get a change of linen herself.

Her fingers were as wrinkled as they had been when she had come out of the sea, and she had rubbed a sore spot on two knuckles, but the clothes were clean and rinsed at last. Wringing them dry was a task beyond her strength, she found, so she dumped the dirty water outside on the shingle, filled the buckets with the wet clothes and trudged up the slope towards the camp fire.

The buckets were heavy and she was panting by the time she

could put them down. 'Would someone who has clean hands help me to—?' Luke was nowhere in sight and she was facing eight men, with Dawkins in the middle.

'Aye, darlin', I can help you,' he drawled, getting to his feet.

'Leave it out, Harry.' Potts looked up from a half-skinned rabbit. 'She's the Cap'n's woman and we can do without you getting the man riled up. He's got a nasty temper when he's not happy and then he'll shoot you and *then* we'll have more work to do with one man less. Besides…' he winked at Averil who was measuring the distance to his cooking knives and trying not to panic '…the lady likes my cooking.' He lifted one knife, the long blade sharpened to a lethal degree, and examined it with studious care.

'Just joking, Potts.' Dawkins sat down again, his brown eyes sliding round to the knife. The cook stuck it into the turf close to his hand and went back to pulling the skin off the rabbit as the whole group relaxed. Averil began to breathe again.

'I'll wring 'em, ma'm.' A big man with an eyepatch got to his feet and shambled over. 'I'm Tom the Patch, ma'am, and me 'ands are clean.' He held up his great calloused paws for inspection like a child. 'Where do you want 'em?'

'I'll drape them over those bushes.' Averil let out the breath she had been holding and pointed halfway up the slope.

'Not there,' Potts said. 'They'll see you.'

'Who will?'

'Anyone in a ship looking this way. Or on Tresco. Put 'em there.' He waved a bloody hand at the thinner bushes close to the fire. Potts, she was beginning to realise, had either more intelligence, or more sense of responsibility, than the other men. Perhaps he had been a petty officer of some kind once.

'Why don't you want anyone to know you are here?' Averil asked as Tom twisted the shirts and the water poured out.

'Hasn't the Cap'n said?' He dropped one shirt into the bucket and picked up another.

'We haven't had much time to talk,' she said and then blushed as the whole group burst into guffaws of laughter.

'Why not share the joke?' Luke strolled out from behind one of the tumbledown stone walls. He had his coat hooked over one finger and hanging down his back, his shirt collar was open, his neckcloth was loose and he gave every indication of just coming back from a relaxing stroll around the island. Averil suspected that he had been behind the wall ever since she had approached the men, waiting to see what happened, testing their mood.

'I said that we had not talked much.' She hefted the bucket with the wrung linen and walked towards the bushes. Any gentleman would have taken the heavy pail from her, but Luke let her walk right past him.

'No, we have not,' he said to her back as she shook out each item with a snap and spread it on the prickly gorse. 'I'll tell you over dinner.'

'Tell 'er *all* about it, will you, Frenchy?' Dawkins said and the whole group went quiet.

Frenchy? Averil spun round. He was French? And that made the men…what? Not just deserters—turncoats and traitors.

'You call me Captain, Dawkins,' Luke said and she saw he had the pistol in his hand, loose by his side. 'Or the next time I will shoot your bloody ear off. Nothing to stop you rowing, you understand, just enough to make sure you spend what is left of your miserable life maimed. *Comprends-tu?*'

The man might not have understood the insult in the way he had just been addressed, but Averil did. And her French was good enough to recognise in those two words not the pure accent of someone carefully taught as she had been, but a touch of originality, a hint of a regional inflection. The man was French. *But we are at war with France,* she thought, stupid with shock.

'Aye, Cap'n,' Dawkins said, his face sullen. 'Just me little joke.'

'Go back to the hut, Miss Heydon,' Luke said over his shoulder. 'I will join you at dinner time.'

'I do not want to go to the hut. I want an explanation. Now.' It was madness to challenge him in front of the men; she realised it as soon as she spoke. If he would not take insubordination from Dawkins, he was most certainly not going to tolerate it from a woman.

'You get what I choose to give you, when I choose,' Luke said, his back still turned. 'Go, now, unless you wish to be turned over my knee and taught to obey orders in front of the men.'

Her dignity was all she had left. Somehow she kept her chin up and her lips tight on the angry words as she walked past him, past the silent sailors and down the slope towards the hut. *Bastard. Beast. Traitor...*

No, she realised as she got into the hut and flung herself down on a chair, Luke was not a traitor. If he was French, he was an enemy. *The* enemy. And she was sitting here, an obedient little captive who shuddered under his hands and wanted his kisses and washed his shirts and trailed back here when she was told. She was an Englishwoman—she had a duty to fight as much as any man had.

Averil jumped to her feet, sending the chair crashing to the floor, and twitched back the crude curtain. There was a navy ship at anchor out there—too far to hail, and probably, unless someone had a glass trained on the island, too far to signal with anything she had to hand. But she could swim. Why hadn't she thought of that before? If she ran down to the sea, plunged in and swam, surely they would see her? And if Luke gave chase then that would create even more of a stir. Someone would come to investigate and, even if he shot her, he would have to explain the commotion.

She was out of the door and running before she could think of any objections, any qualms to slow her with fear. The big pebbles hindered her, but she was clear of them, up to her knees in the water, before she heard anything behind her.

'Get back here!'

Luke! She did not turn or reply, only ploughed doggedly on, fighting through the thigh-high waves.

'Stop or I will shoot!'

He wouldn't. He wouldn't shoot a woman in the back. Even a French agent wouldn't—

She didn't hear the shot, only felt the impact, a thumping blow below her left shoulder, behind her heart. It pitched her forwards into the sea and everything clouded and went dark. Her last thought as she felt the water closing over her head was of shocked anger. *He said he would not kill me... Liar.*

Chapter Six

'**W**ake up.'

It seemed that the voice had been nagging at her for hours. Days, perhaps. She did not want to wake up. She did not think she was dead and this obviously was not heaven unless angels habitually sounded angry and impatient. But even if she was alive, Luke had shot her. Why should she have to wake up and face that? It would hurt.

'Why should I?' Averil asked.

'So I can strangle you?' the voice enquired and became identifiable as Luke.

'You shot me.' She opened her eyes, surprised to find she was not frightened or in great pain. Perhaps she was in shock. Best to lie very still—she was badly wounded, surely she must have lost a great deal of blood?

'I did not shoot you.' He was looming over the bed, tight-lipped and furious. 'I threw a stone at you and you seem to have fainted.'

'Oh.' Averil sat up and yelped in pain. 'It hurts! You could have killed me if you had hit my head.'

'I hit what I aim at,' Luke said. 'It is just a bruise. You might want to cover yourself up.'

Averil glanced down and found she was naked. Again. Her borrowed clothes were draped, steaming, over chairs in front of the fire. She grabbed the edge of the blanket, pulled it up to her chin and sat there glowering back at him.

'What the hell were you doing?' He turned on his heel and walked away as though he was having trouble keeping his hands off her. Averil was not deceived into thinking he was restraining lustful urges.

'I intended to swim to the nearest ship,' she said. 'It was one thing not to try to escape when I believed you were just deserters, but when I realised you are a French spy I had to do something.'

Luke folded his arms and looked at her without emotion or denials. 'Why do you assume I am a French spy?'

'Because you are French, because you have lied to the Governor about why you are here and because you are hiding those men and training them for some nefarious exercise.'

'That is almost entirely correct on all points, Miss Heydon, and you have drawn entirely the wrong conclusion from it.'

'What is not correct?' she demanded, wishing she had her clothes. Defiance was much easier when one was not naked, she had discovered.

'I am half-French.' Luke's shoulders lost their angry rigidity and he sat on the edge of the table and regarded her with what looked like exasperated resignation. 'I am going to have to trust you.'

'Well, you cannot. Not if you are my enemy.'

'I may be that—you seem determined that I am—but I am not England's enemy. I am an English naval officer and I am also *le comte* Lucien Mallory d'Aunay.'

'A French count? A Royalist?'

That produced a bark of laughter. 'Shall we say, a constitutional monarchist? That, at least, was what my father was until Madame Guillotine took his head off and ended his political philosophising.'

He rubbed both hands over his face and through his hair and

emerged rumpled and with no sign of the anger of a few moments before, only a weary patience. 'Averil, will you take my word of honour that what I tell you is the truth? Because if you will not, then I fear we are at an *impasse*. I cannot prove any of it, not here and now.'

'I don't know,' she said with total honesty. He shrugged and suddenly seemed very foreign. 'I wish I had some clothes on,' she added, half to herself.

'Why on earth would that make any difference?'

'I want to look into your eyes.'

'I will come to you then.' He knelt by the bedside and looked steadily at her. 'What can you see?'

'My own reflection. Your cynicism. Weariness.' She made herself relax, let herself sink into the wide grey gaze. 'Truth. Truth and anger.'

'Ah.' He sat back on his heels. 'I will tell you then, but you must swear to keep it secret.'

'Who am I likely to be able to tell?' she demanded.

'You never know.' He got to his feet and went back to the table. 'My mother was Lady Isabelle Mallory and she married my father in 1775. In 1791, when the king was forced to accept the written constitution, I was fifteen. My father was strongly in favour of the new order and believed that bloodshed and revolution would be averted by the more democratic form of government.

'*Maman* insisted that it would be a disaster and said she would return to her parents in England. I wanted to stay in France, but my father told me my duty was to look after my mother and that he would send for us when France became the stable land of freedom and prosperity that he predicted.' He paused and Averil found she was holding her breath. 'She was right, he was wrong and he paid for it with his head during the Terror in '94. Our loyal family servants followed him to the guillotine.'

'Oh, I am sorry. Your poor mother.' He spoke so flatly that she could only guess at the emotions under the words, what he must have felt when the news reached England. 'You speak very good English. I would never have guessed you were French.'

'I have thought in it for years. I was already in the English navy when my father died. I went from being Comte Luc d'Aunay to Midshipman Mr Luke d'Aunay—or Dornay—and I did my level best to be an Englishman. But they called me Frenchy and it stuck—the name and the whispers and the lack of acceptance. I was never *one of us,* never quite English. But I worked and I was lucky and my mother lived long enough to see me gain post rank.'

'She must have been very proud of you,' Averil said. Poor, tragic woman, her husband executed, an exile in her own home country, her son far away and in danger.

Luke—no, she supposed she should say *Luc*—shrugged again, but it was not modesty, she could see that. He knew what he had achieved and against what odds and he was not going to discuss his feeling about his mother's death with her.

'What went wrong?' she asked. She wrapped her arms around her knees, wincing a little as the movement stretched the bruise on her shoulder where the stone had hit.

'Admiral Porthington was what went wrong,' Luc said. He took the knife from his pocket and began to throw it into the tabletop, pull it out, rethrow. 'I was seconded to assess intelligence and I found a pattern of events that pointed to leaks originating from here. The islands are used a lot by navy shipping, and by supply vessels, and they are conveniently close to France. I dug deeper and found that it all appeared to lead back to a certain gentleman who has interests here. I presented my evidence and it was set aside.'

'But why would it not be accepted and the man investigated?'

'He is Porthington's second cousin. I had not dug deeply enough.'

'Oh.'

'Oh, indeed. I was not permitted to investigate any further. Porthington ridiculed the work I had done and refused to countenance any action being taken. I lost my temper.' Averil could imagine, but she bit her lip, unwilling to provoke him now by saying as much. 'I brooded on things, drank rather too much and decided to confront him in his quarters—this was at Portsmouth. I would give him an ultimatum—do something or I would go to the Admiralty and lay it before them.

'I barged in and found he had company—very unwilling company. A young woman who he was about to force.'

'What did you do?'

'Asked him to stop. He laughed in my face and told me to get out. I hit him.'

'Oh, my goodness.' Averil knew what would have happened to an East India Company naval officer if he had done such a thing. 'What happened?'

'Porthington demanded a court-martial, but someone in the Admiralty seems to have had his suspicions, too. I was called in and given one chance—two months to prove my theory right or I would face a court-martial, which, if it chose, could sentence me to death for striking a superior officer. I could not deny I had done it.'

To face death as it stared you in the face at sword point or, as she had experienced, in the form of a towering wave, was one thing. To live with a potential death sentence hanging over you for weeks was a refined form of torture.

'That is terrible,' Averil burst out.

'It was more than I deserved for striking him. I have shot men for less.'

'You were doing your duty by pressing for him to listen to you and you were acting as any gentleman should by defending that woman—surely they saw that?'

'Porthington denied that he had forbidden me to proceed and said I had been told merely to exercise caution while he considered tactics. He portrayed me as headstrong and likely to blunder in and blow the entire investigation. Losing my temper did not help prove him wrong! And as for the woman, she was a servant, not a lady. They seemed to think it made a difference.' He raised one of those slanting eyebrows. 'Don't make me a saint.'

'I am very well aware you are no such thing,' Averil retorted. 'I might dislike you personally—' he raised the other brow '—but I hate injustice. Where did the crew come from?'

'The condemned cells. If I am correct and we track down the source of the leaks, then they are pardoned. If I am wrong, or we fail, they die.'

'They do not have very much to lose by killing you and escaping, have they?' And if they killed Luc, then they would not hesitate to do their worst with her.

'No, they do not. Leadership with men like these is a confidence trick. It is much the same as the way a rider needs to convince a horse that is infinitely stronger and heavier than he that it must obey his commands and bear his weight.'

'But you use brute force when leadership and personality will not work?'

'Oh, yes. And, Averil, do not think I would have hesitated to turn you over my knee up there if you had persisted in questioning me.'

'You would beat a woman?' she bristled at him, outraged. 'I cannot believe any gentleman would!'

'I would if it was necessary, but you had the sense to yield.' Was that the hint of smugness on his face? 'It would have hurt you far less than that stone I was forced to throw at you.'

'It would have been undignified to brangle about it.'

'Certainly undignified, but the more I think about it, the more the idea interests me.' His eyelids drooped, hooding his eyes, and she felt the change in the atmosphere like a shift in the wind. 'You do have a most delightful posterior, my dear. It would be a pleasure to warm it, just a little.'

'You promised...'

'I promised I would not ravish you, Averil, but I said nothing about seduction. You are a serious temptation to a man who has few pleasures in his life just now. A challenge.'

'Well, I am not going to become one of your few pleasures,' she retorted, hauling the blanket tight around her chin. 'Stop teasing me and finish telling me what you are doing over here on this island.' The trouble was, she did not think he was teasing. She must face him down, behave as though such a thing was unthinkable. 'What can you do from here?'

'Wait for a signal. The source who first aroused my suspicions tells me that when the informant—let us not name names yet—has papers for his masters he sends out a brig from Hugh Town which meets a French naval brig beyond the Western Rocks. We take the Scillonian vessel, then we make the rendezvous. The thought of two prizes is a help in motivating the men.'

'I see. I believe you.' He bowed—an ironic gesture, she was sure. 'So now I know the truth you can let me go. Obviously I will not betray you, you have my word.'

'Let you go? My dear Averil, you must see that is impossible.'

'Impossible? By why? Do you not trust me?' Indignant, Averil swung her legs out of bed and stood up. She hauled the blanket around her, ignoring the pain in her shoulder. Luc's eyes widened as she stormed up to him, blanket flapping, and she stopped to yank it tight. 'Stop ogling!'

'There is so much to ogle at when you do that,' he said as he lifted his eyes, full of appreciative amusement, to meet hers. 'You are an intelligent woman—think. Where are you supposed to have been since the ship went down?'

Luc moved around the table and sat on the far side as though to put a safe distance between them before he went on. 'It is four days since the wreck. The navy and the local sailors have scoured the islands, checked every rock that stays above high tide. The population of the Isles is about three hundred souls—there is no-where you could have been undiscovered and yet in as good a con-dition as you are now. So, what story do you tell?'

'I—I do not know,' she admitted. 'Can't I tell the Governor?' He shook his head. 'You think he might be implicated? Then I must stay here, I suppose. For how long?'

'I expect to get the signal within the day, tomorrow at most. There is plenty for the traitor to report on, I imagine, and it would fit the timing of the leaks we could trace.'

'And what now?' She moved to shake out the clothes that hung in front of the fire. 'These are almost wearable.' The thought of being able to dress, to get out of this hut and away from the near-ness of him led to another question. 'Do the men know I tried to escape?'

'No, and it would be dangerous for you if they did. Now, we wait and you and I will emerge looking as though we have been work-ing up an appetite for dinner.'

'I do not want you to kiss me again.' Averil edged backwards, realised it was taking her straight to the bed and stopped, holding on to the other chair back.

'Liar.'

Luc got up and stretched and she found she could not take her eyes off him. She had seen him naked—wasn't that enough? Did she have to do what she accused him of doing and ogle him, just because he was a man? A big, virile, exciting… *Oh, stop it!*

'Tell me why not,' he said.

'Because you are a hypocrite. You condemn the admiral for forc-ing that girl and yet you expect me to kiss you.'

'Am I forcing you?' He came round the table and sat on the edge of it, perhaps two feet from her. It felt far too close for comfort.

'I have no experience of men. I do not know how to deal with the way you make me feel,' she admitted. 'I want to say no and somehow, when you touch me, I cannot. I must be very wanton,' she said, looking away while she fought the blush that was heating her cheeks.

'Not wanton, just sensual,' Luc said. 'Do you not like how it feels when we kiss?'

'Yes, I do. And it is *wrong*.'

'It is perfectly right,' he countered and reached out to turn her face to look at him. 'Natural.'

'I am betrothed,' she said, shocking herself with the way she had lost sight of why she had ended up here. 'I have hardly given that fact a thought since we hit the rocks. I have not thought of Viscount Bradon himself *once* until just now. The reason I was coming back from India was to marry him and I just did not think of him, even when you kissed me.' How on earth could she have ignored something as important as that? How on earth could she have enjoyed another man's caresses as she had? She stared at Luc, appalled at herself. 'That is the most shocking thing of all.'

Luc dropped his hand from where it cupped her cheek. Averil was betrothed? That should change nothing—and yet, subtly, it did. It made him want her more. He had never been competitive with Englishmen for their women. When he married it would be to a French *émigrée,* one of good birth and title. He would not ask for money—he had invested his prize money with care and had few expenses—nor for land—he would be the one providing that once Bonaparte was defeated and he could reclaim what was rightfully his. What he wanted was good French blood to breed back into the d'Aunay line.

Once this episode was over he would either be dead or in a position to court a bride seriously. Bonaparte could not hold out much longer, he felt it in his bones; in three or four years he must be ready to return to France and fight to regain what was his by right.

The woman in front of him knotted her hands into that ridiculous blanket, her face a picture of guilt and confusion. 'Shocking that you should forget?' Given the natural sensuality of her responses he found Averil's expression amusing. 'I do not think so. Surprising, perhaps. I suppose I could find it flattering.' She sent him a withering look. 'But I fancy that being caught up in a shipwreck and almost drowned may account for a little forgetfulness. Do you love him?' Surely not, if she could forget, even when she was being kissed by another man—she might be sensual, but she was not wanton. But then, she had never been kissed before, he remembered.

'Love? Why, no, but then I would not expect to. Love has nothing to do with marriage in aristocratic families, of course.'

'Ah, so you think as I do. Marriage is a matter of dynasty and land. Your father has found you a good match?' It must be if the girl had been sent all the way from India.

'I have never met him, nor had a letter from him, but Papa arranged it all, so there was no need. It is an excellent match,' she added. '*Everyone* says so.'

There was defiance in that statement and under it he sensed doubts. Any woman would have them, he supposed, sent so far from home and family to an unknown husband.

'His father is the Earl of Kingsbury,' Averil added as though playing a trump card.

Yes, on paper a very good match indeed. Luc nodded.

'You know him?'

'I have come across him.' Luc kept his voice carefully neutral. 'I do not know the son.' If Bradon was a spendthrift gamester like his father, then Miss Heydon was in for a most unpleasant shock. What was her own father thinking of? 'Your family are distant relatives of Kingsbury, perhaps?'

'Oh, no.' She smiled brightly. *On the defensive,* Luc thought, wondering what was coming next. 'My father, Sir Joshua Heydon, is a merchant.'

So this was becoming clearer. Kingsbury was doubtless securing a substantial dowry with his new daughter-in-law, money he could well do with. What, he wondered, was Sir Joshua gaining? Influence at court, perhaps, for the earl was one of Prinny's cronies. It was a trade deal, in effect. Luc revised his prejudices a trifle. He had not admired those daughters of cits he had come across so far, not that he had paid them any attention. A d'Aunay did not marry trade. Averil, however, seemed mercifully free of vulgarity.

'Lord Bradon will be anxious when the news reaches him that the ship has gone down,' she said with a frown. It did not seem to occur to her that he was going to be more than *anxious* when he got her back and discovered that his betrothed had been missing, un-chaperoned, for several days. Miss Heydon could well have made a long sea voyage, survived a shipwreck and yet find herself rejected and unwed.

But that was not his problem. *She* was not his problem. He had to capture two brigs, against unknown odds, with the crew from hell, and then pray that with the ships he secured the evidence to expose a traitor and to restore his own career.

Chaperoning an innocent young lady under those circumstances was impossible—from the moment that he had made the decision to take her into the hut and not signal for a navy boat she was as near ruined as made no difference. Averil Heydon was no longer an innocent in the eyes of the world and, if he did not keep a tight rein on his desires and instincts, she would not be one in fact either for much longer. After all, once she was ruined in theory, that was it. She might as well be hanged for a sheep as a lamb.

He looked at her, thinking about it, his body becoming hard and heavy. She was temptation personified and he was in no mood for self-sacrifice.

Chapter Seven

'What are you frowning about?' Averil asked. Lord, but he had to get her dressed again—that blanket was driving him insane. Last night he had been too tired and too distracted to take much notice, although his body had been sending him frantic signals. Now, with it sliding off one shoulder and her hair clean and dry and waving from its tight braid and her face flushed with colour, she was beginning to exude a powerful femininity that he was convinced she had no conscious control over.

'Frowning about? Life,' he said, with perfect honesty. He wondered how much of a bastard he was. Enough of one to ruin this girl in reality? 'And, yes, I have no doubt that your betrothed will be anxious. He will doubtless give you up for dead. Managing your resurrection is going to need some care.' Her expression changed, lost some of its determination, and she caught her lower lip between her teeth as though to force some control over her emotions. Perhaps she could sense his desires—his thoughts were clamorous enough.

'What is it?' He knew he spoke abruptly, and disregarded it; he could not afford to involve himself too deeply with the problems of a young woman who had nothing at all to do with his mission, he told himself. If she thought she had been rescued by a man who was forming some sort of attachment to her, she was mistaken. He had learned not to care the hard way. Averil was a casualty of war and lucky to be alive. 'This can all get sorted out later,' he added. 'A few days is not going to make any difference now.'

'It isn't that. I try not to think about my friends on the *Bengal Queen*,' Averil said. 'But you speaking of resurrection made me think of the burial service at sea. A sailor died during the voyage and the words are different from the words they say on land. But of course you know that...' Her voice trailed away and he saw she was looking back into nightmare.

'When the sea shall give up her dead,' Luc quoted. He had said it more times than he cared to remember as the weighted canvas shrouds were tipped overboard.

'Yes, that is it. And I wonder how many from the *Bengal Queen* died, and how many of those the sea will give up so that families will have the comfort of being able to bury their loved ones.'

'Thinking about it cannot help,' Luc said. 'It will only weaken you. Time enough to mourn when you are safe.'

'And I am not safe now. I understand that,' she said, her voice cool. 'I will try not to bother you with my inconvenient emotions.'

Luc experienced a sudden and quite inexplicable urge to put his arms around her and hold her. Just hold her tenderly to give her comfort. He tried to recall the last time he had comforted a woman and realised it must have been when he had come home on leave after his father had been executed and his mother had finally given up the battle to be strong and had wept in his arms.

Maman had not lived long after that and so he had lost everyone who had mattered: his father, his mother, the loyal servants—they had all died because, in their way, they had done their duty. It was safer not to care, not to form new attachments because they would only lead to pain and distract him from his own duty, to the navy, to his inheritance. Sometimes he thought that if he had allowed himself to form new attachments he would at least have some anchor, some sense of where he truly belonged.

Averil shifted uneasily and he was pulled back to the present. This was not his mother and he had no idea how to console Averil. He did not get involved with women who needed comforting or hugging or cheering up. His relationships were functional and businesslike and, he hoped, involved a degree of mutual pleasure. The women who had been his mistresses had not sat in front of him bravely biting on a trembling lip and making him feel their distress was all his fault.

Damn it, he had not conjured up the storm that sank the East Indiaman and she was not going to make him feel guilty about it. Miss Heydon would have to take him as she found him. He damn well wanted to take her.

'Good,' he retorted. 'Emotions are dangerously distracting under these circumstances.' He got up and felt the clothes hanging in front of the fire. 'These are definitely dry enough now. Get dressed, the men will be wondering why we have not turned up for dinner.'

'I should think their dirty little minds will supply them with an explanation.' Averil did not stir from her chair. 'I am not getting dressed with you here.'

Luc shrugged and got to his feet. It was a reasonable request and he had no need to heat his blood any more than it already was by being in the same room with Averil naked. Even with his eyes closed his recollection was too vivid. 'Try to see, a trifle more affectionate when you appear,' he said over his shoulder, halfway to the door.

'I don't think so.' Averil stood up in a swirl of blanket that somehow managed to be simultaneously provoking and haughty. It was made worse by the fact that he was certain she had no idea of the effect she was creating. 'I think a lovers' quarrel will be far easier to sustain.'

Luc did not bother to answer her. He closed the door behind him, taking care not to slam it, then leaned back against the wind-weathered planks while he got his temper under control. One belligerent, emotional, virginal young lady was not going to get the better of him, he resolved. The trouble was, she had disregarded just about everything he had told her to do, or not to do, and he could not help a sneaking admiration for her courage.

Even if she could swim, to launch herself into the sea, so soon after being almost drowned, took guts and she hadn't complained about the bruise on her back from the stone he had thrown either. It was the first time in his life he had raised his hand to a woman, let alone used a weapon against one, and it had made his stomach churn to do it. Which was another thing not helping his temper, he supposed.

Luc gazed at the horizon and focused his mind on the job in hand. He was a professional naval officer, despite everything, and he was going to overcome this, all of it, just as he had overcome the prejudice and the suspicion and the jibes that had followed him since he had come to England. The *émigré* community was wary because of his father's political views, the English saw him as French and he had a suspicion that his father's marriage had contributed to his troubles in France.

He was a half-breed and he was not going to tolerate it any longer. He would force the damn English navy to exonerate him, he would find a wife befitting a d'Aunay from the *émigré* community and when this war was over, he was going to take back what was his.

A flicker of movement broke his concentration. A brown sail on a small boat that tacked across the Pool as it headed for the narrows between St Helen's and Teän. Now why, with the prevailing wind, was the skipper taking it that way to get to the open sea when the passage to the south, between St Helen's and Tresco, would be so much easier?

Because it was coming to call on him, he realised. It was the expected messenger and that way round took it as far as possible from the navy ships. He felt his mood lift with the prospect of action at last as he strode away from the hut and up the slope, Averil forgotten.

* * *

Averil hardly waited for the door to close before she scrambled into the slightly damp, salt-sticky, breeches and shirt. Her shoulder protested with twinges before it settled down to a throbbing ache around the bruise, but she ignored it as she ignored her painful bare feet. She felt strong, she realised, despite the battering her body had taken over the past few days and the misery at the back of her mind that threatened to creep out and ambush her, as it had just now with Luc.

He thought her an emotional female. Well, there was nothing to be ashamed of in that. But she felt resilient and independent as well, and that was new. Always she had had people to tell her what to do: her father, her aunt, her governess, her chaperones. She had been good and obedient and she had been rewarded by the opportunity to become a countess and to advance her family's fortunes.

And now, through no fault of her own, she was in the power of another man who expected her to do what she as told, and this time she was not inclined to obey him, not in everything—and that was liberating. In some things—kissing, for example—she was far too ready to give in to him and, of course, it was her patriotic duty to comply with Luc's orders in everything relating to the reason he and his men were on the island.

But all in all, Averil thought as she whipped her hair into a firm braid, she was coping. And changing. Whatever happened, the Averil Heydon who left this island was not going to be the same woman who had been washed up on its sands.

She took care to slip out of the door and round to the back of the hut when she left, but there was no sign of interest from the ships riding at anchor in the sunshine. Her frantic dash for freedom and Luc's swift recapture of her must have gone unnoticed.

But there was a strange boat drawn up on the beach below the camp and a stranger stood by the fire, a steaming mug in his hand as he talked. The men were clustered round and they were listening intently, but they were watching their captain. For all their apparent hostility it was clear they looked to him to deal with whatever was happening now. Averil felt an unexpected warmth, almost pride, as though he really was her lover.

She gave herself a brisk mental shake as she walked towards them. Luc d'Aunay was neither her lover nor her love, he was merely doing his job and if he happened to look confident and command-ing and intelligent while he was about it, so much the better for the Royal Navy. There was no excuse for her to get in a flutter.

'Who's this? No one said anything about women.' The stranger spoke with an accent that she guessed must be local. He looked like a fisherman, there were nets and crab pots in the stern of his little boat, and he seemed uneasy with her presence.

'My woman,' Luc said, with a glance in her direction. 'Never mind her—are you certain of the times?'

'I am.' The man grinned. 'Stupid beggar didn't check the sail loft. Still can't work out who he is, mind you. I can't find out where he's coming from and he wears a cloak and his hat pulled tugged low. He keeps his voice low, too—a gentleman, I can hear that much, but if it wasn't for Trethowan not keeping *his* voice down I wouldn't have worked it out.

'He looked to see if he was being followed all right, but it didn't occur to him that someone knew where he was going from last time and got up there first. It's the same brig as before—the *Gannet*— but they've changed the sails, so someone's had some sense. The patch has gone and they've a new set of brown canvas.'

He took a gulp from the mug. 'They'll be slipping anchor at eleven tonight so you'll need to be in position off Annet. The tide'll be right for you to get in behind the Haycocks rocks. I'll signal from the Garrison when I see them leave. It'll be clear tonight.'

'How do we know we can trust 'im?' Harris said and the other men shifted uneasily.

'Because I say so,' Luc replied. 'I know him and he's good reason to hate the French.'

'Aye.' The man scowled at Harris. 'Killed my brother Johnnie they did. And I don't hold with them that'll sell out their country to foreigners.'

'Foreigners like Frenchy here?' a voice from the back muttered.

'Don't be more of a bloody fool than you can help, Bull,' Luc said.

'Sorry, Cap'n, I was only—'

'Don't you go insulting the captain.' The fisherman turned, furious. 'My Johnnie was serving with him when he was killed and he wouldn't have a word said against him. He'd come home and he'd say—'

'Yes, well, spare my blushes, Yestin. You get out fishing now. We'll look out for your lights, six bells on the first watch.'

The man grunted. 'You navy men and your bells. It'll be eleven by the clock on Garrison Gate.' He put down his mug, gave Averil another long stare, then marched down the beach and pushed off his boat. 'You kill the lot of them,' he called back as the wind caught the sail. 'And I'll have lobsters for all of you.'

'Good news,' Luc remarked. 'After dinner, Tom Patch, I want all the dirks and the cutlasses sharpened. Harris, double check the boat. Timmins, come with me and we'll sort out the ammunition and the handguns. The rest of you can take it easy—I need everyone alert and ready to go at two bells on the first watch.'

'Two hours to do that distance?' one of the men queried.

'I want you in good condition when we get there,' Luc said with a grin. 'You'll have some fast rowing and then some brisk fighting—no need to be blown before you start.'

They ate, all of them more cheerful than Averil had seen before. Even Dawkins found discussing the best way to cut a French throat more interesting that ogling her. When they had finished the men with tasks to do went off, leaving nine of them fidgeting around the fire.

'Oh, get away and look for wreckage,' Potts said, exasperated. 'I'm trying to clear up and cook supper and you lot are under my feet. Unless you want to help?'

That sent them off down to the shoreline. Averil watched who went where and then followed, taking the opposite end to Dawkins and Tubbs. There were splintered timbers and cask staves sticking up between ridges of rock, some torn canvas, tangled ropes. Averil picked her way along the shore, gripped by a horrid fascination, half dreading seeing something that she recognised, half as infected by the same treasure-hunting enthusiasm as the men.

Time passed; the sand was warm under her bare feet and the foam at the water's edge tickled her toes. If the cause was not so grim, this would be a delightful way to spend a spring day.

'You found anything?' It was Tubbs.

She straightened up, wary. 'Only shells and rubbish.'

'Aye,' he agreed, sounding almost amiable. 'You found anything, 'Arry?'

'Nah.' The big man was balanced precariously on a low ridge of rock sticking up a couple of feet from the sand. 'I'm for a kip in the tent.' He turned, awkward on the sharp edge. 'Wot's that?'

Tubbs darted forwards and picked something up. Averil saw it as it lay in his calloused palm, a dark oval, smooth and polished, a hinge on one side. 'I know what that is. Give it to me, please—'

'I saw it first,' Dawkins said and made a grab at Tubbs. It all happened so fast Averil did not even have time to step back. Dawkins slipped, fell, crashed into Tubbs, the box shot up in the air, she caught it and was drenched as the two men landed in the shallows. There was a bellow of agony and she saw that Dawkins was not getting up. The water around him was red.

She stuffed the box into the waistcoat pocket and splashed to his side. He was lying awkwardly, cursing with pain; his leg, where all the blood was flowing from, was jammed into a crack in the rock.

'Tubbs, get hold of him, try to get him straight while I hold his ankle!'

The man went to his mate's shoulders and started to heave as Averil got her hands around the trapped foot. 'It'll be 'opeless,' Tubbs remarked gloomily as Dawkins swore, a torrent of obscenity. 'Potts! Get a knife, we'll 'ave to cut it off.'

'Nonsense,' Averil said, hoping it was, as the cook ran down to her side. 'Look, if enough of you can lift him and stop his weight dragging on the leg, I might be able to work it free.'

It involved considerable splashing, cursing and heaving and more blood than Averil ever wanted to see again, but minutes later Dawkins was lying on the beach like a porpoise out of water, moaning and groaning while Averil sent men running for clean water and something to tear up for a bandage.

'I don't think it is broken,' she said when she had got the sand and broken shell washed out of the deep cuts and grazes. The others hauled Dawkins up and he balanced on one foot in front of her, white to the lips. He tried to put his foot down and swayed, gasping with pain. Averil grabbed hold, too, before he crashed down again. 'But I think you've damaged the tendons. You won't be able to walk for a—'

'What the hell?' It was Luc, at the run. 'What have you done? Dawkins, you bastard, get your hands off her!'

Chapter Eight

Averil glanced down at herself and realised what Luc was seeing—Dawkins with his hands on her shoulders, her shirt red with blood. 'It is all right, he has hurt his foot. It is *his* blood,' she said urgently as Luc reached them, murder in his eyes.

'His?' He stared at her, then turned and hit Dawkins square on the jaw, felling the big man.

'I never touched 'er!' the sailor protested, flat on his back on the sand, one meaty hand clamped to his face.

'Why did you hit him?' Averil protested. 'He's the one who is injured. It was an accident.'

Luc pulled her towards him, none too gently, and held her by her shoulders as he scanned her face as though looking for the truth. 'For scaring the living daylights out of me,' he said too softly for the men to hear, then raised his voice. 'The damn fool has probably hurt himself too badly to be any use tonight.'

'I can row,' Dawkins said. The others had hauled him to his feet again and he stood propped between Tubbs and Tom Patch, his slab of a face creased with anxiety. 'I can reload and guard the boat when you're boarding. I can shoot from the brig. Gawd, Cap'n, I've got to go or they'll say I haven't earned me pardon!'

'You haven't,' Luc said. 'You know damn well that the most dangerous part, the part I need the men for, is boarding the brigs and you go and fool around and have an accident—if it is an accident.'

'Tell 'im, Miss!' Dawkins turned to Averil, all trace of the blustering bully gone. 'Tell 'im it was an accident. Could 'ave 'appened to anyone!'

'It *was* an accident,' Averil confirmed. 'Honestly it was, Captain d'Aunay. He wasn't doing anything that the others weren't.'

There was a stinging silence while Luc contemplated Dawkins's sweaty face and the men seemed to hold their breath. 'Miss Heydon is remarkably forgiving, considering the disrespectful way you have behaved to her,' he said at last.

'Yes, Cap'n. She's a real lady and I'm sorry, miss.'

Watching him, Averil thought he probably was genuinely regretful. He was a bully who was used to being kept at a distance; her unforced help seemed to have shocked him.

'Very well. I accept that. If we are successful, then you will get your pardon like the rest. Now go and lie down and stop hopping about like a damned rabbit.'

'Er...miss?' Tubbs was eyeing her like a hopeful jackdaw after a scrap of meat. 'You've got the thing we found, miss. Rightfully mine, that is. Finder's keepers.'

'Yes, it would be, Tubbs,' Averil said. 'But it belongs to me.' It was a lie, but she wasn't allowing the only thing she had left of her friends to fall into Tubb's greasy fingers. 'Look, I'll prove it to you. What do you think is inside?'

'Dunno, miss.' He was looking more intrigued than resentful. Some of the others who were not helping Dawkins back to his shelter stopped to listen. 'Snuff? Money?'

'Tiny carved animals,' Averil said, slipping the box out of her pocket. 'A Noah's Ark. I couldn't have guessed that, could I? If you can find a flat rock out of the wind, I'll show you.'

She opened the lid and there they all were, the minute ivory animals, the ark, Noah himself—the gift Lady Perdita Brooke had bought for Alistair, Viscount Lyndon, in Cape Town. Her hand shook a little as she set them out on the rock with the men crouched down beside her or hanging over her shoulder to look. Where had it been when the ship struck—in Alistair's cabin or on his person? Was it a good omen or a sign that he and Dita were gone?

Averil took herself to task for superstition. It was chance, no more, no less, that this small object should have been washed up on this beach for her to recognise.

'Lovely workmanship,' Luc said behind her as he reached over her shoulder to pick up one of the camels, as small as his little fingernail. 'But very fragile for a child's toy.'

'It isn't a toy,' she said, as she blew grains of sand out of the box before she packed the pieces in again. The men drifted away, back to the beach or the fire, leaving them alone. 'It was a gift. A birthday gift from someone very special to me.' Dita had been her closest female friend and she had loved her like a sister. *I do love her,* she corrected herself. *She is alive, I know she is alive.* 'They bought it in Cape Town,' she added, thinking to explain the craftsmanship.

'I see,' Luc said. 'Lord Bradon would be interested to hear about that, I imagine.'

'You think I had a lover on board? Someone I met on the voyage?' she demanded, shocked and yet curiously gratified. Was he jealous? Not that she wanted him to be, of course, that would presuppose she actually had any feelings for the man, other than a grudging admiration for his leadership and sympathy for the fate that had brought him here.

'I know you did not,' he said. 'At least, if you did, he hadn't kissed you.'

Averil glared. 'It was a gift from a woman, my best friend. Just because you appear to place little importance on fidelity there is no need to assume everyone else is the same.'

'I am always faithful,' Luc protested, all injured innocence, she thought resentfully as he cocked a hip on the rock and made himself comfortable to watch her fiddle the pieces back into place.

'Serial fidelity to a succession of mistresses, I presume?' She could imagine Luc selecting a mistress, negotiating—he would be reasonably generous, she guessed—then… Enjoying her, she supposed, was the phrase. She would not let her imagination go there.

'Exactly.'

'Disgraceful!' She secured the lid of the box and stood up.

'How so? I am generous, I provide well for the woman when the liaison is over, she appears satisfied with the arrangement.'

'There is no need to be smug about your sins,' Averil snapped. Even to her own ears she sounded irritable and stuffy. 'I hope you are not going to tell me you are married *and* keeping a string of mistresses.'

'A succession, not a string,' he said. He appeared to find it mildly amusing, curse the man. 'And, no, I am not married. If I get my head out of this noose then I shall devote myself to finding a well bred, virtuous young lady of an *émigré* family.'

'Really?' Distracted from her anxieties, Averil turned back. 'Not an Englishwoman? You intend to go back to France one day?'

'Of course.' He stared at her as if she had suggested he go to New South Wales instead. 'I have responsibilities in France—that is where my title comes from, where my lands are. Obviously I need a wife who understands that. Once the war is over there will be nothing for me here.'

'Oh. I see. It is just that…you seem so English.' But he did not, somehow. Despite the completely perfect pronunciation there was something under the veneer of the English gentleman and officer, something foreign and unsettling and different.

She pulled herself together. Luc's marriage plans were no affair of hers. 'What will happen to me tonight?'

'You stay here, of course.' He was frowning again. Perhaps it was tactless of her to have mentioned his marriage when he must have feared all that was lost to him. 'There is ample food and water. I will collect you tomorrow. I don't think you need worry about Dawkins. With that foot you can outrun him easily. And I think he knows he is in your debt, although I would lock the door at night, if I were you. Reform is likely to last only so long.'

'And if you do not come back?'

'I always come back.'

'You are not immortal, even if you are arrogant,' she retorted. 'Don't tempt fate by saying such things.'

'I hadn't realised you cared.' Luc stood up and caught her in his arms. His eyes were dark and warm and his mouth was curving and he was just about to kiss her, she was certain.

Averil let herself sway closer, let herself absorb, just for a moment, the intensity of his gaze, the heat of his body, the tempting lines of his mouth that gave such wicked pleasure. 'I do not. Naturally I wish the mission well and that you all return safely, but I am worried about what happens to me if you get yourself killed,' she said, stepping back out of range.

'You wish the mission well?' he mocked, mimicking her starchy tone. 'That is enough to send us all off with a patriotic glow in our breasts, I am sure.' The satirical light in his eyes died and he became serious. 'If I do not come back by nightfall tomorrow, then light a fire on the beach outside the hut and discharge the pistol I will leave with you. I'll show you how to fire and load it now. That will be enough to attract interest from the nearest frigate.'

'A gun?' She had never touched one before and was not at all sure she wanted to start now.

'Here.' Luc pulled the pistol from his belt. 'This is loaded. Hold it.' Reluctantly she curled her fingers round the butt. 'You cock it—go on, it won't bite you—that's half cock, now fully back. Keep it pointing at the ground—no, not at your foot!—until you are ready to fire, then point it out to sea and pull the trigger.'

'Ow!' The bang made her jump, the recoil hurt her wrist. 'Won't that have been heard?'

'The wind is to us.' Luc produced a box from his pocket. 'Here's how to reload—you may need more than one shot.'

He showed her how to reload several times, more patient with her initial clumsiness than she would have expected. When he was satisfied at last he walked with her back to the hut and saw the pistol and ammunition safely stowed on the shelf.

'But you have no handgun now,' Averil realised. 'You will need one.'

Luc was already removing a stone in one wall. 'I have two.' He stuck the spare pistol in his belt and pushed the stone back.

'You would have taken two if it was not for me,' she said, worry fretting at her conscience. 'Here, take this one back, you'll need it. I can attract attention without it, I am sure.'

'I would feel more comfortable if you were armed.'

'Couldn't Dawkins sail your little skiff across to St Mary's? Oh, no, I suppose if you do not come back then he needs to be able to disappear and never to have been here. I see.'

Luc stood frowning at her, thinking about something else and not, she thought, listening to her work it all out aloud. 'There are papers in that cache. You just need to prise the stone out with a knife. If you have to leave without me, take them to the Admiralty when you reach London. Don't give them to the Governor, I am not certain about his loyalties yet.'

'But you will come back.' It mattered, *he* mattered, she realised. Half the time Luc was autocratic and cold as though he was not prepared to let another human being touch his feelings, yet he was fiercely protective. Was that simply the male need to dominate, to fight for possession of anything in his territory?

He could make her so angry—and she was never angry usually. And when he touched her, she wanted him. He had made her want him in a shameful, physical way. And that was not like her either;

she had never had any trouble at all being perfectly well behaved and not flirting, not allowing stolen kisses.

'Ah! You care, *chérie*.' He grinned at her, an infuriating, cocky smile that took years off his apparent age and made him look completely French.

Yes, I care, she wanted to say. 'Do you want me to?' she countered. *I am betrothed. You seek a French wife. I am not thinking about friendship. This is impossible...or sinful.* What on earth was the matter with her? Averil found she had stopped breathing, waiting for his answer.

'I want—yes, what is it?' The bang on the door made him turn, the teasing young man gone, the captain back again.

Harris's head appeared round the door. 'Potts says, do we need to take any provisions with us?'

'Water, some ship's biscuit and cheese. I'll come and sort out final positions.' As the door closed behind Harris, Luc turned back to her. 'I'll be with the men now, up until it is time to go. I don't want to leave them on their own and they need to keep busy. Will you be all right?'

What kind of question was that? Averil thought with a spurt of resentment. All right? No, she was not all right, and she wondered if she ever would be again. The wretched man had made her care about him, so she would worry—and she would worry about that rabble of a crew of his. He had made her think about her marriage in a whole new light and to worry about a lot more than whether Lord Bradon would have a sense of humour, or whether she would remember all her lessons in the duties to be expected of her. Now she was thinking about kissing her betrothed and comparing him with this man who should never have touched her, let alone have lain naked with her in his bed.

But she could say none of that. 'Of course I will,' she said with a smile that was supposed to be confident and which obviously did not deceive Luc for a moment.

'Oh, hell.' He dragged her into his arms. 'One last time, damn it. The Fates owe me that, at least.

'I don't underst—' she began and he kissed her. It was not gentle or considerate or teasing. It was uncompromising, and so was the hard thrust of his body against her and the way he pulled her shirt clean out of her trousers and ran his hand up, over her bare skin, to take her breast and mould it with strong, calloused fingers.

Her flesh seemed to swell as though eager to fill his hand and she moaned into the heat of his mouth, wanting and aching, and both his hands were on her body now and she understood, finally, what her clamouring senses were telling her to do and dragged his shirt out, too, frustrated because his coat stopped her pulling it over his head.

Luc's skin was hot and smooth and she could feel those lovely muscles she had watched with such scandalised fascination. Her hands slipped lower, under the waistband of his trousers and his hands that had been doing indecently wonderful things to her breasts stilled.

'Luc?' His whole body was rigid, then she felt him relax as he stepped back.

'That very nearly got out of control,' he said, passing his hand across his mouth while his eyes held hers. 'I am sorry. It is a good thing you will be sleeping alone tonight, I think.'

Averil found she could, after all, articulate. 'It was my fault, too.'

'No. You are an innocent—you don't understand.'

'I am beginning to get the hang of it, a little,' she ventured, shocking herself.

'Lucky Bradon,' Luc said with a flash of the grin that made her smile back, a trifle uncertainly. 'I'll see you at supper.'

When he had gone she sat quite still for a while on the edge of the bed and tried to think. Luc said she was not wanton, only sensual.

Was that true? He took the blame for that kiss becoming so much more, and yet she wasn't ignorant, or unobservant. She should have stopped him the moment his fingers slid under her shirt. But she had not; she had wanted to undress him and to touch him intimately and—and then what?

Averil got up and let herself out, walked over the rise behind the hut and, once she was out of sight of the ships at anchor, began to climb towards the island's little summit until she was at the top and looking out westward over open ocean. There was nothing between her and America, she realised, thinking of the endless ocean the *Bengal Queen* had ploughed across to bring her here, to this tiny speck on the edge of the Atlantic.

The breeze was brisk and cool, and the sea spread out like crumpled silk with tiny white wavelets all over it and sudden, sinister, patches of foam and disturbed water to mark submerged rocks. She had thought perhaps she would see the wreck of the *Bengal Queen* from this height, but she could not. Was it out of sight behind that big island—Tresco, she thought they had called it—or had it sunk to the bottom?

How could anyone navigate at night through this maze of islands and islets and reefs? She pulled her braid over her shoulder and began to play with the end while she watched the sea. Only a few days since the wreck and so much had happened. She was a different woman. *I have suffered a sea change,* she thought. *I thought I knew who I was and what I wanted. Who I wanted.*

'But it doesn't matter what I want,' she said out loud, as though arguing with someone else. Or, perhaps, just with her conscience. 'There is a contract, an agreement. Papa has said that I will marry Lord Bradon.'

There really was no option, after all. Whatever it was that was happening between her and the man she had met only days before, the man who had saved her life, it was not about the prospect of marriage. And marriage was her purpose in life: to marry well to help her family, then to be a good wife and support her husband and to raise happy, healthy children to carry on his line.

I have had a shock, Averil thought, sitting down, then lying back so she was watching the sky and not the troubling, shifting, sea. *I am not quite steady in my mind.* Almost killed, mourning for her friends... Of course she felt more for Luc d'Aunay than she would have under any other circumstances, she reasoned.

The bright sky hurt her eyes. Averil rolled over and lay on her stomach, propped herself up on her elbows and frowned at the short grass between them. It was starred with tiny flowers she did not know the names of and a minute black beetle was making its way through what must seem a jungle to it.

And what were those feelings when she came right down to it? Luc made her cross a lot of the time. He most certainly aroused wickedly sensual sensations that she was doing her best not to think about. He was attractive, although not handsome—she would not allow him that accolade. He was brave and strong and commanding and ruthless and even if he rescued women from admirals bent on rape he seemed to have no scruples over almost seducing her.

The world was full of strong, confident men like that, she told herself: Alistair Lyndon, the Chatterton twins, to name but three. She bit her lip—they were all right, they had to be. If she could reach land alive, then those men could.

Yes, there were thousands of attractive, courageous, dashing men and she was probably about to marry one. But in the meantime this one, the one she owed her life to, was going into danger. And behind his strength there was a darkness. His family tragedy and his isolation because of his birth would account for some of it. The injustice of the situation he now found himself in would be enough to make any man cynical and angry. She wondered if he would be in this position if he had been fully English or whether prejudice had told against him. Did he really know what he wanted? Did he secretly yearn for acceptance as an Englishman as well as for his French identity and title back again?

Averil sat up and looked down the slope to where the men were gathered round Luc as he stood in the pilot gig on the beach and realised what she had been meaning to do ever since he had pulled her into his arms in the hut.

She was going with them.

Chapter Nine

'Ferris.'

'Yes, miss?' As Averil reached the bottom of the slope the skinny little man looked up from the knife he was sharpening with loving care on a whetstone. She sat down beside him with a momentary thought about how convenient trousers were and how restricting skirts would seem when—if—she ever got back to them.

'With Dawkins injured you are one man down for tonight.'

'Aye, we are that.' He spat on the stone and drew the knife down it again with a sinister hiss. 'Clumsy lummock.'

'Is it all boarding and fighting or does someone have to stay in the pilot gig?' She had been trying to work out the tactics for boarding a brig from a much smaller boat and it seemed to her that they could not just all swarm on board and leave the gig to float away.

'Someone has to stay, miss. If Dawkins wasn't such a big lump, perhaps the cap'n would have taken 'im anyway, but he can't row with that bad foot—you can't get the strength behind the stroke, see—and we can't haul 'im on board, not and fight at the same time, and he's a great hulk of a man.' He tried the edge of his knife with the ball of his thumb and grunted with satisfaction. 'In the gig Dawkins is just that much more weight if he can't fight or row. We've got the extra weapons and the charts and stuff as well—you can't climb up the side carrying that lot *and* fight, so the man in the gig 'as to look after those.'

'So whose job is it to stay on the gig?' That would make them two fighting men down.

'Mine, miss.' He sighed. 'I'm the smallest and the fastest. Pity. I'd like to 'ave a go at them treacherous bastards. I gets to fight when we board the French brig, though. We'll come alongside, tie on and then jump 'em.' He held the knife up to catch the light and grinned with blood-curdling anticipation.

'Ferris, can you get me on board the pilot gig without the captain seeing?' His mouth dropped open, revealing a snaggle of stained teeth. 'I can stay in the gig and then you can go up and fight—you'd prefer that, wouldn't you? I've got a pistol and I can fire it if someone tries to climb down.'

Ferris looked thoughtful, and very much like his nickname. She could almost see his pointed little nose twitching as he scrubbed a hand over his whiskery chin. One benefit of dealing with a cunning, unscrupulous, wicked man like this was that he had no concerns about doing something against orders, if it suited him. And, apparently, the opportunity to kill and be killed tempted him more than any fear of the consequences deterred him.

'Aye, I'll do it. You'll need something dark and warm on your top, and a hat.' He squinted down the beach at the gig. 'I'll be in the prow so I can catch hold and tie us off. Cap'n will be in the stern on the tiller. This is what we'll do…'

'You will be all right.' Luc said it firmly, as though giving an order. He had come back to the hut after all. It was a good thing she had not changed into the dark clothing Ferris had given her yet.

'Of course I will. I know exactly what to do.' Averil smiled up at him with cheerful reassurance, then made her face more serious. It would not do to let the relief that she felt because she was going with him make him suspicious. And it was foolish to think that her presence could keep him safe. But it would give him one more fighting man in Ferris, and one more pistol.

They stood in the hut in front of the fire, suddenly as stiff and awkward with each other as two strangers at a social function. *Kiss me,* she urged him silently, as he stood, bare-headed, his hair disordered from the breeze that was getting up, his body indistinct in the dark clothing he wore, with no trace of white at cuff or throat. Luc showed no sign of wanting to even touch her hand in farewell.

'Will you kiss me goodbye?' She blushed to ask it and he looked, as far as she could see in the flickering light, less than enthusiastic. *How very flattening. I thought men about to embark upon danger welcomed kisses.*

'There is no excuse for a kiss now. We are beyond the need to deceive the men. I wish you well, Averil, and I am sorry if my actions have sullied the innocence you had every right to take to your husband.' He sounded deadly serious and his voice held, for the first time, the faint trace of an accent as he made the stilted speech. He was probably translating from the French in his head, she thought. Was that a sign that his emotions were engaged?

'I have to admit that I enjoyed what we did together,' she confessed. It was hard to resist the temptation to touch his face, caress his cheek, dark with evening stubble. 'I would like you to kiss me again.' *Must I beg?* She was beginning to feel angry with him, and she did not want to feel that, not now.

'I will kiss you when I get back,' he said and smiled suddenly and her heart thumped with an emotion she did not understand, although fear was a large part of it. Her stomach felt hollow with apprehension. Was it fear for his life, or her own? Or for what would happen when they left this tiny island behind them?

'Very well.' She stood on tiptoe and kissed his cheek, the stubble prickling her lips. 'Good luck and fair winds.'

He nodded, abrupt and withdrawn again, and she knew his focus was back with the mission, not this inconvenient female who had complicated his life for five days. 'Goodbye, Averil.' And then he was gone. She waited for ten heartbeats, then dragged the heavy navy wool Guernsey Ferris had given her over her head, making sure her collar and cuffs were tucked well inside. She stuffed her braid down inside it, then wrapped her head in the brown bandana he had found and blew out the lamp.

She knew the way over the slope of the hill now and she ran, higher than the route Luc would have taken moments before. There was jarring pain in her foot when she stubbed her toe on a rock and she swallowed a yelp, hopped a few steps, then fell into a gorse bush, its thick prickly arms enveloping her in a wicked embrace. She hissed curses between her teeth until she was free and then stumbled along, picking tiny spears out of her hands and arms, until she found herself above the small group on the beach.

They were intent on loading the pilot gig and Ferris was where he had said he would be, in the water, holding the nose of the boat steady. Averil walked into the surf beyond the circle of light and crept back to him until he was between her and the beach.

'In you get,' he hissed as the group turned to pick up the weapons that had not yet been loaded. He boosted her up, over the side, and she fell on to the bottom boards. Her ribs found the rowing benches on the way and she clenched her teeth to stop herself crying out. She was going to have a fine set of bruises in the morning.

'Hold it still, Ferret, for Gawd's sake,' someone called as the gig rocked. Averil caught her breath and curled into as small a ball as she could, right up in the prow.

'Crab got me toe,' the man called back. 'Come on then, mates, I've got it and I'm ruddy freezing me wedding tackle off, standing 'ere.'

The boat swayed and rocked as the crew climbed in, muttering and pushing as they got themselves into their rowing positions, the men not at the oars wedged down at the rowers' feet. Ferris heaved himself on board and sat down, his dripping wet legs draped over

Averil's back. With the rest of the crew facing away from them no one could see her; unless she moved or spoke, she was safe.

What she was not, was comfortable. It was necessary to remind herself whose idea this was, because she found it was all too easy to blame Luc for the discomforts of his pilot gig. The trip seemed interminable; her position was cramped, her feet were stuck in the cold water that washed over splintery boards and the little boat seemed dangerously low in the water as it powered through the waves. Every now and again water slapped over the side, drenching her.

What was worse was the waiting once they had got into position. She wriggled so hard that Ferris let her sit up and peer around, but his horny hand pushed down on her head the moment the men began to settle themselves for the wait, turning on the rowing benches to get more comfortable.

They seemed to be in the shelter of some rocks that rose like a jagged crest from the sea, but despite the natural breakwater the pilot gig rocked with the swell, and Averil told herself, over and over, that she did not suffer from seasickness. Not one little bit.

The men were quiet, for sound travelled great distances over water. But Luc was talking, his voice a murmur, barely discernible over the noise of the waves hitting the rocks. Averil could not hear what he was saying, but she felt soothed by it, encouraged. He was calm, so she was, too. *A little touch of Harry in the night,* she thought, recalling her Shakespeare—King Henry walking amongst the camp fires as his troops waited for dawn and the great battle against the French.

She must have dozed as she huddled at Ferris's feet because the whisper from the men took her by surprise. 'The light! He's signalling.' She wriggled round and peered over the edge of the gig and there to the north-east a pinprick of light flashed on and off, on and off, then swung back and forth. Then it was gone for the space of perhaps ten seconds before the pattern was repeated. The men shuffled and bent down, she saw the flash of starlight on metal as weapons were handed around and heard the click as pistols were primed.

Then all there was to do was wait, and now the anticipation in the pilot gig was tangible and her mouth was dry and her heart pounded so much that she did not hear when the order was given. The men fitted the oars back into the rowlocks and began to propel the boat out from the shelter of the rocks.

As they slid into open water she saw the brig, sails dark against the slightly lighter sky, the bow wave a froth of white showing its speed. *'Go!'* Luc said and the gig shot forwards, turned and angled in on the other vessel. She thought they would be rammed, then that they would plough into the side of the ship, but Luc brought her round so they slid alongside with scarcely a thump. Ferris flung himself up, his feet trampling on her as he lashed the ropes to the brig. All along the side other arms were working, heaving ropes, making fast. The pilot gig was tethered, riding alongside as the brig forged onwards. And no voice shouted from on deck. They had achieved surprise, Averil realised and started breathing again.

Luc stood up and she saw him clearly for the first time: a silhouette reaching for the ropes. *Leading from the front,* she thought with a surge of pride that killed the fear for a moment. The men scrambled after him in ferocious silence and then she and Ferris were alone on the tossing gig.

'Check all the ropes,' he whispered. 'And keep checking. Get everything together and bundle it into that net, ready to swing up. You got the pistol?'

There was a shout from on deck, the sound of gunfire, a scream, shouted orders. Chaos. *Luc...* 'Yes,' she said and pulled it from her waistband. 'But you take it. Someone might need it. Watch his back, Ferris, please.'

'You call me Ferret, miss. You're one of us. Yeah, I'll watch your man's back for ye.'

He was gone, swarming up the side like his namesake after a rabbit, and Averil was left in the tossing boat with no idea what was happening above. She got to her feet, was thrown down, crawled, flinched as shots rang out above and voices yelled. Her hands groped until she had collected up everything that was left. A long tube made of some hard material must contain the charts, she supposed. She stuffed it all into the net and tied the neck tight.

A man screamed, there was a splash. More yelling. Her foot found something sharp that she had missed: a cutlass. With it tight in her left hand she worked along the gig, testing each rope, each knot, as though they tethered Luc and his men to life.

A pistol cracked, the brig lost way and they were wallowing, so suddenly that for a moment it was like the awful, endless second when the *Bengal Queen* hit the rocks. The fighting had stopped. Averil shifted the cutlass into her right hand and stared up. Who was she going to see, looking down from the rail?

Then a voice roared, 'Ferris, what the hell are you doing up here?' and she sagged on to a rowing bench in relief. There was the sound of Ferret's voice, making excuses, she supposed, and then the wiry little man came scrambling down the ropes.

'All's well. Nobbut a few scratches all round and a hole in Tom Patch's shoulder and that's just an in-and-out,' he said, as a rope came over the side and he lashed the net to it. 'You better hold on tight to this, miss, and get pulled up with it. And keep yer 'ead down when you get on deck—Cap'n's fit to be tied. 'E says you're to stick with me and keep out of the way or he'll leave you in the gig and cut the lines.'

'He doesn't mean it,' Averil said and saw the glint of white as Ferret rolled his eyes.

'Ha! Most likely drop me over instead. Up you go.'

It was worse than being swung on board the *Bengal Queen* in the bo'sun's chair. Averil clung like a monkey and landed on the deck in a jumble of netting and sharp objects, rolled clear and stood up as Ferret came over the side to attack the bundle and free the weapons.

'Where is he?' she panted, looking round. They had lit a couple of lanterns and in the swaying light she could see that the deck of the brig was crowded. The original crew was huddled around the foremast with three of Luc's men systematically tying their hands and feet and removing hidden weapons. The rest of the men were moving about the small ship with a purposeful air of getting themselves familiar with its workings and she could see Potts at the wheel, feet braced, face calm, transformed from cook to helmsman.

'Cap'n's below in the cabin getting them papers safe.' Ferret dug the chart roll out. 'Be calling for this any minute, I expect—you want to take that down to 'im, miss?'

'Not in the slightest,' Averil said with complete truth, 'but I might as well get it over with.'

'Bark's worse than 'is bite,' Ferret said as he tidied the net away.

'He shot the last person who upset him, I hear,' she muttered as she made her way along the sloping deck and down the steep ladder.

Luc was scribbling on a piece of paper, his head bent over a table spread with charts. In the corner a red-headed man sat scowling in the light of the swaying lantern, his hands tied to the arms of the chair. 'Take this up to Potts,' Luc said, and pushed the note across the table without looking up. 'Tell him to hold that heading until told otherwise.'

'Aye, aye, Captain,' Averil said as she snatched the paper, dumped the chart roll on the table and beat a hasty retreat.

'Then get back down here!' he roared after her.

She had to face the music sooner or later, she thought, as she climbed down the ladder again. Better down there and not on deck in full view, and hearing, of the crew.

But Luc's attention was elsewhere when she peered round the cabin door again, so she slid in and perched in a corner.

'We're smuggling, that's all,' the red-haired man protested. It sounded like a continuing argument. 'Picking up lace and brandy.'

'I am sure you were.' A cupboard door in the bulkhead swung open on its hinges to reveal an empty interior. Luc studied an oil-skin package in his hand, then slit the seals. 'Paid with by this, presumably.'

'Don't know anything about that,' the man said, shifting in his bonds. 'Private letters, those. Mr—er, the gentleman who hires us said they were letters to relatives in France. Personal stuff. I wouldn't dream of looking,' he added with unconvincing righteousness.

'Indeed?' Averil shivered at the cold disbelief in Luc's voice as he spread the papers open on top of the charts. 'They are certainly in French. What an interest his Continental relatives must have in naval affairs. Ship movements, provisioning, rates of sickness, armaments, prizes taken...' He read on. 'Rumours of plans for changes at Plymouth. Interesting—I hadn't heard about those.'

He looked up. That wolf's smile had the same effect on the other man as it had on Averil the first time he had used it on her. 'Treason, Mr Trethowan, that is what this is. You'll hang for it, along with your anonymous gentleman. Unless you cooperate, of course. I might be able to do something for you if I had names to bargain with, otherwise...' He spread his hands in a gesture of helplessness and smiled that smile again.

'He'll kill me. He's got influence, a tame admiral.'

'So have I—and the First Lord of the Admiralty trumps your man's cousin any day. It *is* his cousin, isn't it?'

'If you know it all, why ask me?' The red-haired man hunched a resentful shoulder, then winced as it made the cord dig into his wrist.

'Who else on the islands is involved in this?'

'No one, I swear. That interfering Governor is suspicious—had the brig searched last week, arrested my bo'sun on some trumped-up charge the day before yesterday—and his men are asking questions.'

So, the Governor is in the clear, Averil thought. That would make things easier for Luc.

'Any more papers on board? I'll have the vessel stripped down in any case, but it'll go better for you if you hand it all over now.'

'Nothing. I've got stuff in my house, though.' The man seemed eager to talk now. Averil eyed him with distaste—he had known exactly what he was carrying to pay for those French luxury goods. 'I'll give it all to you, if you'll save my neck.'

'I'm sure you will. And when we come alongside the Frenchman, you'll act as though nothing is wrong or you'll get a knife in the ribs and won't have to worry about the hangman at all.' Luc got to his feet, went out to the foot of the steps and shouted up, 'Two men, down here, now!'

When Trethowan was bundled out Luc turned, finally, to look at Averil. His expression did not soften in the slightest from the way he had looked at the traitor. 'And your excuse for being here is what, exactly?'

'You were a man down.' She wanted to wriggle back against the bulkhead and vanish, but it was solid against her shoulders. Luc neither raised his voice nor came any closer, but her mouth had gone dry and her pulse was pattering as though he had shouted threats at her. 'If I took Ferret's place in the gig then he could come up on deck and fight. I gave him the pistol as well, so you had one more weapon.'

'Very noble,' Luc said.

'There is no need to be sarcastic,' Averil snapped. 'I couldn't bear being stuck back there, not knowing what was happening. But I wouldn't have come if I hadn't been able to do something helpful.'

'Helpful!' The change from cool sarcasm to a roar of fury had her jerking back so violently that her head banged on the wood behind her. 'Do you call shredding my nerves helpful? I saw Ferret, asked him what the devil he was doing on deck and he said you were in that damned gig and I nearly throttled the little rodent. We still have a French brig to capture. You will stay down here. You will not so much as put your nose above deck until I send for you. Is that clear?'

Chapter Ten

What did I expect? To be welcomed with open arms and to be told I am a heroine? 'Yes.' Averil nodded. 'Yes, I promise to stay below deck. Is anyone wounded? Ferret said something about Tom Patch's shoulder. I could dress that if there are any medical supplies.'

'Have a look round,' Luc said as he stuffed the papers into the breast of his coat and strode out. 'And if you find anything incriminating, let me know.'

'How am I supposed to do that without putting my head out?' Averil enquired of the unresponsive door panels. Oh, well, it could have been a lot worse, she supposed. At least no one was seriously hurt and Luc could have been even more angry. It occurred to her after a moment's thought that he was probably more furious than he appeared, but was controlling it well. She could only hope that the fight to capture the French brig would take the edge off his temper.

She began to search the cabin systematically and found several cupboards built into the woodwork. None of them contained any sinister papers, which was a disappointment, but she did find a workmanlike medical kit rolled up in waxed cloth.

'You all right, miss?' Ferret poked his nose round the door, then sidled in. 'Thought I'd keep out of sight a bit.'

'Could you tell the captain that I have found a medical case and

if someone could bring me some water and send anyone who is hurt
down I will see what I can do for them?'

'I'll do that, if 'e don't throw me overboard on sight.' He vanished and a few minutes later Tom Patch arrived with a bucket in
one hand and the other thrust into his bloodstained shirt.

Averil had been brought up to deal with far nastier injuries
amongst the servants or sustained by her father or brothers on hunting expeditions, although Tom was reluctant to take off his shirt
and show his wound to a lady.

'Don't make a fuss,' she said as she poured water into a bowl. 'I
had to dig a bullet out of my brother once when the doctor couldn't
be found.' Actually it was buckshot in the buttocks, the result of
drunken horseplay. Still, bathing and bandaging a simple bullet hole
was easy enough, and it kept her mind off Luc's scathing tongue.

'That's better, miss, thank you.' Tom got to his feet. 'Better get
back up top, we'll be up with them at any moment, I reckon.'

Averil discovered that she could obey Luc's instructions and still
catch a glimpse of what was going on by sitting on the second step
down. It was frustrating, for all she could see was legs, but she could
hear orders being given and listen to Luc's voice.

When it happened, it all happened at once. The brig slowed and
came around. There was a hail, the red-headed man answered in
poor French, then there was a shouted exchange and the brig lost
more way. She almost tumbled down the steps with the bump as
the small ships came together with a grinding of fenders and, suddenly Luc shouted, 'Board them!'

Gunfire, the clash of steel on steel, shouts in French and English.
Averil gripped the steps in an effort to stop herself bobbing up to
see. But if Luc saw her he would be distracted, or think he had to
protect her; it was her duty to stay here, she told herself. Once being
dutiful had been second nature, now it was something she had to
struggle to achieve. Averil held on and prayed.

She did not have long to wait. The gunfire ceased and the voice she could hear clearly was Luc's, in French and then English, giving orders. Averil unclenched her reluctant fingers and went down to the cabin. She was seated at the table, rewinding bandages with mechanical precision when the door opened.

'There you are.' Luc came in and closed the door behind him, then leaned back against it like a man falling on to a soft feather bed, eyes closed. 'Come here.'

So now he was going to shout at her. Averil put down the gauze and went to stand in front of him. 'Is everything all right? Did you get what you needed?'

'Everything.' He kept his eyes closed. 'We got their orders, before they had a chance to throw them overboard, we took the captain and the officers unharmed. *Je te...* I have the proofs.' His educated English accent had changed. He had been speaking and thinking in French, she realised.

'*Très bon,*' she ventured and his lips quirked. Her accent was probably laughable. 'What happens now?'

'This.' He opened his eyes and looked at her and she saw the fire in them, the life, the fierce energy. The desire.

'Luc?' It came out as a quaver.

'Are you afraid of me?' He came upright with a speed that took her unawares, caught her in his arms, turned her and had her pressed against the door before she could say another word. Her nostrils were filled with the scent of man and fresh sweat and black powder smoke; her body quivered with an anticipation she could not control. 'Because you should be. I want to take you here, up against this door. Tell me *no*. Tell me no, *now*.'

One hand was in her hair, the other palmed her breast with possessive urgency. His mouth on her neck was hot, fierce, and her blood responded, all the tension and fear and triumph of the night merging into a fire that consumed the last shreds of restraint.

This is what I want: this, him, now. Nothing else was real, nothing else mattered except the moment, and the next few moments, in Luc's arms. *My hero, my man.*

Her hands were in his hair, trying to bring his mouth to hers, but he was intent on dragging her clothing off and she vanished, blinded and struggling, into the thick wool to emerge, naked from the waist up. She blinked in the lantern's light as she pushed her hair from her face so she could see Luc, reach for him. But he dropped his hands and stepped back, pale under his tan.

'Oh, my God.' He stared at her as if he was seeing her naked body for the first time, then lifted both hands and cupped her breasts, moving close so he could look down at them, as though they were treasures he had found and could not quite believe. Her flesh felt heavy and swollen in his palms, but he did not move more than his thumbs, caressing slowly across the hard, aching points of her nipples.

'Luc.' It was a whisper, but it brought that deep grey gaze to meet her eyes. 'What...what do I do?' Her aunt's lecture on Marital Duties had not included this quivering in her belly, the ache between her legs, the desire and the need. It had included nothing that did not involve lying on her back in the dark and submitting to embarrassing and probably painful intimacies.

His eyes went dark and his hands still and then he released her, turned, slowly, and dropped his hands to the chart table, bent over it like a man in pain.

'Nothing. You do nothing,' Luc said and heard his voice harsh with barely suppressed fury that was directed at himself, not at her. She was probably ruined. Probably. He could not take her until he had tried, and failed, to rescue her from the consequences of all this. He had made her his responsibility, fool that he was.

Behind him Averil was silent for the time it took her to draw in two, very audible, breaths. Then she said, 'Why are you angry? You do not expect a virgin to know what to do, do you?'

She was always thinking—when he allowed her to and was not addling her senses with lovemaking—always, always, courageous. 'I am angry at myself,' he said, wrenching his voice back under control. 'Get dressed before I lose my mind again and forget that you are an innocent.'

'My friend Dita says that men become amorous after danger or excitement. It seemed rather strange to me, when she said it.' Averil's voice faded, then strengthened, and he guessed she had pulled her clothes back over her head. 'Is that what it is?'

'My inability to control myself?' Luc asked. The lines on the chart under his spread hands came back into focus. He was supposed to be sailing this damn brig, and getting it and the French prize and the captured papers back safely, not ravishing virgins in the cabin.

'You seem quite capable of controlling yourself,' Averil said as she came round on his right side and sat down on the edge of the bunk. Her voice was steady, but one look at her white face and the slashes of colour on her cheeks told him that she had sat down because her legs were about to give way. 'Eventually,' she added. For a hideous moment he thought she was going to cry and his stomach, already knotted with guilt and lust, gave a stab of pain.

'You give me an opportunity to excuse myself?' Suddenly it felt as though speaking in French would be easier, for him, but from her accent it seemed unlikely that she would be fluent enough to follow what he was struggling to understand himself. 'I was fired up. I had been fighting and we had won. And, yes, some primitive creature inside me needed to take a woman—*my* woman—in triumph.' *My woman. She is* not *my woman. I do not have a woman. I will not think of her like that. I will not care.*

She was silent and he wanted to drop his eyes from that clear, troubled gaze, but that would be cowardice. 'I had been frightened for you, and angry because you had put me in a position where I might not have been able to protect you. I required, I suppose, to assert mastery and that is one step from forcing you.' *Which is no doubt why I feel sick. That and aching frustration.*

'*Your* woman?' Averil said as though he had not spoken those last sentences.

He could not unsay them. Nor, he realised, did he want to. He wanted her, wanted to be the man who took her virginity. He wanted to keep her and teach her...everything. 'You are not anyone's,' he said at last, making the effort to behave like an English gentleman. 'You are your own woman.'

'Not according to the law,' she pointed out with painful clarity. 'An unmarried woman belongs to her father in every practical way.'

'You are of age.' What was he arguing for? He wanted to make her his.

'I have an obligation,' Averil said. 'A duty. And I have been forgetting that.' And this time a tear did roll down her cheek. Appalled, unable to move, to touch her, Luc watched her dash it away with an impatient hand. No others followed it. 'I don't know—is this, whatever *this* is—' she waved a hand vaguely, encompassing him, the cabin, her own disordered clothing '—is it usual? Is this why unmarried girls are chaperoned so fiercely?'

'I do not know, I have never experienced this before,' he snapped and saw her shock at his tone. 'I have never dallied with an innocent.'

'Oh. Dalliance.' She gave a light laugh and turned her head. He could no longer read her face. 'A pretty word. If that is all it is, then there is nothing to worry about, is there? I must just learn to flirt and not take this all so seriously. Why did you come down here, just now?'

'Why—? Don't you want to discuss this?'

He wanted to, even if she did not. He needed to understand what she felt for him and what it meant.

Averil shrugged, an elegant turn of her shoulder reminding him that she was a lady, despite her seaman's clothing and her tangled hair. 'There is nothing to discuss, is there? We have controlled ourselves, you have remembered that you have a ship to navigate, I that I am betrothed. Don't you recall why you came down?'

'I came to look at the charts,' he said through gritted teeth. How was this little innocent tying him in knots? It was like being outwitted by a kitten, only to discover it was a well-disguised panther.

'Hadn't you better do so?' she asked. 'I don't want to hit the rocks again.' She said it lightly, but he saw the shadows of controlled fear behind her eyes. Despite what had happened the last time she had been on board a ship she had stowed away on the frail pilot gig and then thrown herself into a sea fight. There was nothing wrong with her courage, that was certain.

'We're in deep water now and well clear here of any rocks. I was expecting to sail for the mainland, but now I know I can trust the Governor I can go to him on St Mary's—which will mean we can lay hands on our man without fear of him getting wind of this and escaping. I need to find somewhere for the brigs to hover while I'm rowed into Hugh Town in the pilot gig.'

He smoothed the rolled sheets under his hands and tried to focus. 'I will take you in, too, and leave you with the Governor's wife.' Yes, there was the best place to leave the brigs, in the channel between St Mary's and Gugh. It was a short row into Porthcressa beach and he could send the men back to man the brigs and guard the prisoners until the Governor could get the navy out to them.

'What will you tell her?' Averil swung round, her expression tense.

'That I found you on the beach and locked you in the old isolation hospital away from the men. I am sure she will want to help you. As far as the outside world is concerned there is no need to tell even that. I imagine that there has been enough confusion for us to conveniently gloss over the fact that you were not picked up the morning after the wreck.'

'You mean I should lie?'

'Yes, of course you should lie! At least, I suggest most strongly that you edit the truth. Do you want to be ruined?' *Say yes,* he thought. *Say the world and your virtue are well lost in my arms.*

'No,' she said, looking at him quizzically. 'No, of course not. May I go up on deck now?'

'I don't see why not. The prisoners are all down in the hold.' He turned his back and reached for a rule, pleased to find his hand quite steady. Out of the corner of his eye he saw Averil get to her feet and go to the door. For a moment he wondered if she would speak, but it closed behind her, leaving him alone with the memory of her silence.

Averil climbed up to the deck, found herself a corner out of the way of the crew and watched the French ship, a ghostly shadow that kept station beside them, while she waited for her body to stop trembling and the ache of desire to subside. Lord, how she wanted him—beyond all reason and certainly beyond all decency.

She made herself focus on the ships and what they were doing. The brigs did not seem to need many hands, which was fortunate, with prisoners to guard and allowance to be made for men wounded.

'You all right, miss?' Tom Patch appeared beside her, an unnerving sight with his bloodstained shirt.

'Yes, thank you. Are you? Was anyone else hurt?'

'I'm fine now, thanks to you, miss. And there's nothing much wrong, just the few of 'em with the odd scratch and bang. Cap'n knows what he's about, I'll say that for him, for all that he's a hard devil.'

'Is he? Hard, I mean? I thought all naval officers would be like that.'

'Yeah.' Patch leaned against the mast and sucked his teeth in thought. 'They're all for discipline, but he don't rely just on that, see?' She shook her head, not understanding. 'He can relax, let out the rope, like, because he knows, and we knows, that if we don't come to heel when he tugs it then there's hell to pay. And I gets the feeling that he didn't much care what happened to him, just so long as he could prove himself right and get the bug—um, get the traitors.'

'It was a bit more than that, surely? They had taken his career away. His honour. They could have had him shot. He had a lot to lose and to prove.'

'Aye,' Patch agreed. 'Dead men walking, the lot of us.'

'Not any more,' she said. 'Thanks to the captain.'

'You going to marry him, miss?'

'What? No! I am betrothed to someone else.'

'Oo-er,' Patch said and she could hear he was grinning from his voice. 'He's going to be pleased about all this then, your gentleman.'

'I was not the captain's mistress, that was just a pretence to…to keep me safe.'

That provoked a muffled snort. 'Pull the other one, miss, it's got bells on. I've seen him kiss you. And I've seen him look at you.'

'Captain d'Aunay is a very good actor,' she said stiffly and had to listen to Patch chuckling to himself as he walked away.

At least this motley crew were not going to be acquainted with Lord Bradon! Could she get away with this editing of the truth? Would her future husband guess that she had kissed another man with passion, that he had caressed her, pushed her to the point of reckless surrender? He would know that she had been kissed; Luc had been very confident that he was the first and she supposed she had been getting better at it. That could be explained as the result of flirtations, not anything more serious, she supposed, and frowned into the darkness as the lights of Hugh Town on St Mary's, the largest of the islands, came closer.

But it was not right to deceive the man she was contracted to, the man who would be the father of her children. The man she would spend the remainder of her life with. Should she confess to Andrew Bradon? The thought made her feel sick. She did not think she had even the words to describe what had happened, had *not* happened, let alone the will-power to speak of it to a complete stranger who was not going to be pleased about it, however tolerant he was.

Luc's deep voice behind her made her start. He had come up on deck without her hearing him and was giving the orders to bring them in closer to the beach below the Garrison, high above the town, the place where Yestin the fisherman had signalled to them. That seemed like days ago, not hours.

The men were working the sails, Luc hailed the French brig and it altered course with them. The wind sent her hair whipping across her face.

'There you are.' He leaned against the mast as Tom Patch had done. 'Are you cold?'

'No.' It was not the stiff breeze that made her shiver.

'Tired, then? You can go below and lie down and rest for half an hour. I won't disturb you.'

'I want to watch. I want to see this brought to an end now I have come so far with it.'

'Yes, for you this will be the end of the matter,' he agreed, not looking at her.

'I am sorry I was such a nuisance. It must have been a distraction you could have ill afforded,' she said. It was like speaking to a stranger. She kept her voice polite and formal.

'A distraction, yes, indeed. A nuisance? Never. This will soon become part of a bad dream, part of the nightmare of the shipwreck, and then you will gradually forget.'

'I don't think I could forget Ferret,' she said with an attempt at a joke.

'No, probably not,' Luc agreed with a chuckle. He put his arm around her shoulder and gave her a quick, uncharacteristic, hug. 'Almost there now, Miss Heydon.'

Averil let herself go with the tug of his arm, let her head rest on his chest for an instant and breathed in salt and black powder smoke and damp wool and, under it, the essence of Luc. Her fingers lay on his sleeve and ached with the effort not to close and hold on. *Don't leave me.*

He moved away after a moment, the urgency of her feelings obviously invisible to him, and she clutched the mast for support. What was she thinking of to be clinging to this man, lusting after him? He had no interest in her beyond physical desire—and he would probably have felt that for any reasonably young and attractive female under these circumstances.

I am betrothed. If she repeated that over and over she might, somehow, convince herself it was real, that the shadowy, faceless man she was going to in London was the one she would spend the rest of her life tied to, not this brave, angry, half-Frenchman.

Chapter Eleven

The men swore under their breath as they took the pilot gig into the long sweep of Porthcressa beach. Averil held on to the sides of the pilot gig and stored the colourful language away. It was the early hours of the morning now, no one was about, so there were virtually no lights to guide them in.

Hugh Town was built straggling along a narrow strip of land between two great bites that the sea had taken out of the island, Luc had explained to her. The Garrison, the high mass of land to the east with the Elizabethan Star Fort planted on top and the encircling walls bristling with cannon, grew from one end of the town and the body of the island from the other.

The far side of the strip of town was where the harbour was, but he would not risk going in there and attracting the attention of the traitor. Who knew what watchers he had who would recognise Trethowan being brought back, a prisoner? Or someone might even know the French captain by sight.

But the shallow water and the lack of lights made the men twitchy and their mood infected Averil. She was almost jumping out of her skin by the time the keel ground on sand.

'In you go.' Luc dumped her unceremoniously over the side into water that came halfway up her thighs. A wave sloshed with a cold slap at the base of her belly and she bit back the yelp of discomfort.

Luc followed her over, then Ferret, his long knife in one hand. The remaining crew pushed the prisoners out, jeering quietly as they floundered in the surf with their hands tied behind them.

'Go back to the brigs,' she heard Luc tell the crew as Ferret prodded the two men up the beach to join her on the dry sand. 'I'll send Yestin out with orders. And, Potts, they are both very nice little brigs and if they are not where I expect them to be I will hunt them, and you, down and there will be no prize money, no pardons and either you will hang or I will disembowel you. Or possibly both. Clear?'

'Aye, aye, Cap'n.' Potts sounded as though he was grinning. The pilot gig vanished into the pre-dawn gloom with a faint splash of oars and Luc urged the two captives towards the dark huddle of the town. 'Up there, to the left. The sally port—Trethowan, you'll know it, I have no doubt.'

The man grunted. Beside him the French captain muttered something, low and fast.

'*Capitaine, je parle français,*' Luc remarked. 'I speak also the dialect of Languedoc,' he added, still in French. 'And any further insult to the lady will result in the removal of your ears. You understand me?'

'*Parfaitement. En effet,* you are a traitor to France.' The man reverted to standard French.

'*Mais non,* your France betrayed my family, murdered my father. I will be a loyal Frenchman still when she returns to sanity.' Luc prodded the captain round a corner beside a looming chapel and the road steepened.

'*Ah! Un aristo.*' The Frenchman spat.

'*Absolutement.*' Luc sounded amiable in the face of the insults. Averil trudged up the hill behind him, her wet trousers glued to her legs. They chafed the soft skin of her inner thighs, she was sweating in the heavy Guernsey, the cobbles hurt her bare feet and Luc had forgotten about her with the stimulus of trading insults. She cleared her throat.

'Keep up,' he said over his shoulder. 'It gets darker and steeper here.'

'Good,' she muttered mutinously. 'I needed some exercise.' Just in front of her Ferret gave a snort of laughter, then all four men seemed to vanish into darkness. She baulked at the entrance to the cave, then saw it was simply a narrow way through rocks that lead to the base of a high defensive bank. When she tipped her head back she could see ramparts above her.

'How do we get in?' she asked.

'Quietly.' Luc placed one hand over her mouth. 'There are sentries patrolling the top.'

'How do we get in then?' she repeated, resisting the temptation to either bite or kiss his palm.

'I have a key. Here, Ferret, take it and go first.' The little man vanished into the darkness at the foot of the wall. Luc followed, pushing the prisoners in front of him and Averil, reluctant, brought up the rear.

They were in a narrow twisting stone stairway climbing up through the bank and out by an iron gate that Ferret was holding open, on to a roadway wide enough for a horse and carriage. 'Sentries down there.' He nodded to the left where trees grew thick. And then gestured to the right. 'And I can hear some that way, too.'

'That'll be the guard on the Governor's house. This is where it gets interesting. Don't try to be quiet now or we'll get shot first and questioned afterwards. Just walk along the road so they have plenty of notice we are coming.'

They strode out towards the sounds of voices. Stones crunched underfoot and Ferret began to whistle. Averil smelled wood smoke and bacon. Breakfast. Someone was beginning to cook breakfast. She could eat a horse.

'Who goes there?' The challenge was a shout, then there was the sound of boots approaching at the run.

'Captain Luke d'Aunay of His Majesty's Navy to see the Governor,' Luc said loudly, his accent once more impeccably English. 'With escort and two prisoners.'

'Halt!' A new voice. An officer by the sound of it. A lamp appeared, illuminating black boots, white breeches and a scarlet coat. 'Identify yourself. How the blazes did you get in here?'

'With a key,' Luc stopped and held up a hand to halt them all. 'I have my papers here, if you will permit me?' He reached into his coat, pulled out a slim oilskin package and proffered it. 'Can we discuss this inside? These two are prisoners—one French captain, one English traitor. Their capture needs to be kept quiet.'

The officer looked up from the papers. 'These appear to be in order. Why aren't you in uniform?'

'Clandestine mission, Lieutenant.' There was an edge to his voice that would remind the army man who was the more senior officer.

He doesn't trust us, Averil thought, standing on one leg and rubbing the other dirty, aching foot against the calf while she watched the officer's face. *I don't blame him.*

'Titmuss, Jenkins! Bring them inside under guard until the Governor has seen these.' They were marched forwards, across a sweep of grass and in through the wide front doors of a house.

Civilisation. Averil looked round at polished wainscots, pictures on the walls, heavy silk curtains drawn against the night, and felt weariness sweep over her. Her filthy bare feet sank blissfully into the deep pile of the rugs.

'Keep them here. Sir George is not going to be pleased, being woken at this hour.'

The silvery chime of a clock struck five. Averil looked with longing at the chairs that lined the walls, then set her feet apart, locked her knees to stop herself swaying and resigned herself to wait. Luc caught her eye and tipped his head slightly towards the guards. He did not want them to realise she was a woman, Averil realised. So, it seemed, did Ferret.

'You lean on me, mate,' he said, standing next to her. 'You're in no state to be standing about.' Averil swayed against him until their shoulders were touching. He slipped one arm surreptitiously around her waist and held on. With a sigh of gratitude she let his wiry, malodorous body support her.

'Wake up.' It was Ferret, an elbow in her ribs. 'Here's 'is nibs.'

A big man in a splendid brocade robe, his grey curls still tousled from removing his nightcap, spoke to the officer in the hallway, then took Luc's papers and scrutinised them.

'Mr Dornay, the poet. I see I have been entertaining you on one of my islands under false pretences, Captain.'

'Sir.' Luc was unapologetic. 'I need to speak to you alone as a matter of urgency.'

'Very well. My study. What are we to do with these four, might I ask?' He studied with disfavour the human flotsam dripping sand and seawater on his rugs.

'The two with their hands tied need securing somewhere apart from each other and where there is absolutely no risk of them communicating with anyone in the town. He—' he pointed at Ferret '—needs breakfast and somewhere to rest while he waits for me. That one...' He leaned towards the Governor and murmured in his ear.

'What? Well, I'll be damned. Very well. Better stay in here then. Foster, close the door, let no one in to disturb this, er...person.'

Luc added something else. 'Yes, yes. Foster, fetch a rug so he... er, they can sit down without ruining the upholstery. Now, let's hear the whole of this.'

The officer went out and reappeared with a rug which he threw over a *chaise,* then Averil found herself alone. The room swayed a little as she stood there, but she found if she went with the motion it took her down on to the *chaise* and that was soft and solid and held a faint trace of perfume. With a sigh she let herself drift. It would all be fine now, she thought. She was safe, Luc knew what to do. Safe…

'A female? George, really, you drag me out of bed and some ungodly hour to ask me to look after some disreputable female—'

'Olivia, please! I beg you to keep your voice down.' The door opened as Averil struggled upright and the Governor came in followed by a tall woman, fully dressed and with an expression that, Averil thought hazily, would stun wasps. Luc brought up the rear and closed the door.

'This is Miss Heydon, Lady Olivia. She was washed up on St Helen's after the shipwreck and, because of the extreme secrecy of my mission, I was unable to bring her over here at once. However, as you may know, there is the old isolation hospital there and Miss Heydon was able to sleep there behind locked doors…'

'To which you hold the key, no doubt, Captain.'

'Madam, Miss Heydon is betrothed to Lord Bradon—'

'But not for much longer, I'll be bound. Look at her!'

Averil struggled to her feet. 'Lady Olivia, I am aware that I must present a most disreputable appearance, but—'

The older woman fixed her with a withering look. 'Have you, or have you not, spent five nights in the company of this man, Miss Heydon?'

'Well, yes, but nothing… I mean, it was all perfectly—'

'Your blushes say it all! George, for you to expect me to lend countenance to Captain Dornay's *amours* is outside of enough. Must I remind you that you have two daughters of an impressionable age? They have already seen and heard things that they should not with the house full of half-drowned persons for days on end and whatever is going on up at the Star Fort with Lavinia's friend—'

'Oh, of course! You will know about Dita!' Averil interrupted her. 'Please, can you tell me who was saved?'

Lady Olivia looked down her nose. 'Dita?'

'Lady Perdita Brooke. She is a particular friend of mine.'

'You know Lady Perdita?' The Governor's wife relaxed a trifle. *Old snob,* Averil thought. 'Yes, very well. Please—'

'Lady Perdita was heroically rescued by Viscount Lyndon.' From her expression Lady Olivia obviously approved of Alistair. 'They both left for the mainland yesterday along with most of the other survivors.'

'Thank goodness.' Averil sat down again with a thump. 'And Mrs Bastable, my chaperon? And the Chatterton twins? Daniel and Callum?'

The room went very quiet. 'Mr Daniel Chatterton was drowned. His body was recovered and his brother has taken it back to the mainland for burial,' the Governor said. 'I will have my secretary give you a list of those saved, those known to be dead and those still missing.'

'Thank you,' she said, the schooled politeness forming the words for her while her chest ached with the need to weep. Daniel dead? All that fun and intelligence and personality, gone in an instant. Poor, poor Callum. What a tragic homecoming for him. And Daniel was betrothed—Callum would have that awful news to break to a woman who had been waiting years for her lover to return to her.

'Miss Heydon should rest,' Luc said. 'She has received bad news and she is exhausted. We have been at sea all night.'

'And why it was necessary for her to accompany you out to sea, I really cannot understand,' Lady Olivia interjected.

'And why should you?' Luc said with a smile that would have frozen water. 'All this can wait, surely? Miss Heydon should retire. She will need a bath, some food—'

'Kindly allow me to know what is required for female guests in this house, Captain Dornay or d'Aunay or whatever your name is. Miss Heydon, if you will accompany me, please.' It was an order. Averil did not miss the point that she was a *female,* not a *lady,* in Lady Olivia's eyes. Friendship with Dita might save her from a room in the garrets with the servants, but the Governor's wife had not forgotten the scandalous circumstances of her rescue.

It was an effort not to seek out Luc's eyes, not to send a message— *help me, take me back to our island and make love to me*—but pride stiffened her spine and allowed her to stand, smile at her reluctant hostess and bid the gentlemen good-night as though she was a house party guest.

'Good night, Sir George. Good night, Captain d'Aunay.' She pronounced his surname with care, not that the older woman seemed to notice the implied reproof. She wanted to ask when she would see Luc again, but that would raise Lady Olivia's suspicions even higher. 'Thank you, Lady Olivia.' If a curtsy had not been ridiculous in damp cotton trousers and a smelly Guernsey she would have produced one before she followed her hostess out.

'I will send a maid to you.' Lady Olivia seemed to unbend a trifle now they were away from the men. 'Goodness knows what we can do about clothing. We have had the house full of survivors for days, none of them with so much as a pocket handkerchief to their names, of course.'

A blonde lady in her mid-thirties appeared round the corner, a list in one hand. 'Oh, there you are, Olivia.' She peered at Averil, then raised her eyebrows. 'Another survivor from the *Bengal Queen?*'

'Indeed, Sister. Miss Heydon has fallen into most undesirable company—'

'But at least she is alive,' the other woman said, her warmth reaching Averil like a comforting touch. 'I am so glad for you, my dear.' She held out her hand. 'I am Lavinia Gordon, Sir George's sister.'

'I was just saying that I have no idea what to do about suitable clothing,' her sister-in-law interjected.

'I am sure I have something I can spare—we are much of a size, I suspect. If you tell the maid to come and see me, Sister, I will put out some clothes for Miss Heydon.' She glanced down at the shocking trousers. 'Do tell me, are those as comfortable as they look?'

'They chafe rather when wet, but the freedom is a revelation, Miss Gordon. Thank you so much for offering to lend me clothing.' Beside her, Lady Olivia tutted under her breath and urged her along the corridor.

'The next door on the left, Miss Heydon. I will send the maid along.' Averil found herself in a medium-sized bedchamber. Not a garret then. Perhaps Lady Olivia would unbend still further when she saw Averil properly dressed.

Lord, but she was tired. And hungry. And thoroughly uncomfortable with damp clothes and dirty, tangled hair. As she thought it there was a tap at the door and a maid came in.

'Good morning, miss. I am Waters, miss. There's hot water and a bath on its way up. Would you like some breakfast afterwards? Miss Gordon said you probably would, before you go to sleep. Her woman's bringing a nightgown and fresh linen and a gown.' She ran out of words and stood, mouth slightly open, staring at Averil.

'Thank you, Waters. I would like some breakfast very much. I expect you have been very busy with all the survivors brought here.'

'Yes, miss. None of the ladies had trousers though, miss.'

'Er, no, probably not. But I had to wear something, you see.' There was a knock at the door and Averil made a hasty retreat behind the screens in the corner while thumps and the sound of pouring water heralded the arrival of the bath.

When she looked out there was another maid spreading a nightgown on the bed while Waters tucked items away in the dresser.

'Here you are, miss. You'll need some help with your hair, I expect.'

Averil shed her damp, sandy clothing with a sigh of relief. 'Can these be washed and returned to Captain d'Aunay's man, Ferris? He was sent to the kitchens for some food, but I don't know where he'll be now.'

'Oh, yes, miss.' Waters waited while Averil settled with a sigh of blissful relief in the warm water, then produced soap and a sponge and left Averil to wash herself while she poured water over her hair and knelt to try to rinse out sand, salt and tangles.

It was pure bliss, despite the frequent tugs and tweaks at her hair. Averil lathered up the sponge and washed her hands and arms slowly, luxuriously, as she relaxed. And then she reached her body. The scented bubbles slid down the curves of her bosom and she looked at them as they crested the rosy nipples that peaked at the touch of the suds, ran over the slight swell of her belly, down to the point where the water veiled the dark curls. Her thighs rose above the surface, smooth and pink, marred with bruises and abrasions, and the innocent pleasure she was taking in the bath turned into something else entirely.

While she had been unconscious Luc had washed her naked body. His hands had lathered the strong soap that she had smelt on her skin, his eyes had rested on her breasts as his fingers had washed away the salt and the sand and cleaned her cuts. When she had woken she had felt clean—all over, so his attentions had not stopped with limbs and breasts—and yet, somehow, everything else that had happened, the shock and the grief and the fear, had stopped her thinking about the intimacy of the way he had cared for her.

She could feel the blush colouring her face and hoped the maid patiently working on her hair had not noticed. The realisation should have been mortifying, yet it was not, and she wondered why. Because she had come to trust him? Because she knew with a deep certainty that he had nursed her with integrity and not to gain gratification from her helpless body?

It was more than that, Averil realised as she started to stroke the sponge over her legs. It was erotic, and just thinking about Luc's hands on her body, slick with soap, was arousing her. It had never occurred to her that bathing might be part of lovemaking, but the thought of him kneeling here, beside the tub, produced a soft moan.

'Oh, I am sorry, Miss Heydon! It is such a tangle I don't know that I can do it without pulling a bit.'

'Don't worry, Waters, it was not you. I have so many bruises, I knocked one, that is all.' *I must stop thinking about him bathing me,* she thought as the maid, reassured, went back to tugging the comb thorough her hair. She made an effort and the phantom touch of Luc's hands ceased. *What would it be like to bathe him? Oh, my goodness!* Averil made a grab for her toes and washed them with quite unnecessary vigour. It did not diminish the image of his naked body under her hands, slick with water and soap.

What would it feel like to run her hands into the dark hair on his chest, to follow it down as it arrowed into the water? Would he like it if she touched him there? Of course he would, he was a man. Very much a man.

And I am straying into very dangerous waters. Averil dropped the sponge and wriggled her toes to rinse them. Luc d'Aunay was not for her and Andrew, Lord Bradon, was waiting for her in London. Or, more accurately, he was mourning her; she must send a message as soon as possible

'There, miss. All clean and no tangles. We'd better be getting you dry and into bed before the food arrives.'

'Yes, of course.' Averil got to her feet, dripping, and reached for the towel the maid held out. She had washed Luc from her life as she had rinsed the last traces of soap from her skin. She was going to be Lady Bradon and she was going to start thinking like a viscountess from this moment on. Her throat tightened. It was not going to be as easy as arriving on his doorstep to universal relief that she was not drowned.

Chapter Twelve

'If you feel sufficiently revived, perhaps we should discuss our tactics, Miss Heydon.' The Governor put down his tea cup and the atmosphere in the drawing room changed subtly.

She had slept until woken in the early evening, dressed in her borrowed gown of dusky pink, had her hair coiffed and had walked in Miss Gordon's silk slippers down to join the party for dinner.

Her reception had been gratifying. Lady Olivia nodded approval, Miss Gordon beamed at her and Sir George enquired kindly if she had slept well and felt rested. Luc had looked at her, expressionless, then bowed over her hand with what she could not help but feel was excessive politeness for a small family dinner. She had been entertaining the fantasy that he would be bowled over by the sight of her, elegantly gowned, her hair up, her femininity restored.

But of course, he needed no prompting to think of her as female. He knew, none better, that she was a woman. But it was galling, despite her resolution, to be treated to such comprehensive indifference. Obviously, dressed and respectable, she was no longer attractive to him.

Now she felt them all looking at her. 'Tactics, Sir George?'

'For mitigating the consequences of your belated rescue,' he said.

'I have been thinking about it,' she said with perfect truth. She had thought of nothing else since she had woken and very uncomfortable her reflections had been.

'Indeed,' he said before she could continue. 'And Lady Olivia and I think the best thing would be for us to say nothing publicly about the time you have been...missing. I can write to Lord Bradon regretting that the fact that I was unaware of your betrothal. We will tell him that you have been unconscious for several days being cared for in a house elsewhere in the Isles. Both those statements are perfectly true and will give the impression that you have been with some respectable family all the time. What do you say to that?'

He was so obviously pleased with his solution, and so positive about it, that Averil found herself nodding her head before she realised what she was doing. Then her conscience caught up with her.

'No! I am sorry, Sir George, but I cannot lie by omission and I cannot involve you and others in your household in a deception.'

'Well, in that case,' Lady Olivia said, 'there is only one thing to be done. Captain d'Aunay must marry you.'

Luc's *'Non'* beat her own emphatic 'No!' by a breath. The other three stared at them.

Averil made herself breathe slowly in the long, difficult silence that followed. She felt as though she had been punched in the chest. Of course she did not want him to marry her, but he might at least have hesitated before repudiating the idea with such humiliating vigour! It was incredible how much that sharp negative hurt.

'I have matrimonial plans,' Luc said when it was obvious that she was not going to speak. His eyes were dark and hard and there was colour on his cheekbones under the tanned skin.

'You are betrothed, Captain? Oh, dear, that does complicate matters.'

'I am not betrothed, Sir George. But I am intending to marry a lady of the *émigré* community. A Frenchwoman. I see no reason why Miss Heydon cannot adopt your most sensible solution.'

'Because it is a lie, as I said.' She lifted her chin a notch and managed not to glare at him. That would have revealed too much of her feelings. 'I am contracted to marry Lord Bradon and I intend to honour that contract. I shall go to him and tell him all.'

'All what?' Lady Olivia demanded.

'That I was washed ashore, found by a group of men on a covert naval mission, protected by their officer and returned safely to your care, ma'am.'

'Safely?' There was no mistaking what the Governor's wife meant.

Averil hung on to the ragged edge of her temper with an effort. 'If you are enquiring if I am a virgin, Lady Olivia, the answer is, yes, I am.' She managed, somehow, to say it in a chilly, but polite, tone of voice.

Miss Gordon gave a gasp and Sir George went red. Luc merely tightened his lips and breathed out, hard. 'I am glad to hear it,' Lady Olivia retorted. 'One only hopes that your betrothed believes you.'

'Of course he will. He is, after all, a gentleman.'

The Governor's wife inclined her head. 'He is certainly that and will have expectations of his wife-to-be.'

'I will call on Lord Bradon,' Luc said. 'He will wish to assure himself of Miss Heydon's treatment.'

'I do not think that would be wise,' Averil said. 'It would make it appear that there was something that needed explanation.'

Luc stared at her profile. He could not read this new Averil. The half-drowned sea nymph, the innocently passionate woman, the boy-girl in her borrowed clothes had all gone and in their place was this elegant young lady. The intelligence was there still, of course, and the courage and downright inconvenient honesty. But those attributes lived in the body of this elegant, angry, beautiful creature he did not know how to reach.

And what had possessed him to snap out that one word? In

French, too, which somehow made it worse. A few seconds and he could have been politely supporting Averil. As it was, his reaction had been one of deeply unflattering rejection. He, the last of the d'Aunays, was not going to marry an English merchant's daughter, however well brought up and however elegant her manners, but he could have managed the thing more tactfully.

'I think it would be helpful if I were to speak to Miss Heydon alone.' He had to explain, he could not leave it like this. He no longer had any responsibility for her, he could stop being concerned for her—thank the heavens—but even so, this must be ended properly.

'I hardly think—'

'If they were to stroll in the gardens, Sister?' Miss Gordon intervened. 'I could stay on the terrace as chaperone. The evening is balmy and the fresh air would be pleasant.'

'Very well,' Lady Olivia conceded.

Luc did not wait for her approval. He was on his feet, extending a hand to Averil, even as he said, 'Thank you, Miss Gordon. Miss Heydon? It seems a very clement evening. It would be best if we could agree a mutually satisfactory approach to this, after all.'

'Of course.' Averil got up with grace, as though he had asked her to dance at a ball. 'Thank you, Miss Gordon.'

It was not until they had walked in silence down the length of the path that bisected the long garden that he realised just how angry she was. She turned, slipped her hand from his forearm where it had been resting, and faced him. In the distance, well out of earshot, Miss Gordon strolled up and down the terrace.

'How dare you!'

'Averil, I have explained. You know who I am, what I am. I cannot marry—'

'A merchant's daughter,' she spat.

'An Englishwoman.' Even as he equivocated he felt guilt at not matching her burning honesty.

'That is not what I meant. Of *course* I don't want you to marry me any more than you want to marry me, but could you not have trusted me to refuse? Did you think I want to trap you into marriage?'

'No, I did not think that.' Was that the truth? Why had he been so vehement? It had felt, for a second, almost like fear. Fear of something he did not understand, something that would turn his world on its head. He tried to focus on the important thing, protecting her from the consequences of all this. 'Lord Bradon may not understand. He does not know you as I do.'

'That is most certainly true—no man does!'

'Exactly. Averil, listen to me. He does not need to know about any of this.'

'Yes,' she said slowly. 'Yes, he does. This is the man I have promised to marry. I intend to spend the rest of my life with him and I will, God willing, bear his children. I cannot be anything less than honest with him just because I do not know him.'

He took her by the shoulders and pulled her round so he could see her face in the moonlight. 'You will tell him that I found you naked, that I nursed you for days, that you slept with me in my bed?'

'Certainly.' If he did not know her so well he would have missed the slight shake in her voice. 'It is only right that he knows that I am not quite what he expects me to be. But I am contracted. My father gave his word—'

'You are not a shipload of tea that has been bought and paid for, damn it!' He shook the rigid shoulders under his hands. 'Forget this merchant's obsession with contracts and use some sense. He will reject you out of hand if you tell him all this.'

'I doubt it,' she said, cool as spring water. 'I have a very large dowry and I hope he is able to see beyond his male prejudices and recognise the truth when he hears it. Will you let go of me, please?'

He kept his hands right where they were. 'You know he wants you for your money and yet you will humiliate yourself by confessing all this to him? You talk about a lifetime together, children—do you think *he* thinks about these things?'

'I am sure he thinks about children. This is, whatever you say, a business deal, a partnership with the succession a major factor. Don't tell me that the marriage you are considering will be anything else—a love match, perhaps? You will buy a French bloodline to ally with yours. Would you want your wife to come to you with lies on her tongue?'

She shifted in his grip but he held tight to the slender shoulders. 'Of course I would, if there was nothing serious to confess and if by speaking she ruined everything! Every marriage must contain secrets—and that way lies peace and coexistence. An arranged marriage is not some emotional entanglement.' That was what he wanted. That was safe. No one could hurt your heart and your soul when neither of you cared deeply. He took another deep breath and tried to convince her.

'You are a virgin, you are not carrying my child, I am never going to see you again once you leave this island. It is over, finished. Why ruin the rest of your life for nothing?'

'Honour?' Her tone made him flinch.

'A woman's honour lies in her chastity. You are a virgin.' She gave a little sob that was not grief. Anger, perhaps, or frustration. 'If you insist on this course then I must come with you. Bradon will want to call me out. *That* is a matter of honour.'

He must have jerked her closer without realising. His senses were flooded with the scent of her, the familiar Averil-scent of her skin mingling with the soap she had bathed with and the musk of excited, angry female. His body stirred into instant arousal.

'I have no intention of telling him who you are. This mission will remain secret, I assume? I cannot imagine that they will want it trumpeted that an admiral's cousin has been involved in treason and was thwarted by a Frenchman. Do you think I want you swaggering in, provoking a duel? What if you are killed?'

'I would not be the one killed. And I do not swagger.'

'Ha!' She tossed her head. 'And if you kill my betrothed? Do you think that a duel could be kept secret? You will ruin me—for what? Your honour. Not mine.'

'Damn it, Averil.' What she said was the truth. If she insisted on doing this insane thing then he must stand aside and allow her to do it, at whatever cost to his own honour. 'What will you do if he rejects you?'

'I do not know.' She stared at him, her face black and white and silver in the moonlight. He saw her bite her lip and a tremor ran through her, a vibration of fear under his hands. Then she collected herself. 'He won't. He wouldn't.'

'He might, he very well might. And then you *will* be ruined. Think of the scandal. Where will you go?'

'I don't know.' There was that shiver again. Her brave front was just that—underneath she knew the dangers of what she was intending to do. 'I suppose…I could always go home again.'

'Or you could become my mistress.' Even as he said it, Luc knew it was what he was hoping for. He wanted her and if Bradon rejected her the choices before her were few.

She could travel back to India, a perilous three-month voyage with the shame of her story following her; she could seek, without support, to find herself a less fastidious husband or she could join the *demi-reps*.

'Your mistress?' For a moment she did not seem to understand, then her whole body went rigid with indignation. 'Why, you…you bastard! You don't think I am good enough to marry, but you would keep me for your pleasure!' She wrenched round, fighting his grip. 'Let me go—'

Luc shifted his grip, afraid of hurting her, too aroused to release her. She thudded against his chest and he held her with one hand splayed on her back, the other in her hair, and kissed her.

He told himself it was to stop her creating a scene and bringing the others out into the garden. That degree of rational thought lasted long enough for him to open his mouth over hers and thrust his tongue between her tight lips as though he thrust himself into her virgin body. It was wrong, it was gloriously right, it was heaven. She tasted of wine and fruit and woman and he lost himself, drowning in her, until she twisted, jerking her knee up. If it were not for her hampering skirts she would have had him, square in the groin. As it was, her knee hit him with painful force on the thigh and he tore his mouth free.

'How could you?' she said, her voice as shaky as his legs had become. Luc took an unobtrusive grip on the statue base beside him and opened his mouth to apologise. Then he saw her face in the moonlight. Her eyes were wide, her lips parted, but it was not the face of a fearful woman, a woman who had been assaulted. It was the face of a woman in the throes of passion and uncertainty. There was longing and fear and excitement; she was as affected by that kiss as he was.

'You value honesty and truth,' Luc said, ignoring her question. If he was right her words had been aimed as much at herself as at him. 'Tell me that you did not want me to kiss you. Tell me that you do not want to be my lover. Make me believe you.'

'You arrogant devil,' she whispered.

'Go on, tell me. Surely that is much easier than confessing what happened on St Martin's to Bradon?'

'It would be wrong. Sinful, if I felt like that.'

'I asked for facts, not a moral judgement,' he said and saw her flinch at his harshness.

'Yes,' she threw back at him. 'Yes, I want to be your lover. Yes, I want to give my virginity to you. There—does that make you feel better? Because it makes me feel wretched.' And that time her sob was one of grief as well as anger.

'Averil.' The lust drained from him as rapidly as it had come, leaving him empty. 'Averil,' and he lifted his hand to touch her cheek. He could not take her virginity, he knew that. If she had a faint chance of making this marriage happen, then he had to leave it to her. Somehow he had let himself care that much.

The tendrils of hair that curled around her ears brushed his fingers as she made a little sound that might have been a shocked gasp, that might have been *Yes,* and feeling came back in a rush. A reluctant tenderness and desire and the realisation that she was his for the asking, here, now.

'You will go to London and you will be brave and honest and if Bradon does not take you with open arms, then the man is a fool,' he said. He could not entrap her in the coils of her innocent passion, but he could plan for the inevitable.

'I would rather not marry a fool,' she said, a shaky laugh in her voice. 'I hope he is a good, compassionate man who will forgive all this and makes a kind husband. I hope he makes me feel like this when he touches me.' Luc pulled her into his arms and bent his head. 'No,' she whispered.

'Let me make love to you, Averil. This once. I swear you will go to him as much a virgin as you are now.' And then, when Bradon showed her the door, she would know who to turn to—her desire and her passion would bring her to him.

She tipped up her head, her expression in the silver light eager, all the anger gone. 'You can do that?'

'I can give you pleasure and not harm you if you will trust me.' It was not harm, he told his conscience. The choices were all with the other man.

'Here? But—'

'Here.' He guided her into the arbour that faced away from the house towards the shelter of the slope. 'Here, now.'

* * *

She trusted him. Why, she did not know, for this was her virtue she was risking, not her life, which she knew he would protect at the cost of his. Luc had asked her to be his mistress, he had kissed her until she was dizzy with desire, he was the last man she should yield herself to. And yet she had no will to deny him. Or was it herself that would not be denied?

He pulled her down with him on to the broad-planked seat and kissed her, slowly, druggingly, until analysis was impossible and all that was left was the heat and strength of him and the caress of his mouth and the drift of his hands.

The neckline of the simple gown was no barrier to long fingers sliding under the lace trim to catch and tease her nipples. He rolled them between finger and thumb until she squirmed against him, panting with shocked pleasure. It was as though the wicked play of his fingers pulled on hot wires that led straight to the pulse that beat with urgent insistence between her legs. Averil moaned against his mouth and he stroked his tongue into hers as though to soothe, yet the caress was like pouring oil on to the flames of desire.

'Please,' she gasped against his lips. 'Please…'

She did not know what she was asking for, what to expect. The night air on her legs as Luc's hand lifted the full silken skirts made her stiffen, but his mouth and his other hand on her breast held her in thrall. Her hands were clasping his head, her fingers laced into the dark hair, his skull hard and shapely under her palms.

'Relax,' he said and she almost laughed because she was quivering with tension like an over-tightened violin string and surely she must snap. Luc had her sprawled in utter abandon across his thighs. The hand on her breast held her to him, the other smoothed back the rustling silken skirts until her legs and the paleness of her belly were exposed. In the semi-darkness the dark triangle at the top of her thighs showed stark against the white skin.

'Luc,' she whispered. It was shameful and shameless, but he was looking at her with utter concentration, his palm smoothing down over the quivering skin, and under her she felt the heat and thrust of his erection. He found her desirable, and that was infinitely exciting. But he had promised he would not take her virginity, so what happened now? Surely he would not leave her in this state—aching and needing and so taut that she was trembling?

His big, calloused hand cupped her mound under its sheltering curls as his mouth caught her whimper of protest. One finger slid between the hot, wet folds and began to rub in time to the thrust of his tongue and Averil arched into his palm, pressing against it, instinctively trying to intensify the pleasure.

He had found that tiny knot of sensation where the strange, aching pulse quivered into life every time he touched her and he teased it until he found the rhythm that had her sobbing into his mouth. 'More,' she said, her tongue tangling the word into a groan. 'Oh, more, Luc. More.'

Somehow he must have understood. He lifted his mouth from hers and she saw the glint of moonlight on his teeth as he smiled. 'More like this?' he asked and slid a finger deep into her.

She clenched around him, tight, desperate, as the tension swept through her, an irresistible wave, and she lost all hold on reality and screamed as his kiss swallowed the betraying sound.

Chapter Thirteen

'We had better go in.'

In where? Averil wondered, as she drifted back to reality. Or perhaps it was a dream. She was warm and safe and Luc was holding her and little ripples of pleasure kept running through her body. If they went in, wherever that was, the pleasure would stop.

'No,' she mumbled against his shirt front and heard the laugh rumble in his chest.

'Yes. Come on. Can you stand up?'

'No.' But he stood up anyway and she found her feet were on the ground, even though she had to hold tight to Luc's lapels. Her legs had no more substance than a rag doll's, her pulse was beating wildly and she wanted to do it all over again. Everything, and in a bed this time. But, of course, she could not. This had been once, and never again.

Averil stumbled as Luc helped her outside, his hand under her elbow. 'That was good?' he asked. Somehow she could not resent the thread of amusement in his voice.

'Amazing,' she said honestly. 'What was it?'

'An orgasm,' he explained, still managing to stay serious, although she guessed her ignorance was a novelty for him.

'Don't you need one, too?' Thank goodness it was dark so her crimson cheeks were not visible.

'Don't worry about it,' Luc said. 'It will be all right.'

'Oh.' Presumably that meant he would seek out whatever women in Hugh Town made their living seeing to the needs of the gentlemen of the island. At least they would not ask him foolishly naïve questions.

'You are naturally very passionate,' Luc said, his voice low. They were walking up and down a path parallel to the house; some sense of reality was returning to her. She could make out the shape of Miss Gordon strolling on the terrace, out of earshot: their tactful, ineffectual, chaperone. Was that deliberate on her part?

'You don't really want me to be your mistress,' Averil murmured back. 'I am ignorant and inexperienced.'

'And sensual and natural and very lovely. Of course I want you.' He began to make his way back to the house. Averil dragged her feet—what if the others knew what they had been doing? He seemed to guess at her reluctance. 'Don't worry, it will not be branded on your forehead *I had an orgasm in the summerhouse.*'

'Don't say such things!' she whispered, agitated.

'Pretend to be angry with me,' Luc said. 'That will convince Lady Olivia that we have been discussing the question of marriage and are set against each other and it will explain any colour in your cheeks. If you are determined to go through with this madness, then go to Bradon. I will give you an address. If you need me—*when* you do—send me word.'

'You really expect me to turn up on your doorstep asking to become your mistress, don't you?' she said, reaction turning into something very like anger in reality.

'Yes,' he said. 'I look forward to it.'

Averil whirled out of his light grip and half ran down the path to Miss Gordon. 'It is quite impossible, ma'am, we should never suit, even if it was right that I should break my contract with Lord Bradon. I beg you, please help me to make my way to London.'

'Of course.' The other woman looked past Averil to where Luc stood on the path. 'My brother will advance the money for a chaise from Penzance and your lodgings on the way. You had better take Waters with you as your maid. We will give you instructions to my brother's agent in the port—he will find you respectable lodgings and then hire a chaise and reliable postilions. You must spend at least two nights on the road, I fear, for it is over three hundred miles. Do you think you can manage by yourself?'

'Thank you,' Averil said with real gratitude. The thought of dealing with the practicalities of travel sounded blissfully straightforward after the emotional turmoil of the past week. 'I am used to long journeys in India and a chaise with postilions sounds much easier to deal with than ox carts and elephants!'

Miss Gordon laughed and urged her inside and towards the stairs. There were footsteps on the terrace behind her, but Averil did not turn around.

'Good morning, miss.' The curtains swished back with a rattle of rings.

'Good morning, Waters. Hot chocolate? How delightful.' To wake in a soft bed with light streaming through a wide, clean window: luxury. Lonely luxury. Averil curled her fingers around the cup and inhaled with a shiver of delight as the aroma banished the lingering memory of Pott's evil tea.

'Miss Gordon says, will you come down for breakfast, miss, or would you like to take it in bed?'

'I will come down, thank you.' She slid out of bed, still cradling the chocolate cup, and went to the wash stand. 'Miss Gordon said you might be willing to come with me to London, Waters.'

'Yes, please, miss. I'm a London girl myself, you see, and I came down here because my young man got a job as a footman, but we fell out and I miss my mam and the young ones something awful. And I miss London, too.'

Averil dipped the toothbrush in the pot of powder. 'I can't promise there will be a permanent position for you—that depends on what Lord Bradon, my betrothed, says.'

'That's all right, miss. I can always stay with Mam in Aldgate until I get a new post. Miss Gordon's given me a good character.'

Averil paused at the landing window and looked out over a view of rooftops, then sea and scattered islands with white sand beaches glittering in the sun. Shifting sands. If the *Bengal Queen*'s anchor had not dragged on the sandy seabed, if she had not hit the rocks before the crew could get her back under control, Averil would have landed in Penzance, would have waited patiently until Lord Bradon sent an escort for her and would, even now, be preparing for her marriage.

She would not have met Luc, she would never have discovered the delights of physical love in his arms, she would not have had to make difficult choices. *No, I would still be the nice, well-behaved, dutiful young lady I always was.*

She smiled absently at the servants who met her at the foot of the stairs and directed her to the breakfast room. *Was I always so dutiful? Because if I was, where did this wanton creature come from who only desires to be in Luc's arms and in his bed? Would she have stayed buried for ever if he had not summoned her?*

Her smile was conscious and bright as she entered the cheerful small room and her stomach lurched—relief or disappointment?—when she saw the only occupant was Miss Gordon applying herself to a pile of toast with a book propped up before her on the cruet.

'Good morning, Miss Heydon.' She flipped the volume closed and rang the small bell by her place. 'We are alone, as you see. My brother and Captain d'Aunay breakfasted over an hour since and my sister-in-law prefers the solitude of her bedchamber before facing the hurly-burly of the day. Did you sleep well?'

'Thank you, I was most comfortable.' A footman poured coffee and indicated with a gesture the buffet and its covered dishes.

Miss Gordon nodded to the man and waited until the door closed behind him and Averil returned to her seat with a slice of omelette before speaking again. 'I gather that my brother spent half the night with the captain. The prisoners—although we are not supposed to know of them, of course!—are on their way to Plymouth already.' She took a folded paper from her pocket and handed it to Averil. 'From Captain d'Aunay.'

'Thank you.' Averil eyed the red wax with its impress of a unicorn's head. His seal ring, she supposed, although she had never seen him wearing it. She laid the letter down unopened and picked up her fork.

'Please, do not mind me.' Miss Gordon gave an airy wave of her toast and reopened her book.

Averil put a forkful of egg in her mouth, chewed it for a minute without tasting it, buttered some toast, sipped her coffee. The letter lay there looking as innocent as a snake under a stone.

Impatient with herself, Averil broke the seal and spread the single sheet open.

It goes well, so far, the letter began without salutation. Luc's handwriting was smaller than she imagined it would be, clear and somehow the style was different from the educated hands she was used to. He had been taught to write in France, she reminded herself. *Sir George is convinced, having had his own suspicions, and will tidy things up at his end. I will take the brigs to Plymouth this morning.*

When you need me, send to me at Albany, off Piccadilly.

God's speed on your journey.

L.M. d'A.

When you need me, not *if.* Arrogant man. His certainty that her meeting with Lord Bradon would be a disaster was not encouraging, nor was her complete panic about what she should do if her betrothed rejected her. *Andrew,* she reminded herself. She must begin to think of him as a real person, not an abstraction.

She folded the letter and pushed it into the pocket in the skirts of her borrowed gown. Miss Gordon looked up, closed her book again and cocked her head on one side like an inquisitive bird, but she asked no questions.

'I suggest you rest here another night to recover. It will take the best part of the day to sail to Penzance. I have written out some notes on the road journey for you, and my brother has a letter for his Penzance agent and some money. There is a letter for Lord Bradon as well. It contains no details other than to say that we are sorry we did not know of your connection with him and therefore did not know to contact him after the wreck. That leaves the explanations entirely up to you.' Averil murmured her thanks. 'I have given Waters some changes of linen for you and a cloak and bonnet.'

'You are very kind. I will have everything returned as soon as possible, of course. And Lord Bradon will recompense Sir George.' At least, she sincerely hoped he would. If he showed her the door, he might well forget all about the logistics of her arrival. She must note the amounts so, if the worst happened, Papa could repay her debts.

'Of course. I quite envy you going to London. I miss it sadly, but perhaps we will meet again there later this year. I hope to visit a friend of mine there. She is staying at the Star Fort at the moment, away from the chaos this household has been in this past week, reacquainting herself with a certain gentleman,' she added with a wicked twinkle in her eye.

That must have been what Lady Olivia had been so snappy about, Averil guessed. Miss Gordon appeared to have a *penchant* for assisting lovers. Perhaps she had been disappointed in love herself, or was merely a romantic.

'I should be very glad to see you there,' she said, and meant it.

By the sixth day of her journey from the Isles of Scilly Averil would have been glad to see London, with or without a friendly face.

She was travelling in considerable comfort, although Sir George's agent had been so particular and painstaking that it had taken two days before he was satisfied with all the arrangements and she could convince him that she was well rested enough to undertake the journey, by which time it was Saturday and Averil did not feel she should travel on the Sunday.

Her courses had started on the ship between the islands and Penzance, just to add to the awkwardness of travel, and she confided to Waters that she was not sorry to have the excuse of an extra day in the comfort of a good inn.

But the travelling was comfortable enough once they had set out. The postilions were courteous and steady and both the inn in Penzance and the one she had stayed in the night before at Okehampton had been respectable and clean. Waters was proving sensible, competent and reasonably quiet.

All of which provided not the slightest stimulus, challenge or impediment to her thoughts about what was awaiting her and what had happened in that week with Luc. Her meeting with Andrew Bradon loomed ahead and, like a prisoner awaiting execution, she just wanted to get it over with.

Even the green rolling countryside, so utterly different from India, passed like stage scenery against which the phantoms of her imagination acted out one disastrous encounter after another. There was plenty of time for lurid imaginings. On the first day they had been almost twelve hours on the road; today, it seemed, would be eleven hours.

The chaise slowed for a moment, drew over and another vehicle went past, its bright painted body rocking and swaying. 'Another yellow bounder, and in a hurry,' Averil remarked to Waters, who was pulling up the window against the cloud of dust the other post-chaise left in its wake. 'The passenger must be immune to seasickness!'

'There'll be a lot of navy men on this road, I'll be bound,' Waters remarked.

'Of course, yes.' That would explain the impression she had received of navy blue and the flash of gold braid. 'I shall be glad to stop for the night, I must confess.' Journeys in India took weeks, ponderous affairs requiring much planning, the assembling of trains of creaking ox carts, the hiring of armed outriders, the organisation of the household to shift from the heat of the plains up to the cool of the hills for the summer and back again for the winter. The Europeans moved like the flocks, herding themselves, not for fresh grass, but for relief from heat and dust and disease.

This rapid travel, the ability of a lady to undertake a journey almost at a whim, was novel and rather alarming. As she thought it the chaise slowed to a trot, and she saw they were entering a town. It swerved, passed through the arch into the inn yard and came to a clattering halt.

'Here we are, ma'am.' One of the postilions opened the door. 'The Talbot at Mere. We were told this was the place for you to stop.'

Averil climbed down, stumbling a little, her legs stiff. 'It seems very busy.' As she spoke another carriage clattered into the yard, ostlers ran out with a change of horses and several people walked in from the street. 'Perhaps I had better check they have accommodation before you unharness the horses in case we must try another inn.'

He touched his forelock and she started to cross the yard. From the door a big man with an apron stretched across his belly bowed to her. The landlord, no doubt. On the far side men lounged, talking, several of them in navy-blue uniforms. She kept walking towards the landlord, ignoring them as a lady should, Waters at her heels.

'Good evening, ma'am. Would you be requiring a room?'

'Indeed, and with a private parlour if you have one available.'

'I'm sorry, ma'am. There's just the one bedchamber left—quiet, though on the small side. But all the parlours are taken.'

That would mean dining in the common room. Averil bit her

lip—was it better to stay here where the host seemed respectable and she was sure of a room at least, or carry on and risk another inn?

'The lady may have my rooms,' a voice said. 'I have no pressing need for a parlour.'

She was tired and imagining things. Averil turned. A tall naval officer, his cocked hat under his arm exposing his neatly barbered black head, bowed. 'Your servant, ma'am. Landlord, please have my traps shifted at once. The bed—' the amused grey eyes lifted to Averil's face '—has not been slept in.'

'Captain d'Aunay.' There was no breath left in her lungs for questions.

'My pleasure, ma'am.' He bowed again and walked away without a second glance. The perfect gentleman.

'Well, that's all right then,' the landlord said, his delight at being able to satisfy both customers apparent. 'I'll show you up at once, ma'am.'

My pleasure… The bed has not been slept in. Yet.

'This was fortunate, miss, the captain being here.' Waters looked with approval at the meal the servant had set out on the round table in the parlour. 'Nice rooms, and quiet, too.'

'Yes, indeed.' They were ideal, Averil told herself. A trundle bed for Waters to sleep on in the same chamber as herself and no way to the bedchamber except through the parlour door, which had a stout lock on the inside. What did she think was going to happen? That Luc would stroll in, evict her maid and ravish her? Or that she would lose all self-control and go and seek him out? Either was unthinkable.

Averil eyed the door again, wishing she could lock it now, but the servant would be in and out while they were eating and afterwards to clear the table. She would think Averil had run mad if she had to have the door unlocked every time.

'I didn't recognise Captain d'Aunay for a moment, miss. Scrubs up well, doesn't he?' Waters chatted away. 'Not that he'll ever be handsome, exactly, not with that nose and that stubborn chin. Wasn't it a coincidence, him being here?'

The girl was not making snide remarks, Averil decided, it was simply her own conscience nagging, telling her that this could not possibly be chance.

'He is a fighting man, not a courtier,' she said. 'Doubtless a prominent nose is no handicap at sea. Eat up, Waters, before your dinner gets cold.'

'Yes, miss.' Waters attacked the steak-and-oyster pie with relish. 'What sort of house has Lord Bradon got, miss?' she asked after a few minutes.

'He is the heir, so the properties actually belong to his father, the earl,' Averil explained, trying to recall the details. 'There is a large town house in Mayfair and then Kingsbury, the country seat in Buckinghamshire. And I believe there is a shooting box somewhere as well.'

'And one day you'll be the countess.' Waters pursued a piece of carrot round the plate. 'That's wonderful, miss.'

'Yes.' Indeed it was. Her great-grandfather had sold fruit and vegetables, her grandfather had opened a shop selling tea and coffee and her father had built on that start and become a wealthy merchant with a knighthood. Now he wanted connections and influence in England for his sons, her brothers. Mark and John were not expected to soil their hands with commerce but to become English landed gentry. With her help they would make good marriages, buy estates, become part of the establishment.

Averil had never had to do a hand's turn of work in her life, only to live in the lap of luxury and become a lady. Now it was her duty to make her contribution to the family fortunes. But she could not take marriage vows and deceive her new husband.

A tap on the door heralded the servant who cleared the plates and dishes and left an apple tart and a jug of cream in their place. Averil ate, absently listening to Waters's wistful hopes that Lord Bradon might have a place for her in his establishment.

The door behind creaked open. 'Thank you, we have finished. You may clear now and bring a pot of tea in about an hour,' Averil said as she folded her napkin and stood up.

There was no sign of the servant. Luc stood in the open doorway, filling it.

Chapter Fourteen

'Captain d'Aunay. Is there something you wish to say to me?' How calm she sounded. It was as though someone else entirely was speaking, not the woman whose pulse was racing and whose mouth had suddenly lost all moisture.

He smiled and the maid jumped to her feet. 'I'll go and—'

'Stay here, Waters.' Averil gestured to a chair on one side of the empty fireplace. 'Sit there, if you please.'

'Yes, miss.' Eyes wide, Waters obeyed.

'I merely wished to see whether you are comfortable, Miss Heydon.' Uninvited, Luc strolled into the room and let the door swing to behind him. He filled the cosy, slightly shabby, space just as he had dominated the old hospital hut.

'Perfectly, thank you, Captain. I was on the point of saying to Waters how pleasant it was to have a room to ourselves where we could lock the door.'

'Indeed, that is why I thought you would like this one.'

'You would have me believe you selected this especially for me?' She wished she could sit down, but she would have to invite him to as well and then how would she get him out?

'Of course. Sir George's secretary showed me the inns he had noted for the postilions. I thought, given how busy the roads to London from the ports are, that it would be as well to keep an eye on you if I could.' Luc propped one shoulder against the window frame, quite as comfortable as he would have been in a chair, leaving Averil standing stiffly in the middle of the room.

She sat down and fixed him with a chilly smile. 'Most kind, but I would hardly wish for your assistance when you have your duties to perform.'

'How fortunate that pleasure and duty do not conflict,' Luc said, so smoothly that her fingers itched to wipe the assurance off his face. 'We made good time to Plymouth, I spoke to the senior officer there and was ordered up to London to report to the Admiralty.'

'Then should you not be on your way?'

'I was not required to gallop,' he said. 'Merely to present myself with due despatch to their lordships. Would you care for a stroll to take the evening air, Miss Heydon?'

It was on the tip of her tongue to refuse him, but the room was stuffy, she was stiff with sitting and she had a maid with her. A walk would be very welcome. But if Luc thought she would consent to vanish into the woods with him for further, highly educational, dalliance that would shake her tenuous composure even more, he was much mistaken.

'Thank you, Captain. That would be delightful.'

Oh, yes, that was precisely what he had thought she would say. It was incredible how those cool grey eyes could heat into sensual invitation.

'Come along, Waters, fetch your bonnet. And my bonnet and shawl, please.'

'You think you need protection from me?' Luc asked softly as the maid went into the bedchamber, leaving them alone.

'From the moment my feet touched the mainland I think I have re-entered reality. And my reality is one of respectability, Captain.'

'I see. And you think Lord Bradon will appreciate these geographical boundaries on behaviour?'

'I have no idea, but I will not insult him by risking being seen behaving in any way that is not proper—not here, where I might be recognised later by one of his acquaintance.'

'One hopes Lord Bradon appreciates the sensitive honour displayed by his betrothed,' Luc said as Waters emerged with Averil's bonnet in her hand, the shawl over her arm. Gloves were one thing that she had not been loaned. It was most unladylike to go out without them, but it could not be helped.

'Indeed. Honour is such a very subtle subject for gentlemen—so difficult for a lady to decipher.' She tied her bonnet strings while she spoke and Luc took the shawl from the maid and arranged it around her shoulders, his fingers carefully touching fabric, not skin. The shiver could only come from her imagination. The ache, as she knew well by now, was sheer wantonness.

When they reached the yard he offered his arm. She placed the tips of her ungloved fingers on it and they strolled towards the street, Waters close on their heels. She was within earshot and Averil intended that she stayed there.

It was an effort not to let her mind run round and round their last encounter, like a squirrel in a cage. 'This is the first English town I have seen properly,' she said, determined to pretend it had not happened and this man had not caressed her intimately, brought her wicked delight, seduced her into sin. 'I did not feel I could walk out in Penzance or Okehampton without an escort. Is it usual for so many buildings to be of stone?'

'In parts of the country with good building stone, yes,' Luc said. 'It is the same in France. Otherwise there are brick or timber-framed houses, like that one. It can change within a few miles, depending on the underlying rock.' They strolled on a few more paces. 'The market square,' Luc observed. 'An historic feature, I have no doubt. How genteel we sound. I had no idea a small town could provide such innocuous subjects for conversation.'

'And how fortunate that is,' Averil returned, studying the open space. 'Markets in India are very different. On the way we moored at Madras and I visited the market to buy Christmas presents with Lady Perdita and Lord Lyndon. There was a mad dog and Dita saved a child from it—and me, too. Then Lord Lyndon saved Dita.'

The square was warm with evening light and people going about their business. They moved slowly now, at the end of the working day, stopping to talk with neighbours, to wait for a child's lagging steps.

'How calm and ordered this is. I was so afraid in that market, and I did nothing, just allowed myself to be bundled to safety.' She shivered, seeing a small boy fetching water from the pump, fair-haired and red-cheeked and laughing with his friends, so unlike the small Indian child who had run screaming in terror.

'And you blame yourself for not being in the right place to act,' Luc observed. 'Of course, I have seen how timorous you are, how cowardly, so perhaps you are right.'

'You are teasing me,' Averil observed. There was a warmth in his look that told her it was more than teasing. He thought her courageous? Thinking about it, perhaps she had not done so very badly in the face of shipwreck and capture and a fight at sea.

'As you say,' he agreed with a chuckle. 'Where shall we go now?'

'The church?' That seemed an innocuous destination. If she had been alone she would have liked to go inside and sit for a while, but she felt awkward asking Luc to wait. 'Oh. It is very large, is it not? And a tower with those pointed things on the corners. How interesting—this is the first English church I have seen close to.'

She looked over the wall into the churchyard. 'And so green! In Calcutta, where I used to live in India, there is a big cemetery for the English with massive tombs and dusty paths and trees that look nothing like these at all. And birds and little squirrels and... Oh, dear, I have become quite homesick. How foolish, I thought I had got over that.'

'Come and sit down.' Luc led her into the churchyard and found a bench. Waters perched on the edge of a crumbling table tomb and watched Luc with interest.

She finds him attractive, Averil thought as she caught an errant tear with her handkerchief and straightened her shoulders. *And who am I to blame her?*

'When my mother and I returned to England my English grandfather, the Earl of Marchwood, thought it was best I go to university and then into the church,' Luc observed. He took off his cocked hat, leaned back with his hands clasped behind his head, stretched out his long legs and gazed up at the tower.

'Into—you mean, become a clergyman?' Averil collapsed into unladylike giggles. 'You?'

'You have a very unflattering opinion of me, by the sound of it,' Luc remarked. He appeared lazily indifferent to her mockery. 'Grandpapa was not best pleased to discover that I held the same rationalist beliefs as my father. By the time he had stopped spluttering and threatening me with hellfire and eternal damnation I had joined the navy.'

'You are an atheist?' She had never met one of those dangerous creatures.

'A sceptic with an open mind,' he corrected her. 'I am perfectly comfortable reading services at sea or turning out for church parade. Does that shock you?'

'No,' she said and heard herself sound as doubtful as she felt. 'But you wanted to join the navy?'

'Not particularly. I wanted to kill revolutionaries. I wanted to kill the people who had taken my father's life and my home. It was the navy or the army and I found the Admiralty first.' He shrugged. 'It was fortunate, I suspect. The navy is far less snobbish about foreigners without much money than the army is. Now I have the money and it doesn't matter.'

'Where did you get it from?' A most improper question, she knew. Ladies did not discuss money.

'Prize money and then an inheritance from my mother's side of the family,' Luc said. 'I will need a great deal when I get my hands on my estates again. But there is enough to finance my pleasures very adequately,' he added, so blandly that Waters, swinging her heels and watching the verger locking the church, did not seem to notice anything untoward.

Luc's fingers curled around hers and he began to make circles in the palm of her hand. As Averil stiffened and tried to pull away he half turned on the bench so his shoulder was to the maid and lifted her hand to his lips. As she tugged he opened his mouth and sucked the length of her index finger right in.

His mouth was hot and wet and the suction was strong enough to make her gasp and his eyes were sending her the wickedest of messages. Her other fingers were splayed against his face, the evening growth of beard bristling under the sensitive pads. Then she realised what this was mimicking and her cheeks reddened and his lids lowered as if he was in a sensual dream.

Averil tugged again and he closed his teeth, gently. 'Let me go,' she demanded. 'It is indecent!'

He released her and smiled. 'Such a naughty imagination, Averil,' he murmured and licked his lips. 'Whatever can you mean?'

She got to her feet. 'Waters, come along and stop daydreaming!'

'Yes, ma'am.' The girl scrambled down from the tomb and Averil felt a stab of guilt for snapping at her.

'We must go back now. We have a long day tomorrow. Thank you, Captain d'Aunay, but I am sure we can find our own way to the inn.'

'You will accept my escort, I hope. My intention is to protect you.'

'Your intention is to seduce me,' she hissed as she took his arm. It would create a scene, and questions in Waters's mind, if she made an issue of walking with Luc.

'To protect and seduce,' he murmured back as he opened the gate out of the churchyard.

Averil laughed in the hope that the maid would not realise they were arguing. 'You attempt to reconcile opposites, Captain.'

'Not at all. I believe I know where your best interest lies, Miss Heydon.'

'Then we must agree to disagree. My mind is quite made up on the matter.'

'I had noticed how very stubborn you are, Miss Heydon, and to what lengths you will go to get what you want.'

'What I think is right,' she corrected him. 'For you to lecture me for being stubborn is, I venture, a case of the pot calling the kettle black.'

Luc was silent as they crossed the market square. Averil let herself feel the texture of his uniform jacket under her palm, the rough edge of the gold braid at her fingertips, hear the sound of his boots crunching over the dusty stones.

It felt right to have him by her side, as though they were a respectable married couple walking back to their comfortable home after a church service. There were unspoken words between them, a sensual tension that left her short of breath as though she had been hurrying, yet there was a comfort in being together. Would it feel as natural to walk with Andrew Bradon? Would it be as easy to stroll in companionable silence without the need to make conversation?

The words were there, though, even if neither uttered them. *Kiss me, touch me, stay with me.* They were in the slight pressure of her hand on his arm, in the way he watched her profile, their lagging steps that got slower as they neared the inn.

It had to stop, she knew that, or they would drift upstairs and then—who knew? And even though she could rely on Luc to save her life, she could not trust him with her virginity. Or perhaps it was herself she did not trust.

'Thank you so much, Captain,' Averil said in her brightest society voice as they reached the inn yard. 'I feel better for the fresh air and the exercise.'

'You will set out early tomorrow, I imagine. It is a good twelve hours to London.' Luc stood, hat in hand, showing no sign of wanting to inveigle his way upstairs. Was it all her imagination and he just wanted to flirt?

'Yes, the postilions said we should leave at half past seven. I shall be very glad to arrive, I must confess.' The prospect of stopping this endless travelling, of reaching somewhere—anywhere—permanent after four months, was almost enough to overcome the apprehension about meeting her betrothed.

'Bruton Street, I believe,' Luc said.

'How—how did you know?' A cold trickle ran down her spine. He had promised not to speak to Lord Bradon—surely he would not break his word?

'I checked. Don't look at me like that, I shall not interrupt your arrival with an ill-timed call, believe me, Miss Heydon.'

'Of course. Thank you. It may be a little…strained at first, getting to know each other.' His silence spoke volumes about how strained he expected it to be. 'Well, good night, Captain d'Aunay. I wish you well at the Admiralty.' She held out her hand and he took it, bowed over it and stood aside for her to enter.

'I think the captain's better looking, now I'm used to that nose,' Waters remarked as they climbed the stairs.

'Shh! For goodness' sake, girl, he'll hear you!'

'He didn't come in, Miss Heydon.'

'Oh.' Good. Excellent, in fact. That was that then. She would not see him again, perhaps not for years and when she did she would be Lady Bradon, a respectable society matron and Luc would be a count, or an admiral or ambassador for a royalist France. They would meet and smile and part again and all this agonising would seem pointless.

Unless Lord Bradon rejected her. The cold shiver came back. He

was not going to be pleased, that was certain. But he might be a wonderful, warm, understanding man who would forgive her adventure
and she would forget Luc. No, never forget him. He would always
be part of her memories: his courage, his pride. His lovemaking.

'Time for bed, I think, Waters. Please ring for the hot water.' On
an impulse, she said, 'What is your first name? Waters seems so
stiff.' Probably it was how Lady Bradon should address her maid,
but it was not comfortable.

'Grace, miss.'

'How pretty. I will call you that if you do not feel it lowers your
dignity.'

'*My* dignity, miss? I think calling me by my surname is because
you'll be a great lady and I'm supposed to be a *superior* servant.'
She said it with such a comical expression that Averil laughed. 'Only
I don't think I'm cut out for being a superior abigail.'

She was rather dumpy and snub-nosed, Averil thought, thinking of her aunt's descriptions of how a suitable dresser would look
and behave. But she was warm and sensible and cheerful. Averil
decided she would do her best to keep her—warmth might be in
rather short supply at Bruton Street.

'I think you will do admirably, Grace. I cannot promise anything, because Lord Bradon may already have employed someone
as dresser, but if he has not, then I hope you will stay with me.'

'Oh, Miss Heydon, thank you.' Grace beamed. 'Oh, and, miss,
that means I'll sit with the upper servants, right up at the top!'

And so she would, Averil thought with an inward smile. Ladies'
maids and valets took their employer's rank as far as the hierarchy
of the servants' hall was concerned.

Grace was still bubbling with excitement as they took their seats
in the post-chaise at just past seven the next morning. The yard
was busy already with two private coaches ready to leave and an-

other post-chaise with the ostlers backing the horses between the shafts.

Averil made herself as comfortable as possible and wondered if she would be able to sleep, something that she had signally failed to do the night before, except in snatches. Long intervals, marked by the church clock—which might as well have been the church bells tolling—were spent tossing and turning in an effort to stop imagining scenarios for her arrival in Bruton Street.

What would it be? A warm, understanding welcome, chilly reserve but acceptance or downright anger and rejection? She rehearsed, over and over, what she would say, how she would explain those nights in the company of a gang of condemned men and a half-French officer.

Then, when she did fall asleep, her dreams were full of Luc who was making love to her, fully. And then he appeared in the Bruton Street drawing room and explained that he had to do it, even though she was so inept and naïve in bed and then, somehow, he and Andrew Bradon were standing facing each other with duelling pistols raised and... And Grace had shaken her awake because she was having a nightmare.

The breakfast bacon was sitting uneasily in her stomach. It would be best to be very careful what she ate on the journey, she decided as the postilions swung up and the chaise lurched into motion. It would not do to arrive in fashionable Mayfair travel sick as well as crumpled and uneasy.

As she thought it they passed the other chaise and its occupant who was just settling into his seat. Luc. 'Goodbye,' she mouthed and lifted her hand.

He said something in response and she tried to read his lips. *'Au revoir.'*

Chapter Fifteen

March 29th, 1809—Bruton Street, Mayfair, London

Light flooded out as the front door opened. Luc slowed to a stroll on the corner of Berkeley Square and watched the post-chaise drawn up at the kerb. Averil walked up the steps, paused. There was discussion, too far away for him to hear, then she and the maid went in and a pair of footmen ran down to take their bags.

She was inside, but he had expected that. How long would she stay? That was the question. If she was determined on being utterly frank with Bradon, then what would the man do? He could ship her straight back to India, he supposed, although that would involve cost and Luc suspected that the family was not given to paying cash on the nail for anything if they could avoid it. He might simply throw her out. Or he might accept her.

That would be the action of a trusting, forgiving man. Or a man who wanted Averil's money more than he was concerned about her honour. Luc paced slowly around the periphery of the big square, past Gunther's, past the huge old plane trees, back up the eastern side to the corner.

Well, she wasn't out on the pavement with her bag at her feet so he should take himself off to his chambers in Albany, five minutes' walk away, and try to be pleased about it. Best not to walk along past the house; she might be looking out and feel pursued.

Which was exactly what he was doing, although he did not want to distress her by doing so. Somehow he could not keep away. Perhaps Mere had been a mistake, or simply unkind. He had wanted to help her, make the long, fraught, journey easier. But he had also wanted to see her, touch her, steal a kiss if he could. Like an infatuated schoolboy, Luc thought with a wry twist of his mouth as he strode up the slope of Hay Hill and right into Dover Street.

Bradon would be a fool to spurn Averil. She was rich, lovely, intelligent and patently honest. He would believe her when she told him she was a virgin, surely?

Luc turned left out of Dover Street into the bustle of Piccadilly, his mood sliding towards grim. Averil was not going to be his, it was not right that she should be, and to wish that she would be forced into that position was selfish.

All right, I'm selfish. But I didn't cast her up on the beach at Tubbs's feet. I didn't keep her bedridden for days. Yes, but I could have locked the damned door and slept with the men; his conscience riposted. *I needn't have slept in her bed, kissed her, shown her what lovemaking could be like, taught her desire. But I did not take her virginity*, he thought. *I could have done, and I did not. I could have seduced her.*

It was the same conversation he'd been having with himself since he had left Plymouth. He supposed it was partly mild euphoria to blame for his reckless decision to try to find her on the London road. But the admiral had been enthusiastic about the mission, he was assured of a good reception at the Admiralty; his life, it seemed, was back on course, his honour restored. Porthington, he had been informed by a secretary with a very straight face, would be offered a posting in the West Indies. A long way away, and unhealthy with it, the man had added.

So now Luc would have more than enough to keep himself

occupied until their lordships decided where to post him next. There would be work to be done to tie up the Isles of Scilly leaks, news to catch up on and the Season was in full swing. He could make an effort and start a serious quest for a wife. And he would wait and watch Averil as she ventured into her new life, his hands outstretched to catch her if she slipped from Bradon's grasp.

The image of Averil tumbling into his arms was enough to make his mouth curve into a smile. He walked into the cobbled forecourt of Albany, nodded to the doorman and climbed the stone stairs to his chambers to see what was awaiting him after more than two months away.

At the door he paused, hand on the knob, as a shiver ran down his spine. He was tempting fate, instinct told him—the same instinct that had saved his life at sea before now. He thought he was stepping back into his old life, but in a better, more purposeful way. But now there was someone else to consider—he was not alone any more.

She isn't yours, he told himself and opened the door. *You have to let her go.* The pain was sharp, just as he knew it would be if he was ever careless enough to care about someone. *Too late now...*

'Hughes! Send out for a decent supper. I'm back.'

'Miss Heydon. The earl and Lord Bradon are expecting you. Her ladyship also,' the butler added. His eyes flickered over her travel-stained, borrowed gown, the two small valises, Grace's dumpy figure. 'This way, if you please. The family is in the—'

'I would not dream of going to them in my dirt,' Averil said. 'Perhaps someone could show me to my room and have hot water sent up. And please tell the family that I will be with them directly.'

The butler's gaze sharpened into something like respect. 'Very good, Miss Heydon. This is your woman?'

'Waters is my dresser, yes. When I have something other than borrowed garments, that is,' she added. 'Doubtless there is a room for her?'

'Yes, Miss Heydon. John, show Miss Heydon to the Amber suite. Peters, water at once and have Mrs Gifford send one of the girls up to assist Waters.'

'Thank you.' Averil straightened her shoulders, sent a firm message to her wobbly knees and followed the footman up the stairs. *Start as you mean to go on*, she told herself. And being intimidated by the upper servants would not be a good beginning. Nor would appearing before her future mother-in-law looking like a hoyden.

''Strewth, miss,' Grace said as the footman left. 'It's a bit grand, isn't it?'

'Indeed, yes.' Averil turned on her heel to admire the heavy golden-brown hangings, the tassels, the gilt-framed pictures, the marble overmantel. None of it was new, she could see that, and all of it, in her honest opinion, needed some loving care. It was not exactly shabby, but it was definitely worn.

Hot water came with exemplary speed, brought by a pretty maid with freckles who confided that she was Alice and would Miss Heydon like a cup of tea?

'We both would,' Averil said firmly as Grace attacked her dusty hem with a clothes brush. A large glass of wine would be even better, she thought as she washed her hands and face and began to unpin her hair. But she was going to need all her wits about her now.

'Thank you, Rogers, I am ready now.' The butler looked up as she came down the stairs and she congratulated herself on thinking to ask his name.

He opened a door and announced, 'Miss Heydon, my lady.'

Averil found herself in cool, glittering elegance. White silk walls, gilt details, marble, a pale lemon-and-cream carpet that stretched like an ice flow across dark glossy floorboards towards the chairs and a sofa arranged in a conversation-piece setting at the far end.

Two men got to their feet from the armchairs as she began the interminable walk across the carpet. The taller must be the Earl of Kingsbury, she realised. His brown hair was grey at the temples, his thin face lined more with experience than age. Beside him was his son Andrew, Lord Bradon. Her betrothed. The man she was going to spend the rest of her life with—if he would take her. Shorter than his father, plumper, with the same brown hair and brown eyes. A comparison with another man of the same age flickered through her mind and she forced a smile.

She arrived in front of the sofa and the woman who sat on it. Small, birdlike, dark-haired and dark-eyed: the countess. Her steady regard changed suddenly into a bright smile. The two men bowed. Averil curtsied. *We're like automata*, she thought wildly. A clock would chime at any moment.

'My dear Miss Heydon! What an adventurous journey you have had to be sure. Come and sit beside me. Bradon, ring for wine—we must drink to Miss Heydon's safe arrival.'

Averil sat, expecting an embrace, a kiss or at least a pat on the hand. Nothing. The men resumed their seats, the countess sat beside her, straight-backed, hands folded in her lap.

'You left your family in good health, I trust?'

'Yes, ma'am. My father sends his good wishes and regrets that he was unable to accompany me.'

'Business pressures, no doubt,' the countess remarked and the earl smiled. Rogers brought in a tray with champagne already poured. Averil curled her fingers around the fragile stem of the flute and made herself focus on not snapping it.

'Er. Yes.' No one appeared about to make a toast so she sipped the wine. It fizzed down into her empty stomach. *Mistake. I don't care.*

'And it was an uneventful voyage until the shipwreck, I trust.'

'Yes, ma'am, thank you.' She doubted that her future mother-in-law wanted to hear about mad dogs in Madras, Christmas festivities on board or a joint attempt by the younger passengers to write a sensation novel.

'And the ship was wrecked on the fifteenth of last month, I understand?'

Why were the men so quiet? Averil addressed her answer to Andrew. 'Yes, that is correct. At night.'

'But the letter from the Governor was dated the twenty-first, six days later.' The countess frowned. 'That was very remiss of him, I fear.'

'I was unconscious for three days, on one of the outlying islands. They did not know who I was.' The Governor would have told them that already—her skin began to prickle with apprehension. They were already suspicious. She would tell Andrew what happened tomorrow; she could not blurt it out now, not in front of his parents like this.

'Oh. I see. You were cared for by respectable people, one hopes.'

'A secret navy mission. They rescued me when I was swept on to the beach.'

'Men?' The countess might as well have said *Cockroaches?*

'Yes, ma'am.' Averil took another sip between gritted teeth. She had known this was not going to be easy, but why did her betrothed not utter a word? The earl was watching her from under hooded lids: a calculating, predatory stare. 'I really cannot say much more about it just now—it was very confidential. I will explain all about it tomorrow to Lord Bradon.'

He spoke so suddenly that she jumped. 'I am sure you will.' He might as well have been referring to details of a shopping expedition to buy a new hat. 'Ah, here is Rogers. Dinner at last.'

'You slept well, my dear?'

'Thank you, yes. My lord.' Andrew Bradon had not asked her

to use his given name, so she did not presume. The study was very masculine, very *English*. Was it his taste, or his father's? The earl had excused himself after dinner and she had not seen him since. She suspected that he was not much at home.

The chair Brandon offered her was comfortable, they were alone, his expression was pleasant. What, then, was making her stomach tie itself into knots? This was much worse than she had imagined when she had woken that morning in a bed that seemed far too large and soft and lonely.

'I believe there is something you need to tell me about the shipwreck.' He settled back in his own chair behind the desk and nodded encouragingly. Why, then, did feel she had been called in to explain breaking the best china?

'About the aftermath and my rescue, yes.' This was the right thing to do. Averil took in a breath. 'I was washed up on the beach of an island that is normally uninhabited. I was found by a group of men who were part of a secret mission to intercept messages being sent to the French by a traitor in the islands. Their captain assisted me to shelter in the old isolation hospital on the island.'

'And why did he not return you immediately to the main island?'

'Because I was semi-conscious. He had no way of knowing whether, when I awoke, I would say anything about their presence there. At that point no one could be trusted.'

He did not say much, this man. No exclamations of sympathy or anger, no reaction at all save for a pursing of his lips. Averil guessed he was waiting for her to prattle on out of sheer nervousness and rather thought he was succeeding. 'I was unconscious for two days.'

'Three nights.' Of course, he had to pinpoint the number of nights. 'Who nursed you?'

'He did. The officer.'

'Did he rape you?' Still the same calm, pleasant tone.

'No!'

'Really? Are you certain? You say you were unconscious.'

'I would be able to tell. And besides, he is not that kind of man.' She tried to keep the passion out of her voice, offer an objective assessment, but she was not at all sure she succeeded.

'Did he take liberties of any kind?'

'He kissed me. I slept in his bed.' There, she had said it.

'In his bed?' Everything about Bradon's rounded features sharpened as though he had suddenly come into focus. 'In his *bed*?'

'It was that or sleep outside with the men who were a rough crew sleeping in makeshift shelters.'

'And you kissed him. Did you enjoy it?' He was coolly objective again.

'I have nothing to compare it with. I am a virgin, my lord.' *And I am blushing like a peony and ready to sink.* It was so much worse than she had expected, even though he was so calm and dispassionate. Perhaps because of that. Why was he showing no emotion?

'So you say.'

Averil found she was on her feet. 'I give you my word! Why on earth should I tell you this if it was not out of a desire to be honest with my betrothed?'

'Because you fear you may be with child, of course.' He steepled his fingers and regarded her over the top of them.

'With child?' For a moment it did not make sense. What was he talking about? She could not be pregnant because Luc had not... Then the anger came. He did not believe her. 'It would have to be an immaculate conception then, my lord.'

'Do not blaspheme!' Finally, some emotion.

'I am not lying. I am not pregnant because it is impossible that I should be.'

'Indeed, I hope you are telling me the truth. I will not tolerate a lying wife.'

He was going to throw her out. Something very like relief flooded through her. Averil shook her head. Relief? This was a catastrophe. 'I understand that given the possibilities for scandal you would wish to reconsider the marriage contract. But it was a secret mission, you may rely on nothing of my presence coming out. The Governor gave his assurances that he would say nothing.'

'How you do run on, my dear.' Bradon brought his hands palm down on to the desktop and studied her. 'I did not seek to marry you for your virginity, when all is said and done. We will simply wait and see for a month.'

'Wait? And if I am not with child, you marry me?'

'It seems prudent, would you not say?'

It seemed incredibly cold-blooded. Averil struggled to say so, with tact. 'You do not trust my word or you would not insist on this stratagem. Does it not concern you that I might have lied to you, that I am not a virgin, but I have escaped becoming pregnant? Is such suspicion any basis for marriage?'

'How very innocent you are, my dear—about life, if not in other ways. I am marrying you for the benefits of your very substantial dowry. My father is expensive, I fear. You are marrying me for a title and status. You appear to be a handsome young woman of good address and refined manner, as I was led to believe. What has changed? Has your dowry gone down with the ship?'

'No. Of course not.' So this was how it would be: polite cynicism. He would accept her because he would discover soon enough that she was not pregnant whether he believed it at this moment or not. She must accept him because he had given her no reason not to. He had not struck her or rejected her. He had not even raised his voice to her. She felt more cold than when Luc had carried her from the sea. This man simply did not care about her at all.

'Will it not appear odd that the marriage is delayed?' She tried to match his tone.

'Why, no. No one of any significance knows of it, after all. You are visiting us, we will introduce you into society. After a month I may—or may not—marry you. There will be no expectations, so no gossip, no unpleasant rumours.'

'How civilised,' Averil murmured and he looked pleased, although she did not know how he hoped to keep it a secret. Dita knew. Alistair Lyndon and Callum Chatterton knew. Her chaperon knew. She had made no secret of her reason for travelling to England when she had been on the ship. But something held her back from saying so.

Then she realised why. She welcomed this breathing space. It took little mental effort to calculate that she had three weeks' grace before her mother-in-law knew she was not with child; there was no possibility of hiding such things from the female servants.

'There are some practical matters,' she said. 'I require clothing and I owe Sir George Gordon for my travel here.'

'I assume your father made arrangements with his agents here for you to draw on funds?'

'Yes. Yes, he did.' So, Bradon was not taking on the responsibility of repaying Sir George. Was he mean, penny-pinching or seriously short of money? Her eyes strayed over the ornate furnishing, the silk curtains, the yards of leather-bound, gilt-embossed books. An aristocratic family wealthy in land and property and possessions without a silver shilling to spare, no doubt. The expensive father out pursuing his pleasures while the prudent son ensured the family finances.

Averil tried to keep the judgemental thoughts from her mind. It was not her business how they came to this. It was up to her to try and make sure they were towed out of the River Tick before her children reached their majority, that was all.

'Papa's bankers and lawyers are in the City. May I have a carriage to call on them?'

'Of course.' He got up and came around the desk to stand beside her. Averil felt compelled to stand, too. 'I will accompany you. I assume you will need someone to vouch for you, with all your possessions and papers gone.'

'Yes. I suppose I will. Thank you.'

He took her hand, lifted it, then brushed his lips over her knuckles. She forced herself to stand still and accept the caress, if that is what it could be called. 'We will set out after luncheon. The sooner you can replace your trousseau, the better. Mama will lend you her dresser to guide you to all the best places once you have some money.'

Averil spared a fleeting thought for the silks and muslins, the jewellery and shawls, the piles of linens that she had painstakingly monogrammed as they sailed across miles of oceans. All gone, all lost, along with her dreams.

'Thank you. I will go and put on my bonnet.' He released her hand. *And put any hopes I ever had of love and romance firmly in a box and throw away the key.*

Chapter Sixteen

Luc strolled up Bond Street and turned left into Bruton Street. He had no convincing excuse for coming this way, he admitted to himself. Yes, he was intending to visit Manton's to pick up some new pistols and try a little target practice, but this was a roundabout route by anyone's calculation. He could tell himself he was getting some exercise, but that was purest self-deception. He was worried about Averil and he was missing her like the devil.

He should walk on past and go about his business; there was nothing he could do in any case unless she appeared here and now on the pavement in front of him. However much he wanted her, he had given her his word that he would not turn up on the doorstep and precipitate a crisis.

But despite his resolve some demon had him turning right and then right again into the mews that served the smart houses. He had promised nothing about watching the house and now he grabbed at the loophole. *Damn it, but this obsession hurts. Where's your will-power, man?* He didn't seem to have any, only a sick fear that he was not going to be able to bear it when she married Brandon.

An English gentleman would cut her out of his life: it was, after all, the honourable thing to do. A Frenchman, hot-blooded and passionate, would ignore his own promises and snatch her. But he was neither. God, was he ever going to find where he belonged? What if Napoleon was never defeated and he was stranded here, belonging to no country?

Stop it! Luc exerted years of hard-learned discipline and got his thoughts under control. *Just deal with it, day by day, just as you always have. Concentrate on Averil and whether she is all right.* He forced his attention back to the mews.

It was quiet, so presumably the carriages had gone out for the morning. A man whistled as he came out of a stable with a bucket, nodded to Luc with no sign of curiosity, and strode off.

Luc walked along, counting until he got to the back of the Bradons' house. Where was she? He leaned a shoulder against the wall and eyed the gate that led into the garden as though it could answer the questions that so preoccupied him.

Averil would not be installed in Bradon's bedchamber yet, of that he was certain. The family would do this properly, although without any great fuss, given the bride's connections. But the man might be making love to her even now. What was there to stop him? And unless Bradon was made of stone, he would want her. Jealousy lanced through him. The bastard would take her innocence and that belonged to him, no one else.

As he watched a window opened on the second floor and there was Averil, as though he had called to her. She leaned her elbows on the sill and leaned out, a most unladylike thing to be doing. Luc smiled, the dark mood evaporating like mist under sunshine, and lifted a hand.

For a moment he thought she had not seen him, or perhaps did not recognise him in civilian dress, then she made a flapping gesture with her hand as though trying to shoo chickens. Amused, Luc stayed where he was. He could almost hear the huff of exasperation as she slapped both palms down on the sill and stared at him across the length of the garden and the low roofs of the mews buildings. Now what would his Averil do?

Her face changed and he realised she was mouthing something, although from that distance it was impossible to tell what. *Go away*, probably. They stared at each other for a while, then she ducked back inside and pulled down the window. Luc grinned; she was wearing a pale gown and the glimmer of white behind the glass showed clearly that she was standing watching him. He tipped the brim of his hat down, shifted his shoulders more comfortably and set himself to look like a man with nothing better to do than prop a wall up and watch the world go by for the rest of the morning.

It took ten minutes before the gate opened and Averil appeared. 'Go away! What on earth are you doing here?'

Luc straightened, came across and stood next to her under the shelter of the garden wall. No one looking out of the windows in the house could see them there. 'I wondered how you were.' *I needed to see you so much it hurt.* No, he could not admit his weakness to her. Instinct warned him to hide his vulnerability.

'I was perfectly all right until I saw you,' she retorted. 'I almost had a heart stroke.' She was looking delightfully flushed and flustered, but he saw the dark smudges under her eyes and wondered how much sleep she'd had the night before. Had she been thinking about him, or worrying about Bradon?

'You recognised me.'

'I could think of no one else your size who would be lurking in back alleys.' Despite her tone he suspected she was glad to see him. He hoped she was.

'How was it? What is he like?'

'Lord Bradon is perfectly charming and his parents are delightful. I could not be happier.' Her green eyes were dark and shuttered.

'Liar,' he said. 'Something is wrong. Tell me the truth. Did you confess what had happened?'

'I told Lord Bradon this morning. About the shipwreck and being washed up and being in the hut with you for those days and nights. I did not tell him I was naked, or about…about the summer house in the Governor's garden. He was very calm about it. He is—oh, I don't know!' She threw up her hands and for a moment Luc thought she was going to cry, then she tightened her lips and controlled herself. 'He is very emotionless, very cool. They all are. There is no feeling or warmth. But I expect we will get used to one another soon.'

Luc put his hand on her arm. It was good to touch her and hell, too. He wanted to yank her into his embrace and kiss her sense-less. She shook her head. 'No, do not do that.' He took his hand away, feeling absurdly as though she had slapped him. 'I do not need sympathy. I will be all right.'

'So what did Bradon say? About us?'

'I told him nothing about you. I told him that I could reveal noth-ing about the identity of the officer involved because of the secrecy required for the mission. He appeared to accept that.'

'And you are still here. So he believes you are a virgin.'

'No. Not exactly. He either does not trust my word or thinks me too ignorant to know if something had happened while I was un-conscious. For a month, until he is certain that I am not with child, it will be put about that I am merely a guest of the Bradons. Once he is sure, then we will become betrothed.'

'My God. The cold-blooded devil. You will not stay with him, surely?'

'Why not? What has changed?' She shrugged and he felt a spurt of anger. This was not Averil, not his Averil, this obedient, long-suffering puppet. 'I did not behave well on the islands, I should have been stronger willed. There is a contract. My family—'

'Your family can shift for themselves!' He fought to keep his voice below a quarterdeck bellow. 'They are adult men, the lot of them. You can't behave like a virgin sacrifice, Averil, and they should not expect it of you.'

'Can't I? What will your wife be? She will not be agreeing to a love match, will she? She will be marrying a man who wants her for her bloodlines and her deportment. Will you lie and pretend to a warmth you do not feel while all the time you sneak off to your mistresses?'

The temper and the shreds of restraint that he was hanging on to by his fingernails escaped him. Luc hauled Averil into his arms and lost track of what he was about to say, let alone what he was thinking. She was soft and yet resilient as she pulled back against his arms, she smelled of a meadow in springtime and his mouth knew what her kiss would taste like.

'I do not sneak,' he snapped. 'And I am not such a damned cynic as this money-grubbing Englishman you are throwing yourself away on either.'

'Luc, please...' *Please go,* she meant. Her mouth was soft and under his hands, her body trembled and he knew he should either release her or just hold her, give her the comfort of some human warmth and care. But the devil that had brought him here was strong and the feel and the scent of her was making his head spin with desire so he took her mouth and closed his eyes on the hurt in her green, exposed, gaze.

She was quivering with anger and desire and vulnerability in his arms. She tasted of his dreams and she felt like heaven and he ravaged her mouth even as she twisted in his arms and kicked at his booted shins with her pretty little slippers.

When he lifted his head she stared back, holding his eyes despite the confusion in her own. He remembered the way she had looked deep into his eyes on St Helen's as she searched for the truth in his words.

'Damn it, Averil. Be mine. Come with me—I'll give you all the warmth you'll ever need.'

'You'll ruin me for your own desires, you mean,' she said flatly. 'Let me go. Promise me you will stay away from me.'

Sick at what he had just done, at the look in her eyes, Luc opened his hands and she stepped back. 'There. Free. But I will not stay away, not while you need me. Not while you want me.' *Not while this madness holds me.*

'You—' The effort it took to regain her poise was visible, but she managed it. 'You are arrogant, Monsieur le Comte. I neither need nor want you. Only your absence. Goodbye.'

Luc opened the gate for her and she went past him a swish of skirts without looking at him. He waited until she was through and said, 'Convince me.' The gate shut in his face and he heard the unmistakable sound of a bolt being drawn across. He should leave her to Bradon, forget her. He ran his tongue over his lips and tasted her—passionate, feminine, innocent—and knew he could no more do it than fly.

'That was reasonably satisfactory.' Andrew Bradon replaced his hat and frowned at the traffic fighting its way up and down Cornhill. There was no sign of the carriage. 'Where has that fool got to?'

'There does not appear to be anywhere he could wait.' Averil stared at a flock of sheep being driven down the middle of the street; it was like Calcutta but cooler and with sheep, not goats. Sheep were easier to think about than what had happened this morning. Two men: ice and fire. They both burned the skin.

'He should have kept circling.' Still fuming about his coachman, Bradon extended his crooked elbow. 'Take my arm.'

'Thank you.' She had fled upstairs from the garden and washed her face and hands, brushed out and redressed her hair, afraid that he would somehow scent Luc on her.

'I do not understand why that lawyer wants all your bills sent to him to settle. He could have entrusted a sum to me to deal with on your behalf.'

'Doubtless Mr Wilton will need to give Papa an exact accounting for the purposes of insurance after the shipwreck.' *And I am going to have to go through my married life being this careful and tactful. Mr Wilton saw no reason to put the money into your hands until he was forced to by my marriage. He is a canny man.*

But he was also a dusty, dry and unimaginative man, she decided. She wondered whether to write to Papa and mention this. Wilton seemed to be the sort of person who would carry out orders even if they made no sense—there was a feeling of unyielding rigidity about him. On the other hand, he did appear to be utterly devoted to Papa's interests. Sir Joshua's word, it seemed, was law.

There was a navy blue uniform and a cocked hat in the crowd pouring out of the Royal Exchange. Averil told herself not to be foolish. The City must be full of naval officers; besides, he had been wearing civilian dress. *Oh, my God. It is him. Luc—*

'My dear? What is wrong?'

'That crossing sweeper—I thought he was going to be struck by the carriage with the red panels.'

And Luc was crossing the road, coming towards them. Her heart beat so hard she thought she would be sick. *No!* He was going to speak. He was going to betray her in some way, make Bradon suspicious and her own position more precarious so that she would be forced into his arms. Averil closed her eyes and tried to banish the memory of just how those arms felt around her and how much she wanted to be in them.

'Excuse me. I think you have dropped this?' Luc stooped and straightened with a man's large linen handkerchief in his hand. He made a polite bow in her direction, but his eyes passed over her with no sign of recognition and his enquiring gaze fixed on Bradon.

'What? No, not mine. Obliged, sir.'

'Not at all. Lord Bradon, is it not?'

'Yes.' Bradon pokered up, whether because he objected to being addressed by a stranger or because he was suspicious of anyone in naval uniform after this morning's revelations, she could not tell.

'Forgive me, but someone pointed you out to me the other day as a considerable connoisseur of porcelain.' Under her palm Averil felt Bradon relax. It was a miracle that he could not feel her own pounding pulse.

'You are interested?'

'As a mere amateur. I was able to pick up some interesting Copenhagen items when I was in that area recently.'

'Indeed? I do not believe we have been introduced.' Bradon's manner became almost cordial.

'Captain le comte Luc d'Aunay.'

Averil managed to breathe. Bradon would not suspect a count of involvement with an undercover operation and, thanks to the remark about Copenhagen, he now had a mental image of Luc being posted somewhere in the North Sea. And Luc was very properly not acknowledging a lady to whom he had not been introduced and not, as she had feared, doing anything to make Bradon suspicious. Perhaps this was a coincidental meeting. Had he recovered from that morning's madness?

'...interesting dealer off the Strand,' Bradon was saying as she pulled herself together to listen to the two men. 'Feel free to mention my name.'

'Thank you, I will certainly do that. Good day.' Luc raised his hat, his gaze focused on Averil for the first time. His expression was perfectly bland with just the hint of a query.

Her escort seemed to remember her presence. 'Er, Miss Heydon, from India.'

'Ma'am. India? I thought I had not had the pleasure of seeing you in town before.' The bow was perfectly judged: polite and indifferent with just the hint of masculine appreciation that would be expected.

'Captain.' She inclined her head. 'Lord Bradon's family has kindly asked me to stay with them for a month.'

'I will not delay your sightseeing any longer. Thank you for the recommendation, Bradon.'

As Bradon turned to hail their carriage Averil glanced back, but

Luc was gone, swallowed up by the crowds. What had he been doing there? Surely not following her? He had work to do at the Admiralty, she was certain; it would do his career no good if he neglected that in order to dog her footsteps in the hope she would throw her bonnet over the windmill and decide to become his mistress!

'We will return to Bruton Street,' Bradon said as they settled into the carriage. 'Mama will have given Finch her instructions on where to take you and what you will need. We must have you creditably outfitted before anyone else sees you in that hand-me-down gown.'

'Yes, my lord.' Averil bit her lip and reminded herself of her duty and that tumbling out of the carriage and running up Cornhill in search of Luc would be madness.

Luc took one of the side alleys, went into the George and Vulture, the first tavern he came to, and sat at an empty table in the taproom. 'A pint of lush,' he said to the girl who approached, wiping her hands on her apron. Brandy was tempting, but strong beer was prudent.

He still could not credit that Bradon was waiting a month to see if she was with child. Calculating devil. At least he had seen him now. After what Averil had said that morning he could not rest until he had seen her with her betrothed, seen how the man was with her. The tankard came and he took a swallow. Good London beer, full of hops and dry in the mouth; he had missed that.

Yes, he was a calculating devil who did not believe Averil when she told him she was a virgin. Luc realised he was angry and drank again while he sorted that out in his head. Bradon did not believe her; in fact, he thought she could well be lying. He deserved to be called out for that alone, Luc thought as he drained the tankard.

Getting changed, visiting the Admiralty, had distracted him not an iota from the anguish and confusion that morning's encounter had caused, but he had not had time to think too deeply about the workings of Bradon's mind.

Damn it, Averil was so patently honest, he thought now. Didn't the fool realise that she could have spun him any number of yarns— with the full support of Sir George and his sister? Bradon did not deserve her, but the very fact that he was keeping her, for a month at least, proved that he wanted her, or her dowry, more than he cared about her maidenhead and his own honour.

In a month, possibly much sooner, he would realise that she was not with child and then the marriage would go ahead. She would become Lady Bradon and be lost to Luc for ever.

The fantasy that had been sustaining him since he had sailed from Scilly, of Averil spread beneath him on a wide bed, gasping his name as he drove them both to ecstasy, gripped him afresh, only this time not with a wash of pleasurable anticipation, but with claws of frustration. He snapped his fingers for another tankard. Frustration and loss, if he was to take her at her word and leave her to the other man. Damn it, but he needed her. Where else would he find that enticing mixture of courage and sensuality, beauty and honesty, innocence and spirit?

A group of clerks came in, loudly discussing a prize fight, and called for ale and food as they settled at the next table. Luc nursed his beer and let their argument wash over him until the arrival of their pie reminded him that he had been up since dawn working on his notes about the Scillies traitor. Then he had found his feet leading him to Bruton Street to watch for Averil and to try to find out what had happened with Bradon.

Now he knew. Bradon would marry her and she had accepted that, and his lack of trust in her. The meek way she had stood there just now, her hand on his arm, ignored by the men, waiting to be acknowledged, made his blood boil. Bradon would be satisfied with his bargain, that was for sure, but he doubted it would give Averil any joy.

But her joy, or lack of it, was no longer his business, it seemed. He ordered pie and told himself that he had to stop thinking about her. He had a wife to find. A home to build. Somehow it no longer seemed so straightforward or desirable.

For two days Averil shopped, with Finch the stiff-backed dresser at her elbow and Grace, almost bursting with the effort to behave with as much decorum as Finch, at her heels. She wrote to Mrs Bastable, her chaperone on the *Bengal Queen* and another letter to her father. She wanted to write to Dita, who must now be safe at home in Devon with her family, recovering from her ordeal. But she could not risk to writing what she had to confide to her friend; she must just hope Dita would come up to London soon. She needed her so much.

She took delivery of her new clothes and supervised her borrowed ones being cleaned, parcelled up and returned to Miss Gordon along with a letter of thanks and the assurance that her banker was dealing with the money she owed Sir George.

She arranged flowers for Lady Kingsbury and suffered her purchases to be examined and approved. She thanked her future mother-in-law for the loan of a pearl set and some garnets and sat and addressed invitation cards for a *soirée* in a week's time and she felt as though her heart was weeping in sympathy with the rain that was pouring down outside.

As they drove back from church on Sunday Lady Kingsbury was graciously pleased to compliment her on her walking dress and bonnet. 'You dress with taste, Miss Heydon.'

There was no sign of the earl—he appeared only at dinner and then left. The countess did not appear remotely discommoded by his neglect. Perhaps she was glad of it, as Averil might become glad of Bradon's absence once she was married to him. She shivered.

'Thank you, ma'am.'

'You will accompany me to the Countess of Middlehampton's

reception on Tuesday evening. That will introduce you to a number of people of influence without the necessity to concern ourselves with dancing yet. You can dance, I trust?'

'Yes, ma'am. I enjoy it.'

'Excellent. Tomorrow I will review your new wardrobe with you and give you some guidance on who you will meet in London this Season. Do feel free to ask me any questions about matters of etiquette—I am sure things are different here from what you are used to.'

'Thank you, ma'am.' So, she was to be assessed to make certain she would behave the right way. Averil had no way of telling whether Bradon had told either of his parents the shocking tale of her rescue. She saw virtually nothing of the earl, and Lady Kingsbury, she suspected, would remain poker-faced and cool if she found herself in the midst of the Cyprians' Ball.

Her spirits rose despite the thought of Lady Kingsbury's critical assessment. It was frivolous, but a reception would mean new people to meet, entertainment, a change of scene, noise, human contact, warmth. She needed warmth as a drooping flower needed water. She needed, more than anything, someone to put their arms around her and simply hug her.

Chapter Seventeen

The Middlehampton reception delivered as much noise, heat and distraction as Averil could have hoped for. For the first time since the *Bengal Queen* had entered northern waters she felt warm enough.

Lady Kingsbury introduced her to a number of other young unmarried ladies and drifted off to gossip with her own cronies while Lord Bradon vanished in the direction of the card rooms. That suited Averil very well indeed. She smiled and chatted and one young lady introduced her to another and so on until her head was spinning with the effort of remembering names. Many of them had beaux and the young men flirted with Averil and the girls wanted to know about Indian silks and they all wanted to hear about life in the East and she found herself laughing and talking as if she was back in Calcutta with her friends.

She turned, gurgling with laughter over Mr Crowther's tale of how he had encountered an elephant at some eccentric house party in Hampshire and had been prevailed upon to mount on to its back—'Into a howdedo'—and had fallen off and his hat had been eaten by the elephant. 'They brought it back to me three days later,' he finished mournfully. 'But it was never the same again.'

There was an elegant girl reflected in one of the long mirrors, her face alight with amusement, her gown just like Averil's. *It is me! My goodness. How very* au fait *I look.* And then a figure in a blue tailcoat with gold lace and white collar tabs appeared in the glass behind her and the laughter fled, leaving her wide-eyed and breathless.

'Miss Heydon. Do you remember me? We met in the City five days ago.' Luc stood there, *chapeau bras* tucked under one arm, dress sword at his side, the picture of the perfect naval officer. *Which he is,* she thought, her stomach swooping.

'Of course. Captain d'Aunay, is it not? May I make you known to Miss Langham and Miss Frederica Arthur? And Mr Crowther, who has had much more exciting experiences of elephants than I ever had in India.' She had an instinct to hide him in a mass of other people, even though she wanted him all to herself, alone. If Bradon saw them together he could find no blame if they were part of the crowd, surely? After all, he had introduced them himself.

Lady Kingsbury walked past as the two of them stood talking to half-a-dozen others, separated by the vivacious Miss Langham. She scanned the group with a critical eye and inclined her head in approval.

'That's your mama-in-law to be, I gather.' Luc had come back to her side.

'Yes.' There was so much noise that although they stood just a few paces away from the nearest group they would have had to have screamed before anyone would have picked up their words.

'She looks a cold fish.'

'She is.' Averil shivered. 'They all are.'

'I still have trouble realising that he proposes this month's trial to make sure no little mistake is in the offing.' He sounded comfortingly outraged on her behalf.

'Yes. I was…surprised. I thought that if he did not believe me, the fact he thought I was not…you know…that would be enough to reject me.' Part of her, madly, wished he had. Then she could be with Luc. And ruined, she reminded herself. 'I suppose I have too much money for that.'

'And yet you stay.'

He sounded cold and angry and she bit her lip against the hurt of it. 'Of course. There is an agreement. Why did you follow us into the City? Do you want to risk everything?'

'I had to see you with him. You looked beautiful, but you are unhappy.' Luc moved a little closer, his back to the room, and she found herself in an alcove. It was all right, she told herself, there was no curtain, she could be seen by anyone who looked and all they were doing was talking.

'I never expected happiness exactly. I did not know him after all, let alone love him. Contentment will come—it must. But, oh, I long for some warmth, to be held.' Her voice trailed away. Luc stood like a statue and then reached for her hands. 'No. I cannot. We must not. If there is the slightest suspicion of us, it would be a disaster. I am simply being feeble, I think.' She put up her chin and smiled a determined smile.

'Feeble? My God,' Luc said with a sort of suppressed fury. 'I could shake you, you idiot girl.' He spun on his heel and stalked off. Averil followed the dark head until it vanished through the double doors that opened on to the hall. He had gone and he was obviously angry with her, which was so unreasonable of him. She was doing her best to be brave and dutiful, although that appeared to anger him, and he must realise that she could not flirt, let alone permit anything more intimate.

She had thought that he cared for her, wanted what was right for her, but it seemed that all he wanted was her in his bed until he tired of her and frustration was making him irritable.

Well, she was frustrated too. She almost wished Andrew Bradon would take some liberties, just so she could be held and kissed. But she wanted Luc and it was so unfair of him to teach her to feel passion and then... Then what? He had done what she asked of him and let her go to Bradon instead of abducting her in a thoroughly shocking and romantic manner. Which is what, she very much feared, she had wanted him to do.

Thoroughly exasperated with herself and Luc, and Bradon, Averil swept out of the alcove and rejoined the party. Frederica Arthur came over and linked her arm though hers. 'Oh, has that handsome naval captain gone already?'

'You think him handsome?'

'Well, not conventionally, perhaps.' Miss Arthur lowered her voice. 'But he is very manly, do you not agree?'

'It is the uniform,' Averil said repressively.

'Perhaps.' Her companion's eyes twinkled with mischief. 'And I do so enjoy flirting and making my poor Hugh jealous.'

'You are betrothed?'

'To Sir Hugh Malcolm—see, over there, the tall man with blond hair by the potted palm. We will be married next month. I cannot wait.' The mischief left her face to be replaced with a tender look. 'I want to start a family as soon as possible. I love children, don't you?'

'Yes. Yes, I suppose I do.' Averil realised she had never thought much about the matter. Children were part of family life, part of her obligation to Bradon. But, listening to Frederica's happy plans as the other young woman chattered on, she realised that just because she had taken the idea for granted did not mean it was not important. The abstract concept of children became an image of a real child, a baby. How wonderful. Andrew Bradon seemed steady and responsible, even if he was not demonstrative and his approach to their marriage was coldly practical. He would be a proud father, she thought. A good father.

'There you are, my dear. I was looking for you to take you in to supper.' Andrew Bradon was looking positively animated.

'You have had luck at the card tables?' Averil enquired as he steered her towards the supper room. She realised now that his father was a serious gamester and that was where much of the family fortune had gone. She was not pleased at the thought that her dowry, and their children's inheritance, might be frittered away by her husband.

'Very gratifying. I only play for low stakes, you understand. My father is the gamester in our family.' He found a table and pulled out a chair for Averil. 'You do not play cards, I trust?'

'No, I do not.' She smiled up at him and saw a glimmer of answering interest. 'I am so glad you only play moderately.'

He was still unusually animated when he returned with food for her. 'You look very well, this evening, my dear. In excellent health and looks. Your appetite is good, I trust?'

'Oh, yes, I feel very well, thank you.'

For a moment she did not understand, then he patted her hand and said, 'Excellent', before attacking his own selection of patties, and she realised he thought her robust health indicated that she was not in a delicate condition.

Perhaps he is just shy and hides it behind a façade of indifference, she thought and watched him from beneath her lashes. He would never be Luc—that was wishing for the moon—but perhaps she had misjudged him. *I will be happy. I will forget Luc*, she vowed, and smiled at Andrew again.

Chapter Eighteen

'The reception went very well,' Lady Kingsbury pronounced as they drove back to Bruton Street. Averil could still not think of it as *home*. 'You have already made a number of most suitable acquaintances. We will attend the Farringdons' ball tomorrow night, I think. Brandon, I trust we may count on your escort?'

'Of course, Mama.'

'Unfortunately it is a Wednesday, but we will visit Almack's next week. There are certain to be several of the Patronesses at the ball. I will secure a voucher for you.'

'Thank you, ma'am. Is the fact that it is Wednesday relevant?'

'Of course. A ball and supper every Wednesday during the Season. Do you not know about Almack's?'

'Oh, yes, ma'am. My friend Lady Perdita Brooke told me about it on the ship, I just did not understand about Wednesdays.'

'Perdita Brooke? You know her well?'

'Very well. She is my particular friend. You may imagine my relief when I discovered that she, too, had survived the wreck. She was saved by Viscount Lyndon.'

'He is now Marquis of Iwerne. That is not an acquaintance I would wish you to pursue. The man is a gazetted rake and as for Lady Perdita, there was considerable talk before she left for India.

Shocking behaviour. She eloped and was some time in the company of a most unsuitable young man.'

'But, ma'am, she is my friend! And Lord Lyndon, I mean, Iwerne—I have something of his that was washed up after the wreck. I was going to write and send it to him.'

'I forbid you to correspond with either of them,' Lady Kingsbury said. 'We cannot be too careful under the circumstances.' *So she does know her son believes I lost my virginity.* 'You will promise me, Averil.'

It was the first time the other woman had used her first name. 'I will not write to Dita, if that is what you wish, ma'am.'

'Then that must be the end of it. Yes?'

'I promise.' But Dita would come to London soon; she had not promised not to meet her, only not to write. And somehow she would return Dita's gift to Alistair, that would not be *corresponding.* She could do that without breaking her word.

Averil was enchanted by the Farringdons' ballroom with its swags of spring flowers, fountains and little sitting-out alcoves created with the cunning use of striped canvas. The whole room resembled a *fête champêtre* on a sunny day.

'How delightful! I do not think I have ever seen anything so fresh and pretty.'

'Hush, my dear. One should not appear gauche and over-excited. Do try for more decorum,' Lady Kingsbury reproved as they made their way from the receiving line into the throng in the ballroom. Arriving too early was another fault to be avoided, apparently. Averil felt decidedly provincial.

There were scarlet jackets in abundance amongst the severe black and midnight-blue tailcoats, and several groups of naval officers as well. Averil scanned them and then tried to decide whether she was pleased or not that Luc was absent.

'Ah, there is the dear Duc de la Valière,' Lady Kingsbury said, nodding towards a group on the far side of the room. 'In fact, half the *émigrée* community appears to be here this evening.'

With tacit permission to stare, Averil studied the dozen or so people in conversation around the plump figure with his chest covered in decorations and orders. The ladies were all dressed in what she had come to recognise already as the latest stare and she looked with envy at one particular gown of pale sea-green with azure ribbons.

Its wearer was deploying her fan with her eyes fixed on a tall, dark gentleman next to her. The group shifted a little and Averil found herself staring at Luc wearing civilian evening dress.

Every good resolution to forget him promptly flew out of the window. Averil let out a long breath and tried to understand how she was feeling. Happy, apprehensive, aroused—oh, dear, he still made her ache when she saw him and there were flutters of wicked sensation in the most embarrassing places. Her nipples hardened against the muslin of her chemise. But most of all, seeing him made her happy in a strange, painful way. She wanted to be with him.

'What lovely gowns the French ladies have,' she remarked, searching for a reason for her close interest.

'Smuggled silks and lace,' Bradon said. 'Come, I will introduce you to the *duc*. One meets him everywhere, you know—a great crony of Prinny's.'

It was hard not to look at Luc as they crossed the floor. Averil made her curtsy to the *duc,* salvaged enough of her unreliable French to reply to his rather effusive compliments and stepped back while Bradon continued to talk to the older man. The effort not to look at Luc was making her feel awkward. In fact, she thought, as she felt her whole body stiffening up, she probably looked as though she was too shy, or perhaps too stand-offish, to look at any of the others in the group.

'Miss Heydon?'

Averil gasped, dropped her fan, reticule and dance card and felt

herself blush peony-pink as she bent to scrabble them up. 'Ouch!'
Her head made contact with another and she sat down, hard, on the
floor.

'Miss Heydon—'

'Averil!'

Hands seized each arm and she was pulled to her feet feeling like
a cross between a rag doll and a small child. On one side Bradon
was a picture of disapproval, as well he might be. On the other Luc
was biting the inside of his cheek in an effort not to laugh. At least
the irritation with her that had gripped him last time they met appeared to have gone. She smoothed her skirts while she fought for
composure.

'Miss Heydon, I do apologise.' At least he was speaking English,
thank heavens. She did not think she could cope with this in French.
'First I make you jump, then I almost knock you out. May I fetch
you some lemonade, or help you to a chair?'

'Miss Heydon will be quite all right with me, Captain d'Aunay,'
Bradon said, cutting across her own response.

'Thank you both, I am fine, I assure you.' She spoke to a point in
the air midway between the two men. 'It was the merest bump.'

'In that case, Miss Heydon, might I ask for a dance?'

Beside her she felt Bradon shift as though he was about to in-
tervene, then he relaxed and she breathed out. He could not have it
both ways, she thought with a spurt of amusement. Either she was
his betrothed and he could legitimately bristle at any man wanting
her attention or she was merely a guest and, provided she was not
accosted by an undesirable partner, he really had nothing to say on
the matter.

'I would be delighted, Captain. Or should I say Monsieur le
Comte, as you are out of uniform?' she asked as she proffered her
rather crumpled dance card. Of course, if Bradon only knew it, Luc
was absolutely the most undesirable partner for her.

'Captain is less of a mouthful,' Luc said, his eyes smiling into hers as he looked up from filling in the card in a way that brought the blush back to warm her cheeks. 'I have taken the liberty of marking two sets including the supper dance.'

Bradon stiffened again, then remarked, 'Your very first partner at your first English ball', in such an insufferably patronising tone that she wanted to hit him.

'Oh, no, not my first partner,' she said, smiling wide-eyed at him. 'See.' She turned the card so he could see Luc's initials against the third set and the supper set. The first two sets were free.

'Then allow me.' Bradon whipped the card from her hand, frowned at it, then put his initials against the first set and another after supper. Luc lowered one eyelid in what might have been the ghost of a wink and turned back to the young lady in sea-green, who was, of course, speaking French.

She had auburn hair and was quite lovely. She also appeared to find Luc fascinating. In fact, it seemed mutual, judging by the intensity with which they were making eye contact. Something tightened inside Averil, an uncomfortable twist of what was almost apprehension.

For goodness' sake! Why should Luc not enjoy talking to a pretty young woman? He was, she reminded herself, looking for a wife. A French wife. It would be foolish indeed of her to expect him to reject the company of other women simply because she was not going to become his mistress.

He had probably already taken a new mistress, she thought, sliding even deeper into gloom at the thought. He was not a man to stay celibate for long, she was sure.

The scrape of bowstrings caused the chattering guests to turn towards the floor and the first chords from the orchestra on the dais brought the dancers on to the floor to make up the first set, the country dance that was opening the ball.

Bradon took her arm and steered her into the line of ladies before taking his place facing her. Lady Farringdon, a sprightly blonde, took the head of the line, called the first figure, and they were away. Averil was too occupied in concentrating on her steps to do more than follow Bradon's lead for at least the first fifteen minutes, then they were safely down the line, had executed a complicated figure without her falling over and disgracing herself again and she began to relax a trifle.

Luc was halfway down the line, partnered by the girl in sea-green, who was, of course, dancing with grace and confidence and managing to talk at the same time.

He was courting her, it was obvious in the way he moved, the way he looked at her, the way she coyly avoided looking at him. The sensation in Averil's stomach stopped being a vague discomfort and became a pain she recognised, even though she had never felt it before. It was jealousy. Full-blown, green-eyed, savage jealousy. She should be ashamed. But she was not.

I love him, Averil thought, and turned blindly to follow Bradon's lead through the next figure. *I love him.* It was not simply desire, or gratitude for her rescue. She wanted him body and soul and heart, even if he never touched her or kissed her again. She wanted him as the father of her children. She wanted to grow old with him.

Appalled, Averil looked at Bradon, the man to whom she would be tied for life, who would be, if she was blessed with them, the father of her children. And she could feel nothing except a vague pity for his coldness.

He was well-enough looking, there would be nothing to actively repel her when he came to her bed. He seemed intelligent enough. Until a few minutes ago the fact that she did not love him had not mattered one iota—she had not expected ever to experience that emotion. Now she was dizzy with despair because she knew what it felt like to love a man and she could never have him.

'Are you quite well, my dear?' Bradon bent to murmur in her ear as the measure brought them to stand side by side. 'You have gone quite pale.'

'It is very warm in here,' she lied. Her limbs felt numb with cold.

'I would have thought that after India you would be accustomed,' he said with a frown. 'You are not…unwell?'

'No, I am not,' she almost snapped back. 'And I have been out of India's heat for months now, my lord.'

'We had best sit out the remainder of the set, I think.' He took her arm to guide her out of the line, but Averil resisted. She did not want to have to sit with nothing to do but think, nothing to look at but Luc and the French girl, so absorbed in each other.

Somehow she got through the set, and the next, a cotillion where she was partnered by a shy young man who hardly managed to articulate his request for the dance. Without any need to converse Averil was left to work her way through the complex figures and to brood on Luc.

Even if he knew she loved him he would not marry her. He had made his requirements in a bride quite clear. She must be French and even Averil's spoken French was inadequate. She must be of aristocratic breeding and Averil's grandfather had been a shopkeeper. There was nothing except a physical attraction to make him want her and she had a sinking suspicion that once he had made love to her fully and satisfied that urge, then she would hold no further attraction for him. She was hardly skilled in the arts of love. How long, she wondered gloomily, would he have kept her if she had yielded to his desire and become his mistress? A week, a month?

Shy Mr McCormack delivered her back to Lady Kingsbury with mumbled thanks. The orchestra stopped to retune, the volume of conversation rose. At any moment Luc would come to claim her for the next set and she had not the slightest idea what she would talk to him about, or even if she was capable of conversation.

She was so lost in painful thought that when he appeared in front of her in the flesh she gasped.

'Am I startling you again, Miss Heydon? I do apologise.' Luc stood there, elegant and groomed, a thousand miles from the piratical figure who had hauled her naked from the beach on St Helen's. But that man was still there with the dangerous fire in those deep grey eyes, the jut of that arrogant nose, the set of the determined chin. And the lean figure, all hard-toned muscle and long bones that made her mouth dry with desire when she looked at him. Those were the same.

And so was the mouth that could thin into a hard line of anger or curve into a smile that made her want to follow him into sin and back, that could bark orders in one breath and breathe promises of those sins with another.

'I was momentarily distracted, Count,' Averil said. She got to her feet without a stumble by focusing every ounce of concentration on her deportment. *I stand just so, my hands like this, my back straight and shoulders down. Head up. Fan and reticule—both under control. Chin up. Smile. Put out my hand to him…*

She thought she was succeeding admirably until they took their places for the quadrille. 'What is wrong, Averil?'

'A headache, that is all.' The smile became brighter.

'You no more have a headache than I have. Is it your thoughts that are painful?'

'Perhaps,' she admitted. 'It is not such an easy thing as I thought it would be, to travel so many miles and to learn to live with strangers on such terms of intimacy.'

'Do you think Bradon will become easier with acquaintance?'

'He is not a man who finds it easy to give expression to his feelings,' Averil said, choosing her words with care.

'If he has any,' Luc countered.

There was a slight confusion in a far corner of the dance floor. A young lady had fainted, it seemed. Partners relaxed and began to talk quietly to each other while chaperones bustled about.

'His reactions so far do argue a lack of trust,' Averil said. 'But then, he knows as little about me as I do of him.'

'It is not simply a question of trust.' Luc frowned. 'There is a practical expediency about it that I do not like—it does not seem to matter to him whether you told the truth or not, merely whether there would be consequences if you had not. I could understand him deciding that he would not marry you because you had been compromised, but this is having his cake and eating it, too.'

'I suppose any man might be concerned about such consequences,' Averil murmured. 'You would, surely, if it was a question of the charming young lady in sea-green?'

He looked across the room. 'Mademoiselle de la Falaise? Perhaps I would.'

Indeed you would. 'Is she the one?'

'Perhaps,' he said again. 'She is very lovely, very well bred. Her mother is a distant cousin on my father's side. Her father's estates are in Normandy also.'

'Perfect.' It was true, what they said: the heart did break and you could feel it, a hard, sickening pain like the crack of a bone splintering.

'Time will tell. I do not know if there is any depth or spirit under the elegant little tricks and she does not know me at all. And her father is suspicious of the half-breed naval captain. He, too, wants to return to France, to take his place back at court, to be what he once was. He must choose his sons-in-law with care. Am I French enough for him? Where do my loyalties lie? Am I a dangerous constitutionalist like my father? He wonders about those things.'

'Do you wonder? You sound very French now,' Averil said. Her lips felt numb, but she kept smiling.

'Really?' Luc's voice was sombre. He added something half under his breath and she strained to catch it as the band struck up again and couples straightened up and resumed their positions. *I wish I knew where I belonged, what I was.* Had he really said that? But he seemed so assured, so certain about his desire to return to France.

'Oh, yes. Your intonation has changed, there is the faintest accent.

It is most attractive,' she added lightly, testing her own composure by being a trifle daring.

'And you,' Luc said as he took her hand and the first steps of the dance brought them almost breast to breast. The dark mood seemed to have fled as fast as it had arrived. 'You are even more lovely than you were on my desert island, *ma sirène*.'

She could translate that: *my mermaid*. 'You should not flirt with me while you are courting Mademoiselle de la Falaise.' And that was all it was, flirtation. It came so easily to him, so hard to her. Or perhaps the difference was simply that her feelings were engaged and his were not.

'I do not know how to flirt with you, Averil,' he said as the dance parted them for a wide circle. As they came back together he was frowning. 'With you, I can speak only the truth, it seems.'

'Then you should not speak such truths,' she said and looked up into his eyes. His expression changed, sharpened, and too late she realised that she had done nothing to shield her own. What had he seen in her face, in her gaze?

'Averil, leave him. It is not too late.'

She was silent. The other couples were too close, her heart was beating too hard to find breath for words. When, minutes later, the music stopped and with it the end of the first dance, she stepped off the floor and into one of the little striped tents that were scattered around the room.

'Leave him? For what? My ruin, if you are still asking me to be your mistress.'

'Come to me. I will deal honestly with you, Averil.'

She sat down in a swirl of peach silk and gauze and he stayed on his feet facing her, sombre. Anyone looking in would think, perhaps, that they had intruded on a proposal. And that, of course, was just what it had been. A dishonourable proposal.

'Then let us be entirely honest, shall we? You seek a bride, quite coolly, as though you select the right horse for your carriage.' She paused to get her breathing under control. She must not let him see how this affected her. 'You chose one who will restore the part of you that is not French because, somehow, your identity is compromised by your English blood. You want me, for reasons I will not explore here, and so, just as coolly, you offer me my ruin. Because I am a merchant's daughter, and English, and therefore fit for nothing else. You call Bradon cold and practical. Have you looked in the mirror? That description fits you just as well, I think.'

'You want to marry me?' Luc asked, looking at her as though he had never seen her before.

'I think,' Averil said, finding her anger and with it breath to continue, 'that you should remove yourself before I forget that I am a lady—insofar as a daughter of trade can be, of course—and throw one of these flower arrangements over your arrogant, smug male person.'

Chapter Nineteen

Luc turned on his heel and walked away, not because he feared a bouquet being thrown at his head, but because he was so strongly tempted to turn Miss Averil Heydon over his knee and… Or, strangle her. Or shake some sense into her. But it was he who needed sense knocking into. What had he said? That had almost been a proposal.

Louise de la Falaise saw him from across the room and made a pretty little gesturing motion with her fan. He bowed and walked on. She was very lovely and intelligent, too, as far as he could tell, with her every move and word being supervised by her mama. He should desire her, but he did not, even though she was probably the woman he would propose to. He desired one woman only and she was impossible.

Averil was English. His father had married an Englishwoman and their only child had never known where he belonged, where his loyalties lay, which identity was his. When the time had come to make a decision and take a stand, he had not had the strength to stand up to his mother and to remain in France with his father. The fact that he was just a boy made no difference. If he had stayed, he supposed that now he would be long cold in his grave.

But he had made his choice, he lived and now he had made a decision: as his father's son he could make no other. He had lands and responsibilities to resume and to hand on to a son who would at least be three-quarters French.

Averil was…impossible. The scandal if she left Bradon would be shocking; he could not believe the man would take the loss of such a dowry lying down. She was wrong for him, as wrong as a dangerous drug would be. And he must not compromise her. Bradon had accepted her, she had accepted Bradon for what he was. It would be the action of a blackguard to seduce her away now.

There was Bradon now, talking to a striking brunette. He felt a wave of dislike run through him. The man bristled proprietarily when he saw Averil with another man, but he made no move to touch her except to take her arm formally. His eyes did not follow her with anything in them except a cool assessment. He did not even desire her person, it seemed.

Luc stopped, then swung back, apologising to the officer he almost flattened with the suddenness of his movement. He passed a footman with a tray and lifted two glasses from it as he went. Averil was still sitting in the gay little tent, just as he had left her, her face calm, her hands folded decorously in her lap, her eyes blank.

She looked up as his shadow fell at her feet and went a little pale, but she made no move to throw the arrangement of hothouse lilies on the table beside her as she had threatened.

'Here.' He thrust the glass into her hand and drained his own. 'Does he make love to you?' He sounded like a jealous fool. He did not care.

'Bradon?' Averil looked at the glass as though she had never seen one before. 'No.'

'Does he kiss you? Caress you?'

'No. He kissed my hand, once. He shows no affection and no desire. Why do you ask?' She took a mouthful of the champagne, swallowed. 'What possible business is it of yours what my betrothed does? Please do not tell me you are jealous of him—what right have you?'

'I saved you on that beach and then made a decision that could have—may have—ruined you. I—'

'Oh, so now you are going to tell me again that you feel responsible for me?' Averil got to her feet in an inelegant scramble, tossed back the wine with a reckless hand and stood toe to toe with him, glaring up. 'Well, you are not. I may have been innocent, but I was not addled—I am responsible for the decisions I made. And if you think I should be grateful to you—'

'I think that you are just the right height for me to kiss,' Luc said, ignoring the music and voices and laughter at his back, ignoring her anger. All he could see was her face, all he could smell was the fresh sweetness of her skin, all he could hear was his own blood pounding in his ears and the madness of a need he did not understand, that was so much more than lust, sweeping through him.

'No.' Averil stepped back and the pain deep in her eyes stopped him as abruptly as if she had slammed a door in his face. 'No. I cannot bear this. It may all be about physical pleasure, the fun of the chase, for you. But it is not for me. For me it is a torment. I am not one of your sophisticated matrons or headstrong daughters of the aristocracy. I am a merchant's daughter and I was not brought up for these games. I was brought up to keep my word and to respect and honour my husband.'

'Averil, I am sorry—' He would cut out his heart and lay it at her feet if that would help. It could not hurt any more than the pain in it now.

'Oh, I do not blame you,' she said bitterly. 'You flirt and make love like a hound chases a rabbit—on instinct. If I had not been so weak, Bradon would still have cause for suspicion, but at least I would have a clear conscience and I would not have to be fighting the temptation to give in to you.' She gave a little sob that turned the knife in his heart. 'I would not have known what it was to be made love to as you made love to me, I would have known only him.' Appalled, Luc reached for her. She batted his hands away.

'Go. If you have any concern for me at all, *any,* go and leave me alone.'

Hell. What had he done? She was right, she did not know how to deal with the likes of him and he had no idea how to deal with her, except in his bed. Her chin came up and he could see the effort it was costing her to stand there and confront him like this. His temper, for some reason never far below the surface these days, flared. He wanted to hurt someone, to share the pain that racked him.

'Yes, I will go. As you say, Miss Heydon, I should not be toying with someone who does not understand the rules these games are played by.' He held up his hands in a gesture of surrender. 'Your virtue has defeated me.'

He knew he sounded ungracious, angry, sarcastic, all the things he had no right to feel. He expected her anger in return, was braced for tears. What he did not expect was for the well-behaved Miss Heydon to scoop up the vase of lilies and throw it at his head, just as she had threatened.

Luc caught it before it hit him, but water and lilies went everywhere, showering his immaculate evening clothes. Averil gasped, then turned and slipped through the flap at the back of the little tent, leaving him to shake himself like a wet dog. Lily pollen stained his shirt front as he batted petals from his lapels and water ran down his nose and dripped to the floor.

Behind him the flaps of the tent shifted. 'Ah, there you are!' said Mademoiselle de la Falaise in French. 'It is our dance next, *monsieur.*'

He turned and she stared, her mouth open. '*Mon Dieu!* What has occurred?'

'I was unaccountably clumsy,' he said. 'I tripped. Obviously I cannot stay at the ball. You will excuse me. I regret greatly that I must forgo our dance.'

'I also, but there is nothing to be done.' She shrugged with rueful charm. 'I must go and find a dry gentleman. Goodbye.' Her lips were twitching as she turned and left.

'Goodbye indeed,' Luc muttered. That had done his dignity with the woman he was thinking of courting a great deal of good to be sure. Now what? He could hardly walk out on to the dance floor looking like this. Where had Averil got out? He investigated the back of the tent and found it opened out on to a corridor under the orchestra gallery and it was mercifully empty. Luc gritted his teeth and stalked off to the front door.

'I thought you were engaged for the supper dance, my dear.' Bradon appeared in front of Averil as she sat on a gilt chair in the furthest corner from the little striped tent.

'I was. I gather Captain d'Aunay had an accident and had to leave.'

'I trust he is not badly injured. If no one else has claimed you, perhaps you would care to dance with me.' He held out his hand and Averil put hers into it.

'Thank you, I would prefer that in any case.' He smirked a little, she noticed. She fixed a bright smile on her own face. It was time to face the future as Lady Bradon and convince her betrothed that she was indeed the wife for him. After all, the man she loved was an unscrupulous scoundrel who lost his temper when thwarted. Andrew Bradon's cool equanimity was positively soothing after that scene in the tent.

She wondered what had come over her as she tried to feel remorseful for losing her temper so thoroughly and with such violence. What if she had hit him with the crystal vase?

He deserved it, the angry little voice inside her said. *Just fall out of love with him, that is all you need to do.*

Of course. Fall out of love. She smiled up at Bradon as they took their places. It was a matter of will-power. 'Six days of our month have gone already, my lord,' she said and saw his pupils widen. He was not as indifferent to her as she thought.

'You are a formal little thing, aren't you?' he said. 'You should call me Bradon.'

'Yes…Bradon.' Was she supposed to have known that would be acceptable without being asked? No matter. Provided she made no major breach of etiquette he seemed to like putting her right. Being patronised was just something else she must add to her list of things to become accustomed to. Somehow it no longer seemed of importance, she was so unhappy. The pain could not stay this acute for ever, Averil told herself as she stumbled and Bradon steadied her. When it became a dull ache then she would manage better.

'I am so looking forward to Almack's,' she said.

'Ah, yes, Mama has secured you vouchers. She will explain the rules to you—there is no need to be nervous about it.'

'I wasn't,' Averil said and he frowned.

'You should be. Pay great attention to what Mama tells you—making a good impression at Almack's is vital.'

'Yes, Bradon,' she said meekly and told herself he was only concerned that she was not embarrassed.

Resolutions were all very well, Averil realised at one in the morning as she sat up in bed and lit a candle. She should have gone to sleep half an hour ago when she climbed into bed, but her eyes, hot and heavy, would not stay closed and her mind would not settle.

I love him and I cannot have him. I should not want him. I must learn to forget him. How long would it take? If only she could marry Bradon now, or in a few days' time. Then perhaps her foolish heart would give up, because then being with Luc would be an impossibility.

But it would be another two weeks before the arrival of her courses convinced his mother that there was no danger of her carrying another man's child. Then there would be all the necessary preparations to be made, her drowned trousseau to replace, arrangements to be made. Another month at least.

Averil tossed and turned and finally gave up. The soft pile of the carpet cradled her feet in luxury as she slid out of the high bed, reminding her of her new circumstances. She would go down to the library and find a book, or a fashion journal or something to distract her mind until she could sleep.

The house was quiet as she padded downstairs in bare feet. Her ghostly reflection in her white robe made her jump as she came face to face with a mirror on the first landing and her heart was still thudding as she walked across the hall to the library door.

The fire was burning low in the grate, but candles were still lit and she found the pile of journals on a side table easily enough. Fashion and frivolity to distract her or something serious, sermons perhaps, to make her concentrate?

As she stood with the journals in her hand she became aware of voices. The door to the study was slightly ajar and at least two people were talking in there. Eavesdropping was unladylike and irresistible. Averil put down the *Lady's Monthly Museum* and walked soundlessly to stand by the door.

'…better than I could have hoped. Inexperienced, of course, but there is no vulgarity and she has a certain style. I have high hopes of her once she acquires a little town bronze.' It was Lady Kingsbury and she was talking about her. Averil tried not to bridle at the presumption that she might have been vulgar. 'I just hope that our fears are unjustified and she is not breeding. My instincts tell me that she is not.' Averil rested her hand on the door jamb and leaned closer.

'It will be a pity if she is. The girl has potential, as you say, and of course, there is the money,' Bradon remarked.

'I have been thinking about that, and I agree with you, it would be regrettable to lose her and the money both. If she is carrying a child, then it is not an insurmountable problem, we can deal with that.'

Averil clapped her hand over her mouth to stifle the involuntary gasp.

'End the pregnancy, you mean?' Bradon said conversationally. 'There's that woman in Charles Street that I sent my mistress to when the careless little slut got herself in pup, if you recall.'

Averil dropped her hands to cradle her belly as though there was a real child into there that they were threatening. *That poor girl. He takes no responsibility, he sounds as if he hates her for it.*

'I did think of that, but we do not want to risk anything that might harm her future childbearing,' Lady Kingsbury said with as much sympathy as if she was talking about her lapdog. 'There is always such a risk of infertility and the last thing you want is to find yourself tied to an otherwise healthy young wife who cannot bear a child.'

'She might not stay so healthy in that case,' Bradon said in such a matter-of-fact way that it took Averil a moment to realise he was suggesting murder. Her murder. Soundlessly she slid to the thick carpet, her legs incapable of supporting her.

'Better not to complicate matters,' his mother said with chilling practicality. 'If the chit has got herself with child, then we send her off to the country somewhere for about ten months and *then* you marry her. We can always say she came down with an illness as a result of the change of climate or some such excuse. And at least you will know she is fertile. We can find some couple to take the child.'

'Rather a risk, don't you think? They might talk. But then, small babies are so fragile. It would be best to make sure it never became a hostage to fortune.'

'Yes, that would be best, and so easily done with a newborn babe.'

Averil stuffed her knuckles into her mouth against the rising bile.

Oh, God, what had she done? She was trapped with people who would kill without the slightest compunction simply for money. A baby. An innocent babe. How could they even contemplate such a thing? And then to solve the problem of an infertile wife by murder—how long would they give her to conceive before they decided she was not use to them? A year?

The urge to retch almost overcame her. With painful slowness Averil crawled back away from the door until she could haul herself upright.

She made herself tiptoe across the floor, not run, screaming, as she wanted to. Somehow she remembered not to slam the door, then she fled upstairs, not stopping until she was huddled shivering in her own bed again.

She had thought him cold-blooded to insist they wait a month, but this ruthless expediency, the cold disregard for anything except their own greed and needs was breathtaking in its awfulness.

To send her away and insist the child was given to some kind couple who would love it—that she could understand, even though she would never have agreed to it. But to hope that the infant would die, to help that to happen... They probably did not even think of it as anything worse than letting nature take its course, she thought numbly, hugging herself as though to protect a real child.

Then to contemplate disposing of her like a useless animal... No, that was cold-blooded evil. If there was no excuse for that, then there was no excuse for the other. They were murderers.

If she had not gone downstairs and heard that conversation, she would have made herself marry Bradon and perhaps she would never have understood just what manner of man he was. He would probably be a perfectly good father to his own children, Averil thought. It was just some poor little inconvenient scrap of humanity who got in his way that would be disposable. Only women who were of no use to him who could be discarded like rubbish.

This changed everything. She could not bring herself to speak to

Bradon again; even the thought of seeing him filled her with sick horror. It did not matter that no child was at risk, he had revealed himself in his true colours and she would never be able to forget, never be able to trust him. She would never be able to let him touch her without recoiling.

Papa would not expect her to marry a man like that, nor into a family so callous and calculating and criminal. Bless him, she thought fondly. He was ambitious for the family, but he would protect a grandchild, even a scandalously illegitimate one, with his life.

She would have to go home to India, there was no other solution—and to do that she needed enough money for the return journey. Her courage almost failed her at the thought of another voyage with all its dangers, but there was nothing for her here in England. Nothing.

In the morning she would go to the City and Mr Wilton's office and he would give her the money for her passage. Perhaps Grace would go with her. She must pay her off in any case, and find respectable lodgings while she waited for a ship. She would manage somehow and she would get home to people who loved her and hope they would forgive her for her imprudence.

Her mind was in turmoil. If she had never been shipwrecked, she would not have met Luc. She would not have been compromised and Bradon would have married her and she would have been tied to a ruthless, heartless man. It was the luckiest of escapes, it might even have saved her life. But then her heart would not have been broken and she would never have known what it was to love a man.

Dry-eyed, Averil curled up under the covers and waited, sleepless, for dawn.

Chapter Twenty

'I do not understand. Why can you not give me money to return home?' Averil looked around the dark panelled walls of the office as though she could find some explanation of the man's adamant refusal pinned to them.

'Because I am not authorised to, Miss Heydon.' The lawyer looked over the top of his spectacles at her as though she was a rather stupid new office clerk who could not add up. 'Sir Joshua instructed me on the disbursement of funds for your dowry on the occasion of your marriage to Lord Bradon and for reasonable expenses in the days before your marriage.

'The additional expenditure resulting from the tragic loss of the ship is necessary to accomplish the marriage. But Sir Joshua intends you to marry Lord Bradon, not to return to India on a whim. It is, of course, highly regrettable that you are feeling homesick, but really, Miss Heydon—'

'You do not understand, Mr Wilton. Lord Bradon is not what I thought. I cannot marry him. This is not a whim.'

'Indeed? A false representation has been made?' Mr Wilton sat up straighter and pushed his glasses more firmly on to his nose. 'He is already married? Not of sound mind? Fatally ill?'

'No, none of those things. There is no legal reason why I should not marry him. But I cannot like him.' She could hardly accuse

Bradon of a hypothetical murder of a child who did not exist or of threatening her life.

And she could not say either that she loved another man, that she was compromised. Instinct told her that the lawyer would be entirely in sympathy with Bradon's solution to the problem, at least as far as secretly removing the child was concerned, and that he would dismiss her tale of what else she had heard last night as feminine hysterics.

'Really, Miss Heydon, you cannot in all seriousness expect me to disburse a significant sum of my client's money and to overturn almost two years of discussion and negotiations simply because you cannot like your future husband! On what grounds?'

'He is cold.' The lawyer did not say, *And what does that matter?* But his expression said it for him. 'He is not kind.'

'He has threatened you? Struck you?'

'No…' She had no evidence, only an overheard conversation in the middle of the night with no witnesses. How could she make this practical, unimaginative man understand? She could not, she realised.

'You will forgive me, I trust, Miss Heydon, for my plain speaking. But I would be negligent in my duty to your father if I did anything to encourage this fancy of yours. Young ladies in your position do not marry for love, like the heroine of some fantastical romance novel. And no doubt halfway back to India you would change your mind again on another whim.'

'But what am I to do if I cannot go home?'

'Why, Lord Bradon's house is your home now, Miss Heydon. You can, and must, return there.'

'I will not—'

'Then I will have to inform Lord Bradon that you appear to be suffering an affliction of the spirits and require medical attention. In fact,' he said, frowning at her, 'I wonder if I should not go back to the house with you and speak to his lordship. I am really most concerned. Perhaps you are suffering a brain fever brought on by delayed shock after your ordeal during the shipwreck. Yes, indeed, that must be it.' He got up from behind the desk. 'Now, I will call my carriage and we will get you home at once, my dear Miss Heydon.'

'No!' Averil saw a vision of herself trying to explain to the outraged Bradons why she had run away. She could imagine the scene all too clearly. They would be calm, appear concerned, they would assure Mr Wilton that they had no idea that she was unwell. How sorry they would be that by plunging her into the social whirl they had so distressed her poor, fragile mind. And the moment the door was closed behind the lawyer she would be a prisoner until they discovered it was safe to marry her to Bradon.

'No,' she said, conjuring up every ounce of control she possessed. 'That is very kind, but I have my maid and a carriage.' She pulled a handkerchief from her reticule and dabbed her dry eyes with it. 'You are right, I must be unwell. I have not slept well since the wreck... Such nightmares. Perhaps they will allow me to go to the country estate and rest.' She managed to make her voice tremble a little. 'It will all seem better then, will it not, Mr Wilton?'

'Of course, my dear, of course.' He subsided back into his chair, his relief obvious that she had become a tremulous, biddable female relying on his superior judgement. 'I will ring for a small glass of sherry wine for you. I do not as a rule approve of females consuming alcoholic beverages, but in this case, it may be wise.'

'Thank you,' Averil murmured, wielding the handkerchief again as she sank back into the depths of the chair. At least it would give her a few minutes to think. What on earth was she to do now?

She could go to Lady Perdita Brooke—but Dita's parents would never countenance her sheltering a runaway, especially when Dita herself had a recent scandal to live down. Nor could she ask Dita for a loan, not of the amount of money she would need for lodgings until the ship sailed, the fare, money for three months and wages for Grace, whom she could hardly abandon.

There was one possibility, so shocking that when the sherry came she gulped it down and almost made herself choke. Was it her only option or was it what she wanted to do and she was finding excuses, telling herself she had no other choice?

It took several minutes to shake Mr Wilton off, to assure him she did not require handing into her carriage—which was a good thing as she had come in a hackney—and that she felt much more calm and rational now. She had a sinking feeling that he might write to Papa, but if her plan worked she would be home in India at the same time as any letter.

With the patient Grace beside her she stood on the pavement and looked for a hackney. 'Grace, I need to talk to you, in confidence, about something rather shocking. If you feel you would rather not be involved I quite understand, but in that case we had better go back to Bruton Street now and I will drop you off. All I ask is that you say nothing about it for as long as possible.'

'Of course I'll come with you, Miss Heydon,' the maid said. 'Look, there's one.' She darted to the edge of the pavement and waved down a cab. 'Is it an elopement, miss?'

'No. Not quite.' The driver leaned down for directions. 'One of the main shipping agents, please. I want one who handles the East India ships.'

'Oh!' Grace's eyes were wide as they settled on the worn seats. 'Are we going to India?'

'I am, but not you.' The girl's face fell. 'It is a three-month voyage, Grace. And dangerous—look what happened to me on the way here. And India is hot and unhealthy.'

'I'd like to go,' Grace persisted. 'I've always wanted to travel, honest, miss. If I can survive all the things you can catch in the Rookery, I can manage in India, I'll be bound.'

'I might not be able to pay you for months,' Averil admitted.

'I may not even be able to pay for the two weeks you have been working for me already. I am going to do something very shocking, Grace. I am going to put myself under the protection of a gentleman and hope that he will fund my passage and your wages.'

'I knew it! I knew this valise had more in it than a gown to be altered like you told her ladyship. It's too heavy.'

'It contains everything I own,' Averil admitted. 'Which is not much. And then there are your things—I did not dare tell you about it in the house in case anyone overheard, and I did not know how we could get two valises out.'

'Not to worry, miss.' Grace showed no sign of shock or alarm at Averil's explanations. 'When we find out whether he's up for it I'll take a hackney back to Bruton Street and sneak my stuff out the back way.' She sat in silence for a while. 'You don't want to marry Lord Bradon, miss? Can't say I blame you. Nasty bit of work he is, if you ask me. Like a dead flounder.'

'Grace!' Averil choked on a gasp of laughter.

'Well, he is. He's got hands like one, too.'

'How do you know? He has not made advances to you, has he?'

'Sort of pats and gropes when he's passing.' The girl shrugged. 'Nothing I can't cope with. Some of the gents is like that—they fancy a servant girl because we don't answer back—mostly. Yes, me lud, no, me lud,' she mimicked savagely. 'Lie on me back with me skirts up if you like, me lud. I don't stand for it myself.'

'I am so sorry, Grace. I had no idea—how dreadful.' The hypocrisy of it! Lecturing her on virtue while all the while he was harassing the servants.

'Your gent's not like that, is he, miss?'

'No,' said Averil. 'He asks for what he wants and he takes *no* for an answer.' More or less. 'I think this must be the shipping office.'

They climbed down into the bustling street. It was closer to

Calcutta than Mayfair, Averil thought, finding to her surprise that she could smile. The noise and smells and the mass of carts and porters and hawkers were familiar and unthreatening. 'Wait please,' she called up to the driver. 'We will not be long.'

'Two weeks,' Averil said as they sat back in the hackney fifteen minutes later. She studied the printed sheet in her hand. The *Diamond Rose* for Calcutta. Cabins close to the Great Cabin that would accommodate the two of them were still available, but at a price that was quite impossible to meet unless Luc helped her.

Would he pay that much, plus Grace's wages and some money for her expenses on board, in exchange for her virginity and just two weeks of her unskilled lovemaking?

'Do you love him, miss?' Grace asked as the cab turned into Piccadilly. Averil felt her chest tightening so that she could scarcely breathe.

'Yes,' she said. 'But he does not love me and he does not know how I feel about him. And he must not.'

Grace did not answer, but she changed seats to sit next to Averil and squeezed her hand. Her lover had jilted her, Averil recalled, and squeezed back. The pressure in her chest eased a little.

The hackney swung through a tight opening into a cobbled yard. 'Albany!'

'Veil, miss!'

Averil pulled down the coarse veiling as she climbed down. A porter came out as Grace lifted the valises out.

'Can I help you, madam?' It sounded like, *Go away, we don't welcome your sort here.*

I am a fallen woman, Averil realised. *Or, at least, I am falling.* 'Thank you. Captain d'Aunay's chambers, please.'

The porter went back inside with a curt nod, leaving them standing on the cobbles. After five minutes Averil squared her shoulders and walked towards the door; she could hardly stand there until Luc happened to go in or out.

A dapper little man appeared on the step as she reached it. 'Madam? The captain is not at home at the moment.'

'He told me to send to him here if I ever needed help,' Averil said.

'Ah. Yes, indeed, ma'am. Will you follow me?'

They walked after him down a passage that seemed to Averil as long as a rope walk. The man opened a black door and ushered them into a sitting room. 'If you will make yourself comfortable, ma'am, I will see if—'

'Hughes!' The shout was unmistakeably Luc's voice. 'Something for my damned head and get a move on. I think I'm dying.'

'He's awake. Excuse me.' The manservant vanished through a door at the rear of the room.

They could hear his voice, low and soothing, then, 'A *what?* Who?'

'Hangover,' Grace observed. 'Does he drink much?'

'I have never seen him even tipsy,' Averil said. On St Mary's she had seen him drink and keep up with Sir George's not inconsiderable dinner time consumption, but he had shown no ill effects. In fact, he had made love to her afterwards.

There were more growls from the direction of the bedchamber. Oh, dear. He did not sound like a man who could be persuaded to part with a large sum of money in exchange for a novice mistress's inept caresses. The nerves that had been a flock of butterflies in her stomach turned into bats.

Hughes reappeared, seized a decanter from the sideboard and vanished again. Finally he put his head around the door. 'If your woman would care to join me in the scullery, ma'am, the captain will be out in a moment.'

Grace got to her feet, stopped, whisked off Averil's bonnet, patted her hair into place, hissed, 'Bite your lips. Good luck', and followed him out.

Averil sat watching the door as though a tiger might emerge from it. Every carefully rehearsed sentence fled from her head. When the door did open she was ready to faint through sheer nervous anticipation.

Luc stopped in the doorway and studied her without speaking. His hair was wet and looked as though he had poured water over his head and then run his fingers through the black locks. There were purple smudges under his eyes, which were bloodshot. He was wearing a shirt, open at the neck, and pantaloons; his feet were bare.

'You look dreadful,' Averil said without thinking and stood up. He looked like death and she loved him. She wanted to take him in her arms and fuss over him and soothe his headache and kiss away the strain around his eyes and never leave him. Instead she clasped her hands tightly together and just waited.

'I have seen you looking better,' he rejoined. 'And worse, come to think about it. I am damnably hungover. I am probably still half-cut. Tell me what's wrong, just don't shout at me.'

'I won't.' Averil bit her lip. 'Hadn't you better sit down?'

He gestured at the *chaise* and sat in the chair opposite. 'Does Bradon know you're here?'

'No!' Luc winced. 'Sorry. No. I have run away and left no note. I cannot bear to marry him.'

'And so you have come to me.' The colour was returning to his face and the bleak look in his eyes seemed to fade. Whatever potion the manservant had given him must be working.

'Yes. But—'

'Ah. The *but*. Tell me the worst.'

The door opened to admit Hughes with a tray. 'Coffee, Captain. Your woman said you would take coffee also, ma'am.' Leaving her to pour, he left as quietly as he had entered.

She stirred in sugar, careful not to strike the porcelain and make a noise, passed a cup, black, to Luc and added cream to her own.

'I want to go home, to India. Bradon is a man that my father would not wish me to marry, once he knows the truth about him.'

'Tell me what he has done.'

Averil explained, not at all certain that Luc would believe her. Her father would, she was certain. But would another man?

Luc's face darkened. 'The man contemplates the murder of a woman and child as he might consider destroying a wasps' nest. It would do the world a service to remove him from it. And that harpy of a mother of his. But I suppose one cannot, not without evidence.'

'No,' Averil agreed. 'But you understand why I cannot marry him.'

'Of course. Thank God you ran before they discovered you had overheard.' He rubbed a hand over his face. 'Tell me the *but*.'

Averil bit her lower lip, struggling to find the way to express what she wanted. In the end she simply said, 'I will be your mistress for two weeks in exchange for my passage back to India, Grace's wages as my companion on the voyage and enough money to cover my expenses to Calcutta.'

He was silent, watching her with an impenetrable, heavy gaze over the top of steepled fingers.

'I know it isn't for very long, and it will be a lot of money and I won't be very good, although I am a virgin and men seem to set a lot of store by that, so I suppose that is something, and I will do my best…'

He held up one hand and she trailed to a halt, red-cheeked and breathless with embarrassment and nerves.

'What is your plan if I refuse?' He might have been discussing naval tactics in a meeting except that he had gone white under his tan.

'I have none.'

'So you are desperate and I am your only hope?'

'Yes.'

'Flattering,' he remarked.

But I love you! The words she could not say were bitter on her tongue. What could she say? That if she was not desperate she would still have come to him? No. Nor would she have seen him again if her father's lawyer had given her the money. She would have written to say goodbye, that was all. So he had every right to feel used.

'I am sorry. I thought you wanted me.'

'Oh, I do, my dear. Very much. I was hoping you would come because you wanted me, too—and for rather longer than two weeks.' He closed his eyes and she wondered if his headache was still very bad. 'For much longer,' he said and opened them again.

'But the ship sails then and in any case, the third week wouldn't be…' Her voice trailed away. Possibly it was possible to blush even redder, but she doubted it.

'In three weeks your not-to-be mother-in-law would have known you were not with child?' he enquired. 'There is no need to colour up like a peony, I am aware of how females work, you know.' Luc did not sound at all like a man who had just heard that his physical desires were to be gratified. 'Are you not afraid that two weeks as my mistress will leave you pregnant?'

Yes, it *was* possible to become more embarrassed. Averil studied her gloved hands intently. 'I overheard two married women talking at the reception. They have lovers, I think. And then I asked Grace about what they said and she told me that there is a way if the man…'

'I see. So I have two very expensive weeks teaching you how to make love and I have to withdraw every time?' His voice was flat; she could not tell whether he was furiously angry with her or disgusted and bored. Had she hurt him?

'Yes,' she said. A seam in her glove split and with it her nerve.

'I am sorry. I should never have come here, never have asked. It is quite unreasonable of me, I can see that. I will go away.' The wave of flat despair blacked out even the fear of not knowing what she could do now. All she could think of was that she would never see Luc again, never lie in his arms, never show him how much she loved him even if she could not say the words.

Chapter Twenty-One

'Averil.' She looked up as Luc knelt in front of her and caught her hand. The glimpse of pale skin through the split glove seam was deeply affecting. It was erotic, but it also made him feel a strange tenderness, almost enough to wash away the hurt that she had come to him not because she wanted him but because he was the only person she could sell herself to.

'It is not unreasonable, quite the contrary—it is quite delightful of you,' he said, instinct telling him to keep his voice light. He could not beg her to stay for ever, not when she was so desperate to leave that she would do this thing. 'I must admit that two months would be better and I do hope you will not ruin any more expensive gloves while in my keeping, but I agree to your terms.'

The hazel eyes that looked into his with such earnestness were dark and troubled. There was real fear lurking there. She must have been at her wits' end to have come to him, he knew that. He was her last resort. If he had not taken her in, what would she have done? The options were bleak and the least dreadful of them would be to return to Bradon.

Her desperation put her feelings for him in stark context: becoming his mistress was better than selling herself on the streets, better than throwing herself in the Thames and preferable to returning to a man who terrified and disgusted her. His pride kicked at the realisation. And there was something else, a feeling he could not identify except as an ache. He pushed the pain and resentment to the back of his mind; it was time to put his own feelings to one side and think only of her.

As he spoke her eyes lost focus and he realised she was near to fainting with relief. 'Drink your coffee. Have you eaten today?' She shook her head. Luc got to his feet and tugged the bell. 'Hughes, some food for Miss Heydon.'

As the manservant vanished to the scullery he contemplated his new mistress. His mouth felt dry, his loins were heavy with desire. *Not now*, he thought, willing his clamouring body into some kind of obedience. She was virginal, distressed, determined. Exhausted. He needed to get her safe so she could rest before he so much as kissed her fingertips. That did it all over again; he could only be grateful that she was too preoccupied to notice his rampant arousal and be alarmed even more.

'I'll go and get dressed,' he said as Hughes brought in a tray and began to set an omelette and bread and butter and preserves on the table. 'Eat, you'll feel better.'

In the bedchamber as he changed he worked through the list of things to be done while Hughes jotted notes. 'Book the best cabin you can get—no, make that two cabins, on the next ship for Calcutta. There is one in two weeks, apparently. Go for the best, even if that means settling for one bigger cabin rather than two—I'll leave that to your judgement. On the way call in at the agent for the Half Moon Street house and tell him I want to extend the lease for another month.'

'Staff, Captain? Footman, a cook-housekeeper and a maid?'

'Yes, that will do. Get them round there as soon as possible, I want the place clean and provisioned by tonight.'

He had leased the little house for a new mistress just before the crisis with the admiral blew up and it had never been used for that purpose. Now, although it was in Mayfair and possibly dangerously close to Bradon, he thought Averil would feel comfortable there. It was not as if she was going to be going out much. His body stiffened all over again and he jerked his neck cloth tighter.

'Uniform, Captain?'

'Yes, I need to go down to the Admiralty.' There was his finished report on the Scillies affair to present this afternoon, if he could manage to focus on that. Possibly they would have his new posting. If they wanted him to leave immediately, then they could think again. He found he could smile, his thumping headache beginning to melt away.

'Tell Miss Heydon's woman to make her mistress comfortable in here—she needs to rest.'

He buckled on his sword as he walked through into the main room. Averil had colour back in her cheeks and the plate was clean. She smiled at him as he stood in the doorway. 'How handsome you look in uniform.' She tilted her head to one side and studied him. 'I preferred your hair longer, though.'

Luc grinned at her. 'Flattering me? You do not have to, you know.' He was unprepared for the feeling that hit him when she smiled back. It was as though she had always been there, in his rooms, smiling at him. Only two weeks. Fourteen days. How did you stretch time to make it last for ever? What was the matter with him? He had never wanted to keep a mistress beyond a few months before.

'Do you feel better?' Averil asked. She stood up and came to stand in front of him, frowning a little as she studied his newly shaven face. 'Why did you get so drunk?'

Because he had decided to speak to the Comte de la Falaise today, ask his permission to pay his addresses to Louise, was the honest answer. Because he had contemplated married life and the prospect had filled him with nothing but gloom. An afternoon of brooding had failed to reveal why, when he was within an inch of achieving a major objective in his plans, he should feel so damnably flat and empty.

It was not as though he expected Louise's father to refuse his suit. The man had been unbending subtly over the past few days. He had hinted that he had heard good things about Luc's career prospects, he had made vague, but suggestive, enquiries about the d'Aunay lands in France.

And Louise would do exactly as her father told her. Not that there was any reason why she should not: she had never given any indication of disliking Luc. Nor, if he was honest, of favouring him above any of the other men who paid her the attention a pretty young lady received. She did not care, in effect. Which was exactly what he wanted, of course.

At that point in his mental processes he had begun drinking and had kept drinking, something he never did, not when he was alone. Burgundy had been succeeded by brandy, he recalled vaguely. Brandy had been followed by merciful oblivion and by waking with a head full of hedgehogs, a mouth full of dry hay and a stomach that was achingly empty.

And now he felt wonderful—and fearful, too. 'I had been working very hard to finish my report to the Admiralty about our little adventure. It was late, I was tired, I did not notice how much I was drinking.' He could not tell her about Louise and that proposal would have to wait. Wait until Averil had left, headed half a world away from him. Marrying a woman for whom he felt nothing would not matter then.

Averil sucked in her cheeks as though she was biting the inside of them to keep from saying something. When she eventually spoke all she said was, 'I hope you finished it before you became drunk, if that is where you are going now.'

'Yes,' he said and showed her the leather portfolio under his arm. 'All checked before I touched a drop. I am not going to disgrace myself.'

'Good.' She reached up and tweaked his neckcloth, her face absurdly serious as she inspected him.

'That is very wifely, my dear,' Luc said, enjoying being fussed over. The expression drained from her face.

'I beg your pardon, I had no wish to presume.'

'You are not. I enjoy being looked after. I—' He touched the back of his hand to her cheek and swallowed, forgetting what he had meant to say in the feel of her skin, the way her eyes widened, became greener, the soft catch of her breath. If he wasn't careful he would drag her into the bedroom and neither of them would emerge until tomorrow. And he must go to the Admiralty and she must rest.

'I must go. Hughes is making arrangements for a house for you. Meanwhile use my chamber. Sleep. You are safe here.'

'If Bradon finds out—'

'How should he? I will keep you safe, Averil.'

'I know, you always have.' Her smile vanished in a huge yawn. 'Oh! I am so sorry!'

'So tired, you mean.' He pointed at the bedchamber door. 'Go and sleep.'

The bed smelled of Luc, the familiar scent of him from their little bed on the island all mixed up with clean linen, leather and an elusive, citrusy cologne.

Averil closed her eyes, burrowed into the pillows and let herself relax, finally.

'I'll be outside,' Grace said. 'I won't go for my things until the captain's man comes back.'

That brought her back to reality with a jerk. 'No, go now.' Averil sat up and pushed her hair back with both hands. 'The longer you leave it the more suspicious they will be that I haven't returned. I'll be safe here.'

'Yes, you are right, miss. He's a good man.'

'He is. But he is going to marry a French lady. He has it all planned out. When Bonaparte is defeated he will go back to France and be a Frenchman again.'

Grace simply muttered something under her breath as she closed the door. Averil lay down again, breathed deeply and told herself that two weeks could seem like a lifetime if she lived it as if it was.

Through her thick veil the narrow hall was blurred. Averil pushed it back and looked around. 'This is all for me?'

'Yes, of course.' Luc was still in uniform. He tossed his hat on to the hall table, unbuckled his sword and propped it in the corner. 'Show Miss Smith's woman to the bedchambers,' he said to the footman who had opened the door to them.

At the back of the hall a thin woman bobbed a curtsy. 'Mrs Andrews, ma'am, the cook. And Polly is down in the kitchens and that,' she nodded towards the footman's back as he climbed the stairs, 'is Peter. I had the parcels sent up, ma'am.'

'Parcels?' Averil looked at Luc.

'I did some shopping. You can send your maid out for anything I have forgotten, but I suggest she goes veiled.'

'Of course. Thank you.' Now what? Should she offer him tea? Would he expect to have a conversation in the drawing room that she could glimpse through an open door to the right. Averil's heart thudded and her mouth felt dry. Perhaps she should brazenly walk upstairs to the bedchamber.

'Why don't we go and check what I selected?' Luc said and the amusement in his eyes told her he knew exactly what she was dithering about. 'Dinner for seven-thirty,' he said to Mrs Andrews without so much as a hint of embarrassment.

Presumably he kept all his mistresses here and the staff thought nothing of it. She set her expression into bland unconcern and mounted the stairs. As they reached the top Luc touched her arm and indicated a door that was already open.

Inside the footman was gathering up wrapping paper and Grace was putting away what looked like the contents of an entire shop. Or shops—there were gowns, underwear, shoes, bonnets in the armoire and the chest of drawers, a heap of toiletries on the dressing table.

'Luc, this is too much! Grace—' But the maid and the footman had vanished and the door shut with a soft click.

'No, it is not,' Luc said. 'But just at the moment you are wearing entirely too much.' He began to unbutton his uniform jacket. 'And so am I.'

She had seen him undress before with a total lack of self-consciousness. *I have seen him naked. I have touched him,* she told herself as she tried to get her breathing under control. But this was different and the way he looked at her was different. *Let me do this right,* she thought. *Let me please him.*

She must not be passive, she thought. He had liked it when she had straightened his neckcloth; perhaps he would like her helping him undress. As Luc began to shrug out of the jacket she went behind him and eased it from his shoulders and hung it on the back of the dressing-table chair. Then she stood in front of him and pulled the ends of his neckcloth free and began to work on the knot. He went very still and she looked up to meet hot, dark eyes.

'Go on,' Luc said and made no move to touch her.

The neckcloth seemed endless as she unwound it. He bent his head, but even so she had to keep standing on tiptoe and her breasts brushed against his chest and her hands kept rubbing against the thick silk of his hair and by the time she had the length of muslin free she was as aroused as if he had been kissing her.

'Go on,' he said again as she turned from folding it on top of the jacket.

Her hands were shaking as she undid the shirt buttons and pulled it free from the waistband of his breeches. He bent as she tugged at it and it came off over his head, leaving him naked from the waist up and quite blatantly aroused.

'Touch me.'

'I don't know how.'

'What gives you pleasure? Men are not so very different.'

His hands on my breasts, his hands between my legs. She did not think she could touch him there, not yet. And men did not have breasts. But they did have nipples. Intrigued by the thought she touched the right one with a tentative finger. Hair brushed her palms and tickled, the brown disc crinkled, just as the aureoles of her breasts did. Luc caught his breath. She touched the other one with the same result. Her own nipples hardened and peaked and she gasped.

Averil used finger and thumb, squeezed, rolled and he clenched his fists, his eyes closed—and a startling shaft of pleasure caught her low in her stomach as though he had caressed her.

She moved closer, her hands flat on his chest, and lifted her face to kiss him and then he moved, his arms coming round her to crush her close, his mouth taking her proffered lips without hesitation.

The kiss was demanding, urgent, and his hands worked on her gown as he moved his mouth over hers and stroked his tongue into her mouth, setting up a rhythm that had her licking and nibbling back. Her gown came undone, he moved his hands, it fell off. There was a tearing sound and her chemise and petticoats followed it and Luc raised his head and stepped back.

'Nice,' he purred. 'Oh, yes.'

She was standing there in corset, stockings and garters. She felt ridiculous and exposed and vulnerable in a way that being naked with him had never felt. Averil tried to catch hold of the corset strings, but they eluded her. 'Leave it,' he said and caught her to him again, one hand on her buttocks so she was bent back, her belly against the jut of his erection, as he lifted her breasts free of the constricting corset.

'Aah,' she whimpered as he began to lick and suck and the sensitive, tight nipples hardened and her breasts swelled and ached. 'Don't stop, Luc.'

'I have no intention of stopping,' he said and she felt a deep satisfaction at the way his voice shook, even as he struggled to sound in control. 'I don't think I could if I wanted to.'

She found herself sprawled on the bed without knowing how she got there and Luc had got rid of boots and breeches and was standing over her aroused and magnificent and she wondered if she should feel fear, but all she could summon up of coherent thought was that she wanted him inside her, she wanted to surround him, hold him, be one with him.

He knelt on the bed between her spread thighs and she reached for him as he lowered himself over her. 'Averil, don't be afraid.'

'I am not afraid. I want you.'

He did not answer her in words, only with the caress of his hand as he opened her and the weight of his body as he came down on to her so that the hair on his chest fretted at her sensitive breasts almost unbearably and the heat of his mouth made her lips part, trembling even as she closed her eyes the better to feel and touch and taste him.

Her thighs cradled him and she remembered that moment in the hut when she had realised what her aunt's careful words of explanation had meant in reality and she smiled as he entered her, smiled through the discomfort that vanished into wonder and delight and she was still smiling as his mouth captured her lips and he began the slow, perfect rhythm that transformed the two of them into one striving, passionate creature and finally, finally, broke her into a million shards of pleasure.

She tried to hold him as she felt him leave her, then remembered why he had to and tightened her arms around Luc as he shuddered and groaned and the heat gushed on to her belly and he lay still in her arms at last.

I love you, I love you, I love you. The words kept running in her head as he finally rolled from her, stooped to kiss her and then went to wash. She was still thinking it as he came back with a damp cloth and cleaned her sticky skin. She should not be surprised he was so gentle with her, he had nursed her before. But now she was conscious.

Luc bent over her and brushed the tumbled hair back from her face. 'Thank you.'

'Was it—was I—all right?'

He closed his eyes for a moment and when he opened them the deep intensity matched the seriousness in his voice. 'You are everything I had dreamed you would be.'

'Really? I am so ignorant. I don't know all the things I should know to please you.'

'You do not need tricks to please me. You just need to be yourself and to do what comes naturally.'

'May we do it again?' He was ready for her. 'You cannot hide what you want,' she said, and, greatly daring, reached for him. So hard and yet so smooth. Finest kid leather over steel. She stroked along the length and then curled her fingers round, gauging the size with a purr of satisfaction.

'Wanton.' He did not look displeased. 'We will not do that again today, you will be sore.' She registered the look of satisfaction at her murmur of disappointed protest. 'But there are other things we can do. Let me show you,' he said, his voice husky as he knelt by the bed and pulled her towards him so her legs dangled over the edge.

'Luc?' He parted her thighs and the dark head bent closer. 'Luc!' She had thought she could not feel anything more intense than what she had already experienced. It seemed she was wrong.

Chapter Twenty-Two

'I had not understood,' Averil whispered as Luc leaned back on the *chaise* beside her after dinner and rested his head on the carved back rail with a sigh of repletion. *Sex or food?* she wondered. Perhaps both.

'What did you not understand? You don't have to whisper, no one can hear you.'

'I thought we would make love once or perhaps twice a day. I did not understand that we can do it over and over again.' She managed to raise her voice above a whisper, but it still seemed wicked to be talking about things like this outside the bedchamber. Luc turned his head and smiled that lazy, satisfied smile she was beginning to recognise.

'Am I wearing you out?'

'No, not at all. I still… It is very shocking.' And wonderful. She had not realised that she could speak of love without words, with her body.

'You still want more?'

Blushing, she nodded. How was it possible not to? Perhaps one simply dropped from exhaustion after a while—or burned up with frustration if you had to stop.

Luc slid down until he was lying on the *chaise,* then he unbuttoned his evening breeches. 'If you want more—'

Of course she wanted more. But surely not in the dining room, on the *chaise*. 'The servants!'

'They will not come until we ring.' He had freed himself from his clothing and she could not help but reach for him as he shifted a little. 'Kneel over me, there is room either side of my hips.'

'Me—on top?'

'Then you can be in control, go as slowly and as shallowly as you like. I don't want to hurt you, Averil. You are very new to this.'

But not so new that he had to help her, she thought with a surge of triumph as she looked down at him. Gently she eased him into her warmth and felt the tears start in her eyes because of how perfect it was. She blinked them back in case he thought he was hurting her and bent forwards to kiss him. *Love you*, she murmured against his lips. *So much.*

'You had better stay in today,' Luc said over a very belated breakfast the next morning. 'I will do the rounds of the clubs and see if there are any rumours about your disappearance. I don't think I have done anything to make Bradon suspicious of me, but it will do no harm for him to see me around as usual.'

'I have no idea how he will react,' Averil said. But a cold feeling in the pit of her stomach said otherwise. He would be furious and ruthless, for he would be losing a great deal of money. 'Do be careful,' she added. 'What if he uses Runners?' But he merely smiled and reached for the coffee.

Grace had returned safely with her own possessions to report that she had mentioned to Lady Kingsbury's dresser Finch that Miss Heydon was lying down in her bedchamber with a sick headache. She had locked the door and taken the key away with her, she added with a mischievous grin.

There was a real world out there, Averil reminded herself. And Luc had to live in it—and he had to continue to live in it when she had gone. 'I should have asked before now,' she said, contrite. 'How was your report received at the Admiralty?'

'Well, I believe. They are interested in the methods of analysis I used to trace the leaks and focus on the source. They want me to teach them to a group of lieutenants who have an interest in intelligence work.'

'That is good,' Averil said. His mouth twisted wryly. 'Isn't it?'

'It is flattering and it means they aren't posting me to the far ends of the earth right away.'

'No, of course.' The cold knot inside became a stone. 'It will mean you can continue to court Mademoiselle de la Falaise.'

Luc put down his cup. 'I'm not courting the woman while I am with you! What do you take me for?'

'A man who wanted to set up a mistress,' Averil retorted. 'You have every intention of keeping one when you are married, have you not?'

'I—yes. Yes, I suppose so, after a few months, I suppose, if I am still in the country.'

'Well, then? How is this different?'

'You are different.' He frowned at her and she stared right back at him. 'Don't ask me why. I do not know.' Luc pushed back his chair and got to his feet. 'It just does not seem right.'

'It is less hypocritical to take a mistress after you have married and have taken vows than it is when you are simply courting a woman and making her promises by implication?'

'Damn it, Averil. You are hardly in a position to take the high moral ground on this!' He strode towards the door. 'You had a contract with Bradon that you set great store by, I seem to remember.'

'My father had. I had made no promises to Bradon and you know perfectly well why I could not marry him! I do not like breaking a contract—'

'Stop talking like a merchant!' He spun round and stalked back. 'This is not about some cold-blooded business deal.'

'No?' She found she was on her feet. 'It always was. A mistress provides her body in return for money, does she not? You were clear about that, back in the Scillies—you treat your mistresses well, you said. You provide for them. What would you have done about finding a wife if I had said *yes* then?' He opened his mouth and she swept on. 'You would have gone ahead and courted Mademoiselle de la Falaise and told yourself that she would expect you to have a mistress, that it was part of the expectations in that kind of marriage. And this, now—you and me—is about a financial exchange, so what is different?'

'I don't know, damn it,' Luc said as he came to a halt in front of her. 'It just is.'

'Well, I hope that your analysis of clandestine enemy activity is better than your understanding of relationships, or there are going to be some very confused lieutenants in the near future,' Averil said, standing her ground in the face of over six foot of infuriated male. Oh, but he was magnificent, grey eyes flashing, chest heaving; even that nose of his was designed for nostrils that flared. She wanted him…

He grabbed her by the shoulders and kissed her. He was furious, she could taste it, feel it and the excitement flared through her veins. What had come over her? She rocked back on her heels as he released her and she realised she was fizzing with energy and desire and excitement. All her life she had been well behaved and quiet and had avoided conflict like the plague. Now all she wanted was to rouse Luc to kiss her like that again.

'You brute!' Wanting to provoke, Averil picked up the first thing that came to hand, the coffee pot, and to her surprise Luc gave a bark of laughter.

'Oh, well done—perfect mistress behaviour! But you should choose something more valuable and then, when you have smashed it, you must wheedle an even more valuable replacement out of me—' He ducked as the pot flew past his head and splintered into shards against the door. 'Ah well, at least it was empty. That flower vase soaked me.'

With his amusement her own excitement ebbed away. Averil just stood there, her hands pressed to her mouth. What had she done? Twice she had thrown things at him, behaved like a hoyden, and now he was laughing at her as though that was amusing. She loved him and all she was to him was a convenient body, a female to amuse himself with, a predictable creature with grasping habits and a tendency to make scenes.

Appalled, she felt the hot tears welling up and running down her face, unstoppable.

'Averil!' Luc's feet crunched through the ruined coffee pot. 'Stop it. You do not cry, you never cry.'

'I don't mean to,' she said. 'They won't stop.' He reached for her and she batted at his hands. 'Go away. Please, just go away.'

She meant it. Luc backed towards the door, reluctant to leave her with those great tears running silently down her cheeks, but he had no idea how to stop them or what to say without making things worse. How had their leisurely, contented breakfast turned into this? His crime, he decided as he picked up hat and gloves and let himself out, was that he was not continuing to court Louise.

As he cut diagonally across Green Park for St James's Street he puzzled over why Averil was not pleased that he was staying faithful to her. She had his undivided attention for two weeks—and she was showing every sign of thoroughly enjoying those attentions. There was something wrong, some hairline crack in the pattern of what Averil had told him and how she was acting, yet he could not put his finger on it. And what had made her cry? She had faced far worse on St Helen than a row over the breakfast table and yet she had never once given way to tears. Why was he able to untangle the subtle pattern of a spy's actions and yet he could not understand a woman who was sharing his bed?

His heartbeat slowed as he walked and his thoughts became more coherent. She was sharing his bed. He had got what he wanted, but at what cost? He had ruined her. That she seemed to enjoy his love-making mattered not at all. He had corrupted her.

But I have agreed to help her, the inner demon protested, but he thrust away the easy excuses. Now, the hangover gone, his lust slaked, he could see clearly. What he should have done was to in-stall her in the house, buy her what she needed and protect her until the ship sailed. He should not have laid a finger on her whatever either of them wanted.

Luc felt sick. Sick with guilt, sick with the knowledge that the moment he had her alone again he would not be able to stop him-self from taking her again, caressing her, making love to her until they both collapsed with exhaustion. Sick with the knowledge that when she left him he had no idea how he would stay sane.

The walk was long enough, and brisk enough, for him to have regained a semblance of calm by the time he reached White's. Which was fortunate as the first person he saw as he entered was Lord Bradon.

'Ah, Bradon, this is well met. I have been hoping to run into you.' He kept his voice cheerful and his hands relaxed even though in his imagination he had the man by the throat and was pounding his brains out on the elegant marble floor.

The other man turned, his already frowning countenance turn-ing darker when he saw who was addressing him. 'Were you, indeed!'

'Yes, although this appears not to be a convenient time to dis-cuss porcelain. You seem distracted.'

'You want to talk to me about porcelain? Is this a joke?'

'Well, it might be a forgery,' Luc said. How interesting that

Bradon should react so badly to seeing him. Given that Luc had done nothing to anger the man there could be only one conclusion to be drawn: he was suspicious that Luc might have something to do with Averil's flight. 'I am not experienced with Meissen and I wondered if—'

'To hell with Meissen.' Bradon shouldered past him and out of the doors.

'Damn bad form,' Percy Fulton remarked, strolling past the porter's desk and joining Luc as he went into the library. 'He was prowling round here like a bear with a sore head last night and back he comes this morning, asking who had seen you. I suggested he went round to your chambers and had my head bitten off for my trouble and now that he finds you he doesn't want to talk. Done something to upset him? I'm always ready to stand as second, you know. Can't abide the man.'

'A misunderstanding, that is all. But thank you.' Luc retreated behind a copy of *The Times*. So, Bradon had put two and two together and come up with the only naval officer who had been paying Averil any attention. It never did to underestimate the opposition and it seemed that he had done just that with Averil's betrothed.

So now he had to be very careful indeed or he would lead the man to her doorstep and, while he had no objection to facing him at dawn over the matter, it would do Averil's reputation no good at all.

Half an hour later he realised that he had been thinking about Averil and had not given a thought to protecting her from Bradon. Restless, he got up and walked out, back up the long slope to Piccadilly and Albany. He turned into the court yard and caught a movement from the corner of his eye. A man in dark, ordinary clothing moved down the side of the yard and out on to the street. Nothing so unusual there, but the way he kept his head averted had the hairs rising on the back of Luc's neck.

He had felt like that before now and had found a sniper with his sights on him. 'Who was that?' he asked the porter.

Jenks shook his head. 'No idea, Captain. I've been out the back for a few minutes.'

'Hughes,' he said as he let himself into his rooms, 'I have a problem. How do you fancy a game of hide and seek?'

'Has to be better than blacking your boots for the rest of the morning, Captain.' The manservant began to untie his green baize apron. 'What's the plan?'

Half an hour later Luc strolled out of Albany at a leisurely pace. If they couldn't keep up with this, they deserved to lose him. At the bottom of St James's Street, with the warm red brick of the Tudor palace in front of him, he opened the door of Berry Brothers and Rudd and walked into an atmosphere redolent of wax polish, coffee and wine.

'Captain, welcome back!' The wine merchant came out from behind the counter. 'Are you here to be weighed or to restock your cellar?'

'The latter.' Luc moved around the great swinging coffee scales that most of the aristocracy of the day were weighed on. 'I am deplorably short of Burgundy.'

'Not easy to get just now, as you no doubt know.' The man shook his head as he steered Luc towards the head of the stairs down to the cellars. 'We are buying up what private holdings there are in the country, but naturally, we cannot countenance smuggled wines...'

'Indeed not.' Luc paused and peered at racks as he passed. Behind him the bell on the door rang as someone came in. 'I have a long list, I'm afraid, Humphries.'

At the bottom of the stairs Hughes appeared, a valise in his hands. Humphries said, 'Mind the shop, John. I'll be a while with Captain d'Aunay', and a young man put down a ledger and hurried up the stairs.

Luc stripped off tail coat and pantaloons and changed into buckskin breeches, a riding coat and a low-crowned hat, then followed the wine merchant back through the labyrinth of cellars and up another set of stairs.

'There you go, sir.' Humphries heaved open a trapdoor. 'Pickering Place.'

'Thank you—there will be an order coming your way in the next few days.' Luc walked briskly down the narrow passage back to St James, round the corner into Pall Mall and signalled for a hackney.

Averil rang for the maid and apologised for the state of the dining-room carpet. The girl, Polly, seemed surprised that she should do so and went calmly about her business picking up the pieces and sponging the thick pile.

Presumably such tantrums were only to be expected of a kept woman. Averil bit her lip. That was what she was: ruined, wanton and an outcast from decent society and there was no point in deluding herself that this was simply an idyll with the man she loved.

She had sold herself to him. The fact that Luc seemed to like her and that he also appeared to find their lovemaking satisfying, was beside the point, she lectured herself as she walked moodily up and down the pretty little drawing room. He had appeared quite happy that this was a financial transaction. What had she expected? That he would refuse to sully their relationship with money?

He had been gone a long time, but that was only to be expected. He had business of his own and no incentive to hurry back to a mistress who treated him to scenes over breakfast.

At last, after picking at her luncheon and mangling some embroidery for an hour, she rang for Grace. 'I am going out.'

'Is that wise, miss? What if someone recognised you?'

'In a hackney and wearing a veil?'

'Very well, miss.'

With both of them shrouded in sufficient black veiling for heavy mourning the two stepped out on to the pavement. 'There's a cab,' Grace said, but as she stepped forwards another figure emerged from behind the railings and hailed the hackney.

'Ferret!'

'Afternoon, miss. You hop in now. Where are we going?'

'We?' Beside her Grace was taking a firm and threatening grip on Averil's parasol.

'Cap'n said I was to go with you everywhere, miss. What'll I tell the driver?'

'Round Hyde Park,' Averil said at random and climbed in.

'Miss Heydon?'

'It is all right, Grace. I know this man.' Ferret settled opposite her and began to peer out of the windows as the vehicle moved off. 'When did the captain say you were to go with me, Ferret? He didn't tell me.'

'About noon, it was. Turned up down at the docks at me auntie's beer house. We're all down there while he sorts out the pardons and work and ships for us. Says there's a gent means you no good, so we're to guard you.' He flipped back the front of his frieze coat to reveal a collection of knives and a small club. 'Don't you be worrying about anything.'

'I feel very safe,' Averil said, her mind reeling at the thought of Bradon confronted by Ferret. 'All of you?'

'Well, Tubbs and Dawkins are watching the Cap'n's lodgings to sort out the men who are watching that, and Bull's following the Cap'n to see who is following him.' Ferret looked remarkably clean and tidy, although his gap-tooth grin was as disreputable as ever.

'What will they do with whomever they catch?'

'Sell 'em to the press gang, miss. Nice park, ain't it?' He settled back as the hackney began to trot along the perimeter track, but his eyes flickered from side to side and Averil did not believe for a moment that he was as relaxed as he pretended to be. Beside her Grace kept a firm grip on the parasol; it was not going to be a calming ride, but at least it had the charm of novelty. Then Ferret's words sank in. Bradon had someone following Luc—he was in danger and all he had to protect him were the rascally crew from the island.

Luc turned the key in the door of the Half Moon Street house with a degree of caution. In his experience once a mistress had acquired the taste for throwing things she was likely to retain it.

The sound of running feet had him bracing himself, but Averil threw open the drawing room door and cast herself on his chest with no sign of a weapon. 'Are you all right?' She looked up into his face and the worry drained out of hers. 'Oh, thank goodness, yes, you are. I was so worried when Ferret told me about Bradon.'

'Bradon can go to the devil,' Luc said and kissed her with enjoyable thoroughness. Life was hideously complicated but this, at least, was perfect in its simplicity.

'Yes, but how does he know?' Averil, most satisfactorily pink and flustered from the embrace, dragged him into the drawing room. How easily she had slipped into this role, into his life. And how easily she would leave it.

'The man is not an idiot. He knows you were compromised by a naval officer and the only naval officer who has been paying you any marked attention since you arrived in London is me. Once his suspicions were aroused it wouldn't take much to discover that I have been out of town for some time, that no one can be very positive about where I have been and I returned just as you arrived.'

She had gone very pale. 'Averil, there is no need to worry. The whole crew are covering you.'

'I am not worried about myself!' She turned on him, fierce and passionate, and his breath caught and something he did not recognise jolted, deep inside. Not lust, not desire, although they were there, too. This was something warmer and deeper, this was what had been churning inside him ever since she had walked into his chambers at Albany. Puzzled, he caught at her hands as she twisted them into an anguished knot.

'He could harm you, he is vindictive and calculating. He could have you stabbed in some dark alley or go to the Admiralty and make trouble for you there. I must leave, now.'

'Over my dead body!'

'That is what I am afraid of, you stupid man!'

Luc produced his best quarterdeck frown. He needed to distract her, and fast. 'Might I remind you that you are my mistress and as such I expect obedience and respect. You have twice thrown things at my head, you have ruined a shirt, my best evening coat may never be the same again, that coffee pot was Dresden and now you say I am stupid. That little catalogue calls for chastisement, I fear.'

'What? You do not mean that you would—no!'

Averil gave a scream of protest as Luc picked her up and threw her over his shoulder, just as he had that first day on the beach. This time she fought, drumming her fists on his buttocks and thighs as she dangled upside down, kicking her heels as he carried her up upstairs and into the bedchamber, but it was hopeless. He twisted her round as he sat down on the edge of the bed and she found herself face down across his lap.

'Let me go, you brute! You dare beat me! I'll…I'll…'

Cool air touched her thighs, her buttocks and the world went dark as her skirts flew over her head. One large warm hand spread over her exposed backside, lifted—and she was rolled on to the bed with Luc scrambling after her, tickling her until she screamed with laughter.

'Oh, you beast,' she murmured when they finally lay still, gasping and tear-stained and still hiccupping faintly with hilarity.

'I know. Shall I be more beastly still?'

'Yes, please,' Averil said. 'I would like that very much.'

Chapter Twenty-Three

Eight days had seemed endless when she was staying with the Bradons. Now thirteen seemed to have sped by. Tomorrow she would sail for India. Tomorrow she would say goodbye to Luc and never see him again, possibly never hear what became of him. She had counted off the passing days with the dread of a prisoner awaiting execution, prayed that this evening would never come, but of course, it had.

Ferret had escorted a heavily veiled Grace to do their shopping, but as that had been spread over many days it had been possible to pretend it was still not all complete.

The only thing that had changed with time had been Luc, she realised, watching him as he lay asleep beside her. It was three in the morning, the watchman had passed only minutes before, but the candles were still burning. They had been making love half the night.

As the days had passed he had become quieter, more introspective. She had thought at first he was worried about Bradon, but then realised that he was too courageous to let the other man bother him once he had put measures for her protection in place. Then she wondered if he was working too hard at the Admiralty, but he seemed to enjoy the sessions he was having with his students and returned energised from them.

His lovemaking had grown more intense, more passionate, as the days and nights had passed and sometimes she would catch him watching her, his eyes dark and troubled as though she was a mystery he could not solve.

Now he lay sprawled face down, naked except for a twist of sheet that did nothing for decency. Averil resisted the temptation to touch him again or he would wake and she wanted him to sleep now so she could look at him and fill her memory with the images that would have to last her for the rest of her life.

For the first time she wished she could draw. 'I love you,' she whispered, over and over. It was a delicious, heart-breaking luxury to be able to say it. 'I love you.' Her lids drooped and she wriggled down the pillows to lie close beside him, soothed by the scent of his skin and the musk of their lovemaking. If she could just stay awake, the night would never end....

Luc woke slowly, smiling as he seemed to every morning, waking next to Averil. Eyes closed, he reached out a hand to where she would be lying curled up, her hair in her eyes, warm and soft and sleepy. She would come to him, still waking and they would kiss and then—then his hand touched the hollow in the mattress and it was cold. She was gone.

Puzzled, he opened his eyes and remembered. Today was the day she was leaving. The ship was sailing, Averil was going home. Leaving him.

That was what they had agreed and he had deceived himself for days that time would stand still. But it had not and he knew she had been fretting for this morning to come; he had just not admitted it to himself. He had moved a book she was reading and a scrap of paper fell out, a page torn from an almanac with the days crossed off. She had grown quieter and yet more restless and there were dark shadows under her eyes.

He closed his eyes again. *Coward. Get up and face it.* But there was something else to face, the fact that he had taken her innocence, had used her as his mistress when he could have simply hidden her away, given her the money she needed. That it had never entered his head until it was too late was no excuse. Neither was the fact that Averil enjoyed their lovemaking and had suggested the arrangement in the first place any justification.

There were no excuses for seizing what he wanted without thinking about Averil. But he was being punished for it now. He was missing her already. *I've grown accustomed to her*, he thought. *Accustomed to her touch and her laughter, to her scent and her company, her courage and her kisses. Accustomed, that is all. She will be gone and I will propose marriage to the de la Falaise chit and find another mistress...*

He rolled over on to his back, eyes wide open now. It was barely light. No, when he married he would make himself be faithful. Averil would not approve otherwise. But what did it matter what she would think? She would be thousands of miles away making a new life, trying hard to forget him and the bargain she had made to free herself from Bradon. By the time she came back to England, if she ever did, he would be in France, being a Frenchman at last, with his French wife and his French children at his side.

He tried to sink into the familiar dream that had sustained him so often in the past. But for the first time he could not picture the scene. Instead of a vivid picture of the château and laughing children and an elegant chatelaine there was nothing, just the black-and-white ghost of the house as he remembered it.

With a curse Luc rolled off the bed, dragged his robe around his shoulders and went to look for Averil. She was sitting in the dressing room, folding small items, placing them in one of the trays that would fit into the trunk that stood open next to the clothes press. Her face was shuttered, intent.

Luc thought to stand there for a while and watch her, but she looked up and the scrap of silk and lace fell from her hands. 'I was finishing packing,' she said.

So eager to be gone. 'Yes, of course,' he said. 'You will be happy to see your father and brothers again.'

'Yes. I miss them.' She bent and retrieved the camisole. 'This will all seem like a dream. The voyage, the shipwreck.'

'Me.'

She nodded, not meeting his eyes. Yes, she could let it become a dream, find a husband in India, pretend none of this had happened. With any luck and a little acting the man would never know. He felt faintly sick and guessed that it must be jealousy of that unknown, unsuspecting man. She would make the choice herself this time, he knew. She would choose with care, someone she would get to know before she committed herself, someone she could trust.

'You'll marry,' he said, almost welcoming the knot of pain in his gut.

'Yes,' she agreed, picking another garment from the drawer. 'I would like children.'

'Come back to bed.' Luc heard his own voice, rough, demanding. Impatient. He could have kicked himself when Averil put down the garment she was folding and rose obediently to come to him. *Obedient to the man who is paying her.*

'Come,' he said, more gently and saw the tears glimmering in her eyes. The tears he had put there because he was selfish and thoughtless and had taken what he wanted. 'Come back to bed and let us say goodbye.'

At nine o'clock Averil stood on the dockside shielded from the press of the crowd by Tubbs's bulk behind and Tom the Patch at her side. Ferret was with Grace, making sure the last of the baggage was safely on board. The other men were scattered along the quay, watchful and armed.

She searched in her reticule for a hair pin and found the Noah's Ark box. She had forgotten all about it. 'Tom, can you write?'

'Yes, ma'am. Learned at dame school.'

'Then can you please make sure this is posted for me?' she asked and scribbled Alistair's name and title on a slip of card and handed them both to him. 'He is sure to have a town house.'

'No message, ma'am?'

'No.' She could not think of a thing to say. She could hardly think.

Her protectors clustered around her. The only person missing was Luc. He would be making himself visible in Mayfair, he had told her. 'I daren't go with you to the ship,' he said as he held her in his arms in the battered hackney carriage. 'I can't be veiled, I'm too big and I can't hide this damned nose of mine. You will be safe. Ferret will stay with you until the pilot is taken off at Tilbury.'

Of course she would and it was the practical, sensible thing for him to do, she knew that. And Luc had probably had enough of her emotions by now and wanted to avoid a tearful scene on the quayside.

He was right to fear it. She had been on the verge of losing all control ever since she had woken. The urge to kiss him awake, tell him she loved him, had been so overwhelming that she had slid from the bed and gone to pack her last remaining things, just so she was a safe distance from him.

And then he had stood in the doorway and looked at her with something like anger in those dark grey eyes and the roughness in his voice when he had asked her to come back to bed had been like a blow.

But their lovemaking had been almost silent, slow, so tender and gentle that she thought she would weep and then found that she was and that Luc was kissing the tears from the corners of her eyes before they could fall. 'You never cry, Averil,' he said.

Now she thought he had drunk every tear. Her eyes felt hot and dry, but she managed a smile for Grace and Ferret when they came to say it was time to board and words of thanks for the men who were guarding her.

Then she was at the rail and the ship had cast off and was slipping down river on the falling tide and she searched the quayside for a tall man, a dark head, the face that she loved. The man who had cupped her face in his hands as he looked at her with something in his eyes that she had never seen before. '*Au 'voir, ma sirène,*' he said as he climbed out of the carriage without looking back.

'*Au 'voir, Luc. Je t'aime,*' she whispered now as the docks slid away and the river widened. Ferret and Grace left her alone. Ferret, she knew, was scanning the passengers, checking, double-checking for anyone taking an interest in her.

Time passed, London passed, the river widened into an estuary. Soon they would drop the pilot, and Ferret would go with him.

The clocks rang the half-hour. Luc stared blankly at the open newspaper in front of his face. *Diamond Rose* was casting off now. She would slip down the Thames on the falling tide leaving nothing behind to mark her presence, only the ache in his heart.

The print blurred and he blinked, appalled to realise there were tears in his eyes. What the hell was the matter with him? It felt as though something—someone—had died.

And then he realised. Something had. He loved her. He loved Averil and he had let her go, sent her out of his life. The image of the château came back, in colour now, and the children were there and the woman by his side and the laughter was Averil's and the smiles on the faces of the children were hers, too. He had killed that future, those children, and it was too late. Too late.

But he had to try. Luc threw down the paper, ran from the library and down the stairs into the hall of White's club, thrust past the indignant members by the porter's desk, out on to St James's Street. 'Cab!'

Behind him he heard the porter. 'Sir! Your hat, sir! Your coat!' but the hackney stopped. 'Get me to the nearest livery stables in five minutes and there's gold for you.'

It would be too late, but he had to try.

Averil watched the banks as Tilbury came into sight. In a few minutes it would be too late, there would be no turning back. Perhaps it was already too late and this was madness, but quite suddenly, she knew what she must do. And with the resolve the blanket of misery that had seemed to stifle every breath lifted. 'Ferret!'

'Yes, miss?' The little man materialised by her side.

'I am going back with you.'

'What—back on the pilot boat? To London? To the Cap'n?'

'Yes. To the Cap'n.' For as long as he wanted her, for whatever he wanted her as. She loved him, she was his. *Papa,* she thought. *Forgive me, but he is my life now. I ruined your plans the moment I left Bradon. I cannot live without Luc.*

'Right, miss. Don't know as we can get your stuff off again, though.'

'It doesn't matter, just so long as we don't forget Grace.'

'I wouldn't do that, miss,' Ferret said with an emphasis that cut through her preoccupation with Luc. *Ferret and Grace?*

It took some argument and several guineas before the captain agreed to put another two passengers and their hand baggage off, but at last, as the ship lost way and the pilot boat came alongside, she was scrambling down the ladder with Ferret's hands on her ankles guiding her safely. 'If you'll excuse the liberty, miss.'

'Of course.' And Grace seemed to be positively enjoying it when her turn came.

The cutter cast off and headed for shore. 'What's that?' the pilot said, scratching his head and pointing at an identical craft heading out towards them. 'Late passenger, I reckon.'

There was a man standing up in the bows, rock-steady, at home on a ship. A man she would know anywhere. *'Luc,'* she whispered.

Hands reached out to stop her as she fought her way forwards amongst sailors and coils of rope. Then she was standing on the prow as he was and as the boats lost way and came together he reached out and caught hold of her and swung her across to him.

'Averil. You were coming back to me?'

'Yes. To you.' She stood there in the circle of his arm and everything vanished, the onlookers, the tossing boat, everything but him. 'You were coming for me?'

'I love you. Why did I not know before? I love you.' He looked down at her, and for the first time she saw real uncertainty on his face. 'Do you think you could…? You came back. I thought I would be too late. I rode harder than I ever have in my life and yet I thought I would be too late. But you are here for me…'

'Because I love you, too. More than anything, more than everything. I love you, Luc.'

'Thank God.' He closed his eyes and pulled her tight against him and she could hear his heart thudding as though he had been running. 'Let's go home.'

Luc was so silent beside her in the carriage on the long drive back from Tilbury that Averil wondered if he had changed his mind. But his arm as he held her against his chest was rock steady and his breathing was even, like that of a contented man. After a while she felt pressure on the top of her head and realised he was resting his cheek on her hair. She wanted to close her eyes and just luxuriate in being loved, but there too many things to worry about yet.

'Should I go into the country for a while until Bradon gives up looking for me?' she asked after twenty minutes.

'He is going to know soon enough,' Luc said.

'But he will call you out!' Averil wriggled free and twisted on the seat to look at him.

'He'll humiliate himself if he does—you were not known to be his betrothed, so if he fights me over you it will become common knowledge that he was jilted. If there was a chance he could get you back without a fuss, then that would be one thing—that was what I was afraid of, that he'd snatch you if he found you—but he won't be able to do that now.'

'But why not? We know he is ruthless and cold-blooded—'

'A married woman is of no use to him,' Luc said so calmly that for a moment she missed his meaning.

'Married? You mean to marry me?'

'Of course.' His smile as he saw the realisation hit her was pure, unclouded joy. 'There is no need to worry about banns—I can swear the allegation and get a licence from the vicar at St James's church just opposite Albany. I can prove residence easily enough, even though I am hardly a regular churchgoer. You do not mind St James's?'

'Mind? But you cannot marry me, Luc. You want a Frenchwoman. And my grandfather was a grocer, for goodness' sake!'

'So you came back to be my mistress?' It was his turn to stare now. 'You love me enough to do that?'

'Of course,' she said, impatient that he did not understand. 'For as long as you want me.'

'I want you for ever.' He shook his head, as frustrated as she by their mutual incomprehension. 'I did not understand what it was to be in love. I made all those stupid conditions, set up barriers that mean nothing. Yes, you are English, but you can learn French, we can divide our time so the children can grow up in both countries. Our first son, of course, will inherit the title, so he must always feel more French than English, but I know you will support me in that.'

'Children,' she murmured, and nodded, too moved for words. Their children. She wanted to kiss him because the look in his eyes answered every doubt she could ever have that he loved her.

'D'Aunays *do not marry trade,*' Luc said bitterly. 'I can just hear the words in my head. I was a fool, a prejudiced fool. Well, this d'Aunay will marry for love. All that matters is that I have found an intelligent, brave, beautiful woman whom I adore and who will stand by my side.'

It was a dream come true, and like all dreams, nightmare lurked on the edges. 'Bradon could sue you for alienation of my affections, the loss of my dowry.'

'Then he can have your damn dowry,' Luc said. 'How much does your father love you? Will he settle for a French count with a promising career in the navy while the war lasts and a foothold in two countries when it ends? Will he pay off Bradon if I do not ask for any dowry with you and settle my own money on you? He still gets a son-in-law with some influence and standing, after all.'

'You would do that?'

'Of course. I would hand over every penny I own to keep you. Averil, you have turned my life upside down. I thought I knew what I wanted and now all I want is you. You will marry me?' The sudden uncertainty in his voice caught at her heart. He was so strong, so confident and yet he was so unsure of her.

She swallowed, trying to find the right words to reassure him, but he got to his knees on the floor of the rocking carriage, caught her hands in his and said, 'Averil Heydon, I love you. Marry me and I swear you will never regret it. Marry me, because I do not think I can live without you.'

'I shall have to,' she said as she lifted their joined hands to her lips and kissed his knuckles. 'Because I cannot live without you either. *Je t'aime.*'

'Now that,' Luc said as he sat down beside her and pulled her into his arms, 'that is all the French you will need for a long, long time.'

The carriage rocked on its way towards Piccadilly and the old church, but Averil did not notice it, for Luc's arms were strong around her and his mouth was tender on hers and the words he spoke, although she did not understand them with her head, she could translate with her heart, because they were all of love.

* * * * *

HISTORICAL

Novels coming in August 2011

MARRIED TO A STRANGER
Louise Allen

When Sophia Langley learns of her estranged fiancé's death, the last thing she expects is a shock proposal from his twin brother! A marriage of convenience it may be, but Sophie cannot fight the desire she feels for her reluctant husband…

A DARK AND BROODING GENTLEMAN
Margaret McPhee

Sebastian Hunter's nights, once spent carousing, are now spent in the shadows of Blackloch Hall—that is until Phoebe Allardyce interrupts his brooding. After catching her thieving, Sebastian resolves to keep an eye on this provocative little temptress!

SEDUCING MISS LOCKWOOD
Helen Dickson

Against all advice, Juliet Lockwood begins working for the notorious Lord Dominic Lansdowne. Juliet's addition to his staff is pure temptation for Dominic, but honour binds him from seduction…*unless, of course, he makes her his wife!*

THE HIGHLANDER'S RETURN
Marguerite Kaye

Alasdhair Ross was banished for courting the laird's daughter, Ailsa. Six years later, toils and troubles have shaped him into a man set on returning to claim what's rightfully his. When Ailsa sees him, she knows a reckoning is irresistibly inevitable…

HISTORICAL

Another exciting novel available this month:

UNMASKING THE DUKE'S MISTRESS

Margaret McPhee

The Mysterious Miss Noir…

With trembling hands Arabella dons the mask of Miss Noir for her first night at Mrs Silver's House of Pleasures. Thinking of her young son, she prepares to smile prettily at the next gentleman who enters…

Dominic Furneaux, Duke of Arlesford, is stunned to see that the woman who shattered his heart has fallen so low. He offers her a way out—by making her his mistress!

The temptation to reacquaint herself with Dominic's body is hard to resist, but Dominic needs only to look into the Furneaux-blue eyes of her son to uncover Arabella's deepest secret…

GENTLEMEN OF DISREPUTE
Rebellious rule-breakers, ready to wed!

HISTORICAL

Another exciting novel available this month:

TO CATCH A HUSBAND…

Sarah Mallory

"I am off to London to seek my fortune!"

Impoverished husband-hunter Kitty Wythenshawe knows what she must achieve by the end of her London season— marriage to a wealthy gentleman will save her mother from a life of drudgery. After all, love doesn't pay the bills.

Wealthy landowner Daniel Blackwood is proud to be an industrialist, even if it means he's not quite what the *ton* expects. And as for young ladies like Kitty, who care only for a man's fortune – well, they just ought not to feel so temptingly irresistible when you kiss them…

HISTORICAL

**Another exciting novel available
this month:**

THE HIGHLANDER'S REDEMPTION

Marguerite Kaye

Reluctant Saviour, Willing Seducer

On her first night in Scotland, Madeleine Lafayette is rescued
from danger by brooding Highlander Calumn Munro…

Why Calumn agrees to take Madeleine under his protection, he
doesn't know—the unconquerable demons of his warrior
past are burden enough without adding the demands of
one bewitchingly brave Frenchwoman!

Yet her innocence soothes the jagged edges of his soul,
and her beauty fires his blood…

He might be her reluctant saviour, but he'll be
her willing seducer…

HIGHLAND BRIDES
Warriors take a wife!